Lock Down Publications and Ca$h Presents

# EMBRACING THE LOVE OF A BOSS 2

Written By

**MEESHA**

First Edition 2026

Printed in the United States of America

This is a work of fiction. Names, characters, places, and incidents either are products of the author's imagination or are used fictitiously. Any similarity to actual events or locales or persons, living or dead, is entirely coincidental.

Lock Down Publications
P.O. Box 944
Stockbridge, GA 30281
www.lockdownpublications.com

Like our page on Facebook: Lock Down Publications
www.facebook.com/lockdownpublications.ldp

## Stay Connected with Us!

Text **LOCKDOWN** to 22828 to stay up-to-date with new releases, sneak peaks, contests and more…

Like our page on Facebook:
Lock Down Publications

Join Lock Down Publications/The New Era Reading Group

Visit our website:
www.lockdownpublications.com

Follow us on Instagram:
Lock Down Publications

Email Us: We want to hear from you!

# Chapter 1

Koko was happy to be back home. Being in Chicago was bittersweet just as she predicted. Daniyah put the icing on the cake when she stepped to her at the ice cream shop. It was Koko's cue to leave that part of her life right where she had left it, in Chicago. The flip side of her trip was the fact that Stephan did just what he said he would. Got her name out there. Koko had so many order invoices on her website and she was ready to fulfill them.

Entering her apartment, she turned on the light by the front door and something felt off. She glanced around trying to see if anything was out of place. Koko didn't notice anything so she grabbed her luggage and headed to her bedroom. When she flipped the light switch, the first thing she noticed was a piece of paper on the dresser that she hadn't placed there. Walking slowly, she picked up the note as she observed Cyrus' handwriting right away.

*Love,*

*I've called and texted the entire time you were away. You may not want anything to do with me after everything you found out about me. Like I told you before, CJ is my son and he will forever be in my life. You will too. There is no getting out of this relationship. You are my wife, Koko. I know soon as you come home you will be trying to work at the studio. That can't happen if you can't get in that muthafucka. Come to my house and I'll give the keys to you.*

*I love you,*

*Cyrus.*

"This muthafucka got me all the way fucked up," Koko said aloud.

She wasted no time leaving her apartment, heading straight to Cyrus' home. Her adrenaline was at an all-time high because she couldn't believe he was trying to play with her like she was a goofy bitch. As Koko hopped in her vehicle, she thought about the day Cyrus placed the set of keys on the table at her studio. She laughed because she realized the nigga must have gotten another set made. That was cool, because soon as she retrieved her shit for the studio, she was calling a locksmith to change the locks in both places.

Koko was tired of the back and forth she had going on with Cyrus. She was ready for all the shit to be over and done. He never appreciated her when they were together, and the minute she said she was done, Cyrus wanted to do right by her. Back in the day, everything he said made her reconsider leaving but that ship had sailed because there was no coming back from him having a child. The imaginary relationship she thought was real was a fucking joke.

When Koko pulled up to his apartment, she barely turned the car off before jumping out. She passed a vehicle and stopped in her tracks. The SUV with tinted windows caught her attention instantly. Koko was pissed at herself for not packing her gun. With Cyrus being in his feelings and the possibility of her having to fight just to get what was rightfully hers, Koko took a deep breath before advancing toward his place. All she wanted was her belongings and she was out.

Walking up the stairs to the second floor, Koko stood outside the door and could hear music playing loudly inside. She knocked a few times without anyone answering. In turn, she knocked harder thinking it would for sure cause Cyrus to open the door. Her knocks went unanswered. That didn't stop what she came to do because just like Cyrus' ass, she had access to his place too. Shuffling through the keys in her hand, she inserted the one that would give her access inside. There was no one in the front room as Koko quietly closed the door behind her. She moved further into the apartment, and in her mind, she heard a voice say, *"Go back out the door, Koko."* Of course, she kept pushing forward because she had to see for herself what was going on.

The words Horace said about Jackie and Cyrus rang loudly in her ears. "*There's more to their relationship, Koko. It's either she wants what y'all had or she already had it."* The way her heart was beating in her chest, Koko kept going. Whatever she saw behind the door would be what it was, but she needed the last slap in the face to drive home while she walked away. The closer she got to the bedroom, the more Horace's words became true. The sounds of a sexual encounter blended in with the R&B music well. The door was closed but she twisted the knob and the scene was one Koko never expected to see. No wonder she was left in the dark about the shit that was going on right under her nose.

Cyrus was drilling the fuck out of Jackie from behind while she had her face buried between his baby mama's thighs. It wasn't a surprise because the shit explained why Jackie snapped on the bitch at the club about being in another nigga's face. Feeling sick to her stomach as she witnessed the man she'd slept with unprotected for years, do the same to the *friend* Koko knew slept with any and everybody for a buck. She laughed lowly and at that point she knew she was mentally stronger than ever before. Koko looked to her right and spotted her chocolate bar keychain lying next to Cyrus' on the dresser. She grabbed it making sure she shook the keys in the process announcing her presence. Cyrus' head whipped in the direction of the noise and his eyes almost popped out of his head.

"Don't allow me to stop your action. Keep going. I just came to get my shit like you asked." As Koko talked, she worked the key for his apartment from her keyring. She made eye contact with Jackie and she could read the panicky expression on her face. "You're a nothing ass bitch, Jackie. I've seen you do so many people wrong but never thought you would do the same to me. Karma is a bitch and she works quickly. Remember that." Placing the key on the dresser, she turned and walked out.

"Koko!"

"Fuck you, Cyrus! Kiss my ass, nigga." She laughed.

"It's not what you think," he said, following behind her.

Koko turned and laughed harder. The nigga chased her to the door, dick slanging and all. But it wasn't what she thought. Yeah, okay.

"You've been fuckin' that bitch Jackie the entire time we've been together. Had me fuckin' behind that nasty bitch and you say it ain't what the fuck I think. Nigga, I saw you raw doggin' the hoe with my own eyes. The shit don't matter because I been told you I was done and I meant what I said! Go back in there with your hoes and leave me the fuck alone!"

Back peddling toward the door, Cyrus reached out and grabbed her wrist. The look of disgust displayed on Koko's face instantly as she snatched away.

"Don't ever touch me again! You probably had that same hand on that bitch pussy and your thumb in her ass! Nigga, you ain't shit and never will be. You muthafuckas deserve one another. I promise, if you ever call my phone or approach me, I'll shoot yo' ass," Koko growled.

Cyrus smirked. "Like I did yo' lil rich boyfriend?"

Koko's neck snapped at what he revealed but she had no clue what he was talking about. Then realization clicked. He was talking about Kazimir. That was impossible because the last she knew he was still in Chicago.

"Yeah, I got yo' muthafuckin' attention now, don't I? You thought you were about to be happy with this nigga after I told you it was me and you forever? Stop playing with me!"

"You know you sound stupid, right? Aren't you the same nigga that got two stupid bitches back there in your bedroom waiting for me to leave so y'all can go back to swapping bodily fluids? *We* ain't shit!" Koko looked behind Cyrus and couldn't believe her eyes. "Y'all trifling as fuck! How the fuck you muthafuckas in here doing the sexual tango with that baby here? Is this the way you're teaching your son to be a man? You know what? This is not my business. Live your life however you choose because I won't be part of this foolishness."

"Call and check on that nigga. Oh, he may be too dead to answer."

Koko left, slamming the door behind her. She made her way to the car and the thought of Cyrus hurting Kazimir was heavy on her mind. Soon as she drove out of the parking lot, she decided to call his phone to make sure he was okay. When he didn't answer, her heart started beating rapidly in her chest. Koko pulled over to calm her nerves because again, there was no way Cyrus could have come into contact with him. They didn't run in the same circle and Kazimir was in Chicago.

She drove home with a lot on her mind. Koko was getting hit with blow after blow, and she was tired; to be honest. All she wanted was to succeed in what she loved, and that was her business. Her personal life was stressing her out to the point her focus was off. The masterpiece she crafted for Stephan and the trip to her hometown was supposed to be her breakthrough; happy days were meant to follow. Instead, she was being harassed and made a fool of by many who proclaimed to love her. The shit was overwhelming, to the point Koko just wanted to pack up and leave without telling anyone her whereabouts.

"I have to separate myself from the very people who are trying to bring me down. I've come too far to fail by the wayside of ignorant folks. By the looks of things, I'm going to end up killing somebody and serving time in prison." She said aloud.

Arriving home faster than expected, Koko found an empty spot outside of her apartment and got out hastily. She was tired as hell because the drive from Chicago was long and uncomfortable. Her bed was calling her name, but she had to shower before getting any type of rest. As she walked through the door, Koko kicked off her shoes and headed straight to her bedroom. She would find a locksmith first thing in the morning. Turning on the TV to drown out the voices in her head, she started taking her clothes off when a news segment caught her attention. There was a shooting being broadcast, but Koko didn't pay it any mind; the shit was common.

*Earlier this afternoon, there was a shooting in North Minneapolis. The update about the incident confirms the victim has been identified as business mogul Kazimir St. Claire.*

Koko's spine went rigid as soon as the name came from the reporter's mouth. She realized at that moment Cyrus wasn't just trying to get her riled up when he said he had killed Kazimir. Her hands shook uncontrollably as she sat on the edge of the bed to watch the rest of the segment.

*There aren't any suspects in custody for the shooting, and Mr. St. Claire was taken to the hospital by an acquaintance. Law enforcement was informed that St. Claire wasn't the intended target of the incident. Gun violence in Minneapolis has increased over the past couple of years, and it's something police are trying to crack down on.*

Muting the TV, Koko didn't want to hear any more about what happened. She was more concerned about Kazimir's condition. Sitting in deep thought, she tried to think of someone who could give her an update. The entire situation took place on account of her. Cyrus was mad because he saw her with another man, not knowing it wasn't what he presumed it to be. What baffled the fuck out of Koko was the fact that Cyrus didn't even want her; he was doing all this extra—for what? Cyrus was a selfish muthafucka who wanted Koko so nobody else could have her. The days of her being the woman who overlooked his cheating and disrespect were over.

Kazimir wasn't in the streets, but he was caught up in bullshit that had nothing to do with him. Koko felt bad for getting him tangled in her tainted web; he didn't deserve to be shot. A few minutes passed before she jumped up to rustle through her luggage. She paused, then hurried back to the bed for her cellphone. Stephan would know what was going on; she was sure of it, as she anxiously waited for him to answer.

"Miss Simmons, how are you? To what do I owe the pleasure of this call?"

Koko swallowed the lump in her throat. She could tell by the tone of Stephan's voice he had no clue about what happened to Kazimir. Not wanting to be the bearer of bad news, she had to spill it if she wanted information on his condition.

"Um, you told me if I ever needed anything to call. I'm taking you up on that offer."

"Yeah, what's up?" The professionalism went out the window; he could tell she was emotional. Stephan was ready to jump in and help any way he could.

"Kazimir was shot—"

"What?" Stephan shouted as he shuffled around hastily. "I haven't received any calls. What happened, and how did you find out? Where is he?"

"Apparently, it happened here in Minnesota. The only information I have is what was shared on the news. You were the only person I thought of to find out his condition and the hospital he was taken to. According to the segment, Kazimir was driven to the hospital by an acquaintance." Koko made sure to answer all questions best she could.

"Definitely. Thanks for bringing this to my attention. I'm going to reach out to a few people, and I should have something for you once I'm able to gather the information."

"No, thank you for checking on him for me."

"I'll try my best to have answers for you soon."

Stephan ended the call, and Koko regretted not telling him everything she knew. He helped her in a major way by bringing attention to her business, and she didn't want to be judged by people who were no longer in her life. The truth would come to light eventually, so she planned to play it safe until it was brought to her. Koko would be ready to explain the situation between her and Cyrus. Hopefully, Kazimir and Stephan would understand the relationship was one she never intended to rekindle.

Soon as she placed her phone on the bed, it rang again. Koko snatched it up and answered immediately when she saw who was calling.

"Horace—"

"I know the news reporter got the name wrong, right?" he asked. "We just left Chicago, and Kazimir was still there."

"That's what I thought too," Koko sighed. "Cyrus shot him."

"What did you say?"

"You heard me. He was in my place at some point while I was away. I found a note saying to come to his apartment to get the keys to my studio. The nigga is stupid because he had the spare key. I went because I wanted to let him know one last time; I was done with him for good. Cyrus doesn't seem to understand what the fuck I've been saying over and over. When I got there, he didn't answer after I banged on the door like the police. So I used the key I had to his place. This muthafucka was engaged in a full-blown threesome with his baby mama and Jackie."

"Bitch, I told you!" Horace clapped and screamed into Koko's ear. "Jackie ain't never been shit! Nasty, no-good ass hoe! What time are we ridin'? I'm ready."

"We won't need to do shit to Cyrus, but I'm stomping Jackie's ears closed whenever I see her. The universe is going to handle Cyrus."

"Wait, so he shot that man for real?" Horace asked, shocked.

"There was no way he could've seen the news before I did; it was breaking. Cyrus did it because I told him if he didn't stay away from me, I would shoot him. His rebuttal was, *Like I shot your rich boyfriend?* I rolled my eyes and left because I figured he was talking out the side of his neck to get a reaction. And Kazimir is not my boyfriend. I didn't believe Cyrus until I heard the man was shot on the news. Cyrus is crazy. For the first time since I've met him, I'm scared. The way his eyes turned black let me know he's psycho."

"Did he put his hands on you, though?"

"Cyrus knows better. I would've stuffed his dick up his ass. The entire time he was talking about how it wasn't what I thought, he was butt naked with cum dripping on the floor."

"Eww! Nasty ass. Cyrus has some nerve being mad about who he thinks you're dealing with. He don't have a leg to stand on—he's been cheating, had a baby, and got caught red-handed fucking his 'sister/friend.' Cyrus needs somebody to beat the fuck out of him. A lot of women have brothers for that type of shit. You're lucky to have me."

"That's why I love you, Horace. But do not approach Cyrus. The last thing I need is for you to get hurt protecting me."

"Koko, the feelings are mutual. Everyone who's ever talked to me knows I'm beyond gay; I'm not ashamed of who I am. So fuck him for disliking a real one. Cyrus is going to realize soon that being gay has nothing to do with masculinity. *I ain't a killa, but don't push me* is a saying I'm willing to put into play on his ass."

"Stay away from him, please," Koko pleaded softly. "Look, I have to take a shower. I may need you to ride with me if Stephan gets information about Kazimir tonight."

"Call me. Even if it's tomorrow, I'll be there when you need me."

"Okay. We have to discuss the details of your new position soon. With everything going on, I can't do it now."

"That's fine. Business sales aren't going to be a problem. I want you to go run a hot bath, get some wine, and relax your mind. Kazimir is going to be okay. You have to get yourself together first and foremost. He isn't dead, and that's a plus. Now get off this phone and do what I suggested. I love you, boo."

"I love you too. I'll talk to you later."

They said their goodbyes, and Koko gathered everything she needed for her bath. Horace made a valid point; she needed to relax. Walking down the hall to the bathroom, Koko started bawling out of the blue. She used the wall to balance herself as her knees suddenly went weak. Even though she and Kazimir weren't romantically involved, he didn't deserve to be hurt. Her heart hurt even more for Alessia; she loved that man.

Koko ran her bath while cleansing her face. She couldn't figure out how Kazimir ended up in Cyrus's presence. The connection wasn't making sense at the moment, but the truth would reveal itself in due time. As she eased into the hot water, Koko moaned lowly. She forgot to grab the wine and wasn't getting out of the tub to retrieve it. Instead, she laid her head back and closed her eyes, letting the hot water wash away the worries of the day.

# Chapter 2

Cyrus walked around his living room with his hands on top of his head. He didn't ever want Koko to find out about him and Jackie. Let alone for her to actually see them in the act. There wasn't anyone he knew of who would forgive for that type of deceit. So, he knew Koko wouldn't either. Cyrus knew Koko was going to show up for her keys; he just didn't think it would be so soon. He left the note the night prior and hadn't heard from her. That alone told him she wasn't back from Chicago. Communication was one-sided between them, and Cyrus found himself doing all the reaching out. The shit made him feel like a bitch because he never chased a woman down to stay with him. And there he was doing exactly that with Koko.

He knew what he was doing when he told Sheree to come over with CJ. Cyrus wanted Koko to see him being a father to his son, and he planned to treat Sheree like she was just a baby mama. It would've proved there was nothing going on between the two of them outside of parenting. That shit didn't pan out the way he thought it would.

When Sheree showed up, she and Cyrus ate and chilled with their son. Things took an unexpected turn when Jackie came over unannounced. Far as everyone knew, Cyrus and Jackie were just cool; including Sheree. CJ was put to bed shortly after, and the party started with the adults. Liquor was flowing, and the music blasted through the sound system. The environment went from kickin' it to turned up soon as

Jackie pulled pills from her purse. That was all it took for one of Cyrus' fantasies to be fulfilled.

Sheree, with her curious ass, wanted to try one of the pills; Jackie didn't hesitate to give it to her. The drug and alcohol mixture had both women feisty as fuck. Cyrus didn't indulge in anything more than marijuana, so he sat back pulling from the blunt he had flamed up while watching the scene play out in front of him. It didn't take long at all for the action to begin.

Jackie's kicked shit off by massaging Sheree's breasts. At first, she appeared uncomfortable, but she didn't pull away. Cyrus smirked as he cupped his penis through his basketball shorts. The sight before him had his dick on brick. Easing her shirt up so she could get to Sheree's nipples, Jackie latched on like a baby. Sheree's low moans were music to Cyrus' ears as he cupped the back of Jackie's head. When he saw his friend rubbing his baby mama's mound, he knew there was no turning back. He stubbed out the blunt, then stood to his feet.

"We gon' take this to the bedroom. Y'all not about to leave me on the sideline watching. Hell, we're all about to cum together."

Jackie pulled back at the sound of Cyrus' voice. She had forgotten he was even there while she seduced his baby mama. Jackie had been with her share of women, but it wasn't something she did on the regular. The pill had her feeling adventurous, and trying her hand with Sheree was easy. She'd been eyeing her for some time. Giving Sheree the pill was part of Jackie's plan all along because she knew there would be a high chance of tasting her nectar. Cyrus reached for both their hands, and they all made their way to his bedroom.

Thinking about how he got caught in such a compromising predicament, Cyrus was snapped back to reality when Sheree and Jackie entered the room wearing T-shirts. They had been fucking for hours; Koko hadn't truly interrupted anything. The trio had just continued where they left off after a quick nap.

"What was she doing here?"

"Sheree, not now," Cyrus said, still pacing.

"I wanna know too. Why was she here? Koko is the last person I wanted to see me the way she did. That bitch is going to tell anybody who will listen about what she walked in on!" Jackie shouted.

Cyrus' head snapped in Jackie's direction. "Do you really give a fuck? We've been doing this shit for years behind muthafuckas' backs. Now they won't have to speculate no mo'."

"What do you mean y'all been fuckin' for years?" Sheree asked angrily. "I was under the impression we were all doing this for the first time."

"You heard what I said."

"How the fuck is that when she's supposed to be like family?" Sheree asked angrily.

"Me and Jackie been more than friends for the longest. She knows her place in my life, and I know mine in hers. We don't compromise each other's relationships and do us when the time presents itself." Cyrus shrugged like it was nothing. "I'd never participated in a threesome until today and that shit was good. You didn't have a problem getting yo' pussy ate by another bitch until you heard I'd already fucked."

Sheree stood dumbfounded, unable to find the words. Jackie, on the other hand, was mad as hell that Cyrus didn't give a damn about how she felt. Just because they'd been having sex all along didn't mean she wanted the world to know about it.

"Nigga, I don't want nobody in my business!" Jackie yelled. "What we do behind closed doors is only for the parties involved. How do you think that's going to make me look?"

Cyrus was tired of the noise. He was ready to be alone and think about his next move. "Both of y'all get the fuck out! Sheree, don't think about taking my son with you. I'll bring him home in a couple days."

He left them standing in the living room and went to shower, slamming the door and locking it behind him. Cyrus relieved his bladder before stepping into the tub. The water beat down on his head, forcing his eyes closed, but relaxation was out of the question. His mind replayed the interaction he had with Koko. He realized he told her about shooting that nigga Kaz, and he never intended to do that. It wasn't a secret; everybody present at the trap saw what happened in real time. Koko was his only concern. She was mad and would for sure go to the police. Cyrus wasn't worried. The only proof she had was his word.

After showering, Cyrus checked on his son. CJ was sound asleep despite the chaos that had taken place in the apartment. He kissed the top of his head then left the room. As he entered his bedroom, Sheree was lying in bed, but Jackie was nowhere in sight. He stood by the door with a towel wrapped around his waist. All he wanted to do was sleep, but Sheree's expression told him that wasn't happening anytime soon.

"Are you ready to talk like adults?" Sheree asked calmly. "Jackie went home, so we should be able to communicate without the hostility."

"Even if Jackie was present, I still wouldn't want to discuss the shit," Cyrus retorted as he walked into the room.

"Well, I do. You had me involved in a threesome with your sneaky link. Not to mention, the bitch had me believing she was like a sister to you."

"Don't raise yo' voice at me, Ree. What type of relationship me and Jackie have got nothing to do with you. Nobody held a gun to yo' head and made you open yo' legs. Hell, you enjoyed the shit like the rest of us. We had a good time exploring each other's bodies, and it felt right. Tell me I'm wrong." Cyrus crossed his arms over his chest.

"It doesn't matter how I felt in the moment. You and the bitch played in my face! On top of that, Jackie was friends with your ex, and y'all was fuckin' behind her back. The shit is fucked up on all levels. No wonder she was so quick to talk down on that woman to me. Jackie wants whatever the fuck you were giving Koko. Right now, I'm glad she did whoop her ass."

"Don't forget she whooped yo' ass too," Cyrus smirked. "I need to know, what does any of that have to do with you? I didn't lie about shit. Just to clear the air, I don't like explaining myself, and that's part of the reason I'm single. You're my baby mama, not my woman. The sooner you accept that, the better off you'll be. You opened the door for another woman to step in with us sexually. Let's go with that and do it again."

"Whatever, Cyrus. You're selfish as hell."

"How? Because I told the truth? Man, gon' with that shit. You can leave now. I need some sleep; I got things to do tomorrow."

"If that's the case, me and my son will leave you to sleep."

Sheree huffed as she scrambled out of bed to get dressed. She moved slowly, like she was waiting for Cyrus to tell her to stay. It didn't happen. He didn't argue about her taking CJ either, even though he'd told her not to. The ache in Sheree's heart was heavy, but she didn't let it show. She left without a goodbye, giving Cyrus the opportunity to lie down alone, thinking about everything that transpired in a single day.

***

Cyrus woke up to the sun beaming in his face. He felt refreshed and rejuvenated, which surprised him after the night he'd endured. Jackie and Sheree deserved credit for that. They drained the fuck out of him mentally and physically. Without a doubt, Cyrus planned to get them to run that shit back one more time. If Koko was true to her word about not reconciling, he had plans to convince Jackie and Sheree to be sister wives. They were both attracted to each other and had love for him. To Cyrus, it was a win-win situation.

After taking care of his hygiene, he chose a pair of black khaki shorts and an olive-green T-shirt, finishing the look with matching olive-green-and-black Nikes. He dressed down because where he was headed, the whole fit would need to be trashed afterward. Securing his Glock in the small of his back, Cyrus grabbed his wallet and keys, then headed to his whip. He was on his way to holla at Sheree's people. JoJo and his cousin had muthafuckas believing he had something to do with their fuckery.

One thing for sure and two for certain, Cyrus had never been a thief, and he wasn't about to let a narrative tarnish his name. Yeah, he shot Kaz because he was, in fact, a muthafuckin' killa; Cyrus would stand ten toes down on what he'd done. He was ready when the heat came his way. Still, he wasn't too worried. Kaz wasn't as tough as he portrayed to be. Cyrus saw through the entire façade. He wasn't new to that type of shit; he was true to it.

Parking in front of Debbie's crib, Cyrus stalked to the door. He rang the bell repeatedly, hearing movement on the other side before everything went silent. Sheree's mama was watching him through the peephole but didn't open the door. Cyrus leaned into it, keeping pressure on the bell and pounding heavy knocks in between.

"What the fuck you beating my door down for?" Debbie barked as she snatched the door open.

"Where's JoJo?"

"He ain't here! Don't come to my house with that bullshit, Cyrus! Leave what happened in the past. Y'all fought, now it's over. Nobody was going to shoot you."

"I'm gon' deal with that shit in due time. That's not why I'm here. JoJo and Jerrod stole a substantial amount of money from somebody, and they want all three hundred thousand back. You and I both know what's gon' happen when they catch up with them," Cyrus chortled.

"I need to holla at them niggas because, for some reason, they decided to drop my name in this shit. Putting me in the middle of a theft conspiracy was the wrong move. I'm fuckin' them up. I had nothing to do with them stealing from the plug."

The color drained from Debbie's face. Her dark skin turned damn near gray as she processed his words. She knew he wasn't lying. She'd seen the bag of money up close. Hell, she'd helped JoJo bury it behind the shed and even took twenty thousand for herself. Still, she wasn't about to reveal that. Instead, she did what any mama would do; she stood ten toes down for her son.

"JoJo didn't steal nothing! He don't have a reason to take money from nobody. If anything happens to him, you'll be the first son of a bitch I mention to the police. I'll make sure my grandson is taken care of while you rot in hell."

"You can call the pigs and say whatever you want It'll be hearsay because you don't know a damn thing about me. I ain't worried, not by a long shot. But you should be. JoJo's broke ass got every reason in the world to steal; he's a fuckin' bum," Cyrus laughed. "Not only is yo' son on the choppin' block, but yo' ass is too. Three hunnid G's is a lot of money. When that muthafucka come to collect, he gon' kill you to bring yo' bitch-ass son to the forefront. Just so you know. And far as my son goes, I'll be the one taking care of him. Locked up or not, ain't shit gon' stop me. So stop threatening me with a good time, you can't even take care of yo'self, let alone CJ. Tell yo' punk-ass son I'm looking for him."

Cyrus turned and headed for his whip while Debbie watched from inside. Once the door closed, she collapsed onto the couch, replaying the confrontation. She gasped and snatched up her phone.

"Fuck. I gotta warn my sister. Cyrus is about to look for Jerrod next," she muttered.

"Sista, you been on my mind—"

"Not today. Where's Jerrod?" Debbie asked, her voice shaking.

"He not here. What's wrong?"

"Cyrus came here talking about JoJo and Jerrod stole some money."

The line went quiet before Daphne whispered, "Oh my God."

"What?"

"They did that shit, Deb. Jerrod gave me fifty thousand the other day and told me to act like we were broke. He wouldn't say where it came from."

"Shut up! Don't say another word on this phone," Debbie snapped. "Cyrus is on his way to your house. I'm sure of it. If he asks, you don't know shit. We gotta protect our kids. JoJo and Jerrod can get killed behind this."

"We can just give the money back."

"The money we got don't even match what they took! That would prove they stole it. We ain't giving back a dime. Act dumb and do what I said!"

"Okay. Let me talk to Jermaine before your son-in-law start harassing us."

Daphne hung up with shaky hands, nerves jumping like a stripper on her first night on the pole. She stepped into the hallway, searching for her son. When she saw Jermaine standing by the window with his fists clenched, she knew she was already too late. He stormed outside seconds later.

It took Cyrus half the time to reach Daphne's house. He hopped out of his car on a mission just as Jermaine charged down the walkway.

"Nigga, you got some nerve coming here on bullshit," Jermaine barked.

Cyrus smiled, ignoring his rant. "Tell yo' pussy-ass brother I need to holla at him. Stay in yo' lane unless you had something to do with the shit they pulled."

"Watch yo' muthafuckin' tone. Get the fuck on, Cyrus. I don't know who you thought was scared of you; but it ain't me. Whatever beef you got with my brother, you got with me."

"Aight."

Cyrus rushed him without another word, raining punches to Jermaine's face. He didn't give him time to react. Jermaine swung wildly, as Cyrus took hold of his arm snapping it at the elbow like a twig. Cyrus blacked out with the intent of killing him. When Jermaine hit the pavement, Cyrus stomped his head repeatedly. Daphne's screams echoed from the doorway.

"He gon' kill him! Get him off my baby!"

"Freeze! Put your hands above your head now!"

Hearing the police only pissed Cyrus off more. He knew Daphne's trick ass had called them. It didn't matter because he'd be out before sunset. Next time, he'd finish the job. After one final kick, officers tackled him to the ground.

"Get the fuck off me!" Cyrus yelled as his face was smashed into the concrete.

"Gun!"

Cyrus laughed. The Glock was registered; he was licensed to carry. No felonies, no reason to panic. He hadn't even pulled it.

"Oh, there won't be any getting the fuck off you," the officer sneered. "Assault with a deadly weapon and resisting arrest. I can't wait to run your background. You're toast, buddy."

"Good luck with that, *buddy,*" Cyrus shot back. "I whooped his ass without a gun. You pulled the muthafucka from the back of my pants. That's simple assault.

The officers yanked him to his feet, cuffs biting into his wrists. Cyrus gritted his teeth and let them drag him to the patrol car. Through the window, he watched paramedics kneel beside Jermaine. Daphne glared at him, cigarette dangling from her lips. Sirens wailed as an ambulance pulled up. He laughed when she gave him the finger on the sly.

The officer who had a hard on after finding the gun climbed into the driver's seat, he glanced into the rearview mirror, then took off fast; slamming the brakes and snapping the seatbelt tight around Cyrus' neck. The cop laughed.

Cyrus memorized it all: *Officer Christopher. Badge 0110.* He could laugh now, but his family would cry later.

# Chapter 3

Kaz was ready to get out of the hospital so he could find Cyrus. He was a dead man walking. Kaz couldn't believe the bitch-ass nigga shot him. Instead of being mad about seeing him with Koko, Cyrus should've been mad at his damn self for fumbling a good woman. The shit Cyrus pulled only motivated Kaz to make her his. Koko was going to need a muthafucka like him by her side with an ex like Cyrus. It wouldn't be long before Cyrus' punk ass crashed out when he realized she would never take him back.

Sitting on the edge of the hospital bed, Kaz waited patiently for the nurse to return with his discharge papers. According to the doctor, he was lucky; the bullet went through his shoulder and out his back. He received a tetanus shot and antibiotics. His arm rested in a sling, but it was nothing a little physical therapy couldn't fix. Kaz would be back to his old self in no time.

Steelo tapped away on his phone. He hadn't said a word since entering the room. Kaz could only imagine what he was doing, but he needed to know for sure. After a few minutes of silence, Kaz finally spoke.

"Lo, what you doing over there?"

"I'm trying to dig into this nigga's life, but I need a last name. Cyrus ain't getting away with the shit he pulled today. He fucked around and shot the wrong muthafucka. You can't touch him, Kaz. Plenty people can, including me."

"I won't stop whatever happens to him, but I'm not sitting this shit out. Before I was a businessman, I was the nigga to be feared. If I sit back and allow others to handle my problems, the next muthafucka will try their hand at taking from me."

Steelo leaned back, shaking his head. "You've come too far from the streets, Kaz. As your friend, I can't let you jeopardize everything you built. On top of that, you got Pax to think about. If you kill this nigga, who's going to take care of him? Not David's money-hungry ass. Use yo' head and let me handle it."

Kaz's phone rang, and Steelo handed it to him without hesitation. Stephan's name flashed on the screen, making Kaz sigh. He knew word hadn't traveled that fast to his people, but instead of declining the call, he answered.

"Yeah, Steph. What's up?"

"What do you mean, what's up? How the fuck did you get shot?"

Kaz laughed. "You're in Chicago and already know? Tell me this shit ain't on the news there."

"It's not, but I hear everything. What happened?"

"Wrong place, wrong time," Kaz replied casually. "You know how it goes. Innocent bystanders get caught in the mix."

"For some reason, I don't believe you. I'm glad your cool ass is okay. Call Kameeko; she's worried. She saw the shooting on the news and reached out to me."

Kaz smiled. Koko was the reason he got shot, but none of it was her fault. Knowing she checked on him told him everything he needed to know. The interest between them was mutual, and Kaz planned to explore it beyond business. How she ever got involved with a nigga like Cyrus didn't matter. Kazimir St. Claire would be the last man to capture her heart.

"I'll call her," Kaz said.

"Were you in Minnesota to see her? She lives there, and you two were already acquainted before I introduced you."

Kaz wanted to tell the truth but couldn't do that over the phone. He settled for a white lie.

"Yeah. I came to see her. I just didn't make it to my destination."

The door opened, and Nurse Taylor entered with a smile. There was a glimmer in her eye Kaz recognized instantly. If Koko wasn't heavy on his radar, he'd have her moaning in an empty room. Taylor waited quietly as Kaz wrapped up his call, though Stephan's voice faded into background noise while Kaz mentally undressed her. He snickered lowly before cutting Stephan off mid-sentence.

"Aye, I'ma hit you back." "The nurse is here with my get outta jail free papers."

"You're way too happy for a man who was shot today."

"I'm good, Steph. Trust me."

"Okay, Axel Foley. I can hear the devilish grin through the phone."

"Bye, man. You holdin' me up," Kaz chuckled and hung up, giving Taylor his full attention.

"Mr. St. Claire, I have your discharge papers," she said. "Dr. Stevens wants you to stay overnight for observation."

"No need. I'll follow up with my physician in Chicago. I appreciate the concern, but I'm good."

"Well, I tried," Taylor shrugged. "Here are your prescriptions. Pain meds as needed, antibiotics three times a day for seven days. Instructions are included. Any questions?"

"No."

"Take care of yourself, Mr. St. Claire."

"You do the same. Thank you."

Taylor hesitated like she wanted to say more, but she must've read the expression on Kaz's face, then thought better of it and left. Kaz watched her hips sway and the jingle of the wagon she dragged behind her until the door closed.

"You ain't shit," Steelo laughed. "She wanted you bad. The lust in your eyes scared her. Nicolette gon' fuck you up one of these days."

"Nicolette ain't gon' do shit," Kaz replied. "She know what it is. Until she files for divorce, I'm doing me. Let's go, I'm tired of this hospital smell."

They left the hospital; silence filled the car. Kaz took the time to rest his eyes until Steelo interrupted his relaxation.

"Do you want to stop at ol' girl crib?"

"No, I just need to fill my prescription and get to the hotel.

Steelo nodded as he gripped the steering wheel tightly. Kaz could've been killed and his life would've never been the same. Minnesota wasn't his stomping ground but he was dead set on getting revenge. Driving along the highway, Steelo jerked the steering wheel to the left. The blare of horns, followed by the sound of crumbling metal, he was able to avoid the collision ahead.

"What the fuck happened?"

"The stupid muthafucka in the red truck was switching lanes like a madman and clipped the silver Sentra. It spun out hitting the car two cars up," Steelo explained. "I saw that shit before it happened. This is what *you have to drive for yourself and everybody else* means. Had I not been paying attention, this rental would be fucked up."

Kaz scanned the chaos. "You can bypass this shit. Get on the shoulder. I need to get to the hotel and take something for this pain."

"Ion know, Kaz. That shit gon' be tight."

"You got it. Just get me outta here. This shit got me feeling some type of way. Two near death experiences in one day. Yeah, the man upstairs is trying to tell my black ass something.

After maneuvering through the chaos, Steelo was able to head to continue onto the highway without incident. Kaz paid attention to the route they were going then stared at Steelo to see if he was going to follow his instructions.

"Stop looking at me like that, nigga. Hotel first, then I'll grab your meds," Steelo said. "You grumpy and it's only gon' get worse with you having to sit and wait. I'm not trying to hear that shit."

"Fuck you," Kaz laughed as Steelo pulled in front of the hotel's entrance. "Tell them to hurry up with that shit. Oh, and bring me back some catfish filets and fries from Captain Hooks, or J&J's."

Kaz tossed him two hundred-dollar bills. Steelo took it shaking his head. It was nothing for him to pay for whatever his friend needed because Kaz looked out for him when he had nothing. He wouldn't see it that way though. Steelo waited until he was safely inside before pulling off.

The elevator ride to the room felt endless. Kaz leaned on the rail as he watched the digital numbers rise. Kaz exhaled when the doors finally opened. He searched for the keycard as he walked down the hall. Inside the suite, he headed to the bedroom then collapsed onto the bed. His shoulder throbbed and there was nothing he could do about it until Steelo returned. The thought of Koko entered his mind causing him to fish his phone from his pocket. Before he could find her contact, her name appeared on the screen. The pain faded instantly.

"Hello, beautiful," Kaz said putting the phone on speaker.

"I'm glad you're okay. Stephan called and told me to look out for your call. I had to hear your voice. So, I called."

"You can call me anytime. I'm alright. Thank you for checking on me."

There was a pause. "I need to talk to you about something."

"Go ahead."

"Not over the phone. Can I come to you?"

Koko's angelic voice gave Kaz's soul a sense of peace and a hard on. He squeezed his wood to calm himself in order to respond to her request. It would be nice to be in her presence for a short while.

"Are you there?"

"Yes, I'm still here," Kaz said sending his location. "I'm at the Marriot on 7th Street. Drive safely and I'll see you soon."

"We don't have to hang up."

"I want you focused on the road. Call me when you're close."

"Okay. I have another call coming through. I'll be there in twenty."

Koko glanced at the unknown number. She didn't know who was on the other end and didn't think anything of it when she answered. Slipping on her shoes, she cradled the phone with her shoulder then spoke.

"Hello?"

"Is this Koko?"

"Yes. Who's this?"

"This Don. Cyrus told me to call. He's locked up. He wants you on standby to bail him out."

Koko paused midway through tying her shoe. She knew damn well Cyrus didn't have anybody calling her to do anything for him. He was locked up, and that shit had nothing to do with her. That alone made her wonder why Don was calling her phone. He was usually with Cyrus in the streets, but he never said more than two words to Koko.

"Don, you know Cyrus better than anybody besides me. Y'all been friends longer than I've known him, so it's ironic for you to call on his behalf. The fact that we're no longer together should be something you're aware of. Cyrus sent you off coming to me with this bullshit because I don't give a fuck what he has going on. The bitch you should be bothering with his problems is his baby mama or Jackie's hoe ass; not me."

"Koko, how you gon' turn yo' back on him during a time like this? That shit foul as fuck after all he's done for you. This yo' chance to prove the love you claim to have for my nigga."

Koko couldn't believe what she was hearing. It was obvious Cyrus hadn't told anyone in his circle they'd gone their separate ways. Don was talking like she planned to walk away just because Cyrus was in jail. What stood out even more was the fact he had nothing to say about the baby mama.

"No, I'll tell you what's foul. Cyrus having a baby while professing his love for me. Talking crazy, breaking into my house while I'm gone, and fucking the bitch who was supposed to be my best friend. Before you come at me with false accusations, I left Cyrus alone over a month ago. As far as proving my love for him, I did that throughout our relationship. His ass was the one running around acting single. And for the record, Cyrus has never done a muthafuckin' thing for me. I've always held shit down on my own. With that being said, don't call me again. Have Cyrus recite the numbers of his hoes. He's their problem now."

Cyrus really had the audacity to think she would run to his aid after everything he'd done. Koko chuckled after hanging up. She didn't snap on Don intentionally; he put himself in the line of fire when he dialed her number. Guilty by association. She didn't care how he felt. Grabbing her purse and keys, Koko left the apartment. Soon as she settled into the driver's seat, she entered the address Kaz sent into the Carplay GPS.

Most people would think it was a shame she still needed help navigating the city after years of living there. Long as she knew the route to her studio and back home, everything else wasn't that important. Koko opened Apple Music and queued up **"My Way"** by Fetty Wap.

*Baby won't you come my way*
*Got something I want to say*
*Cannot keep you out my brain*
*But first off, Ima start by saying this*

*Aye, all headshots if you think you can take my bitch*
*Aye, and I'm too turnt when I shoot, swear I won't miss*

She used to love the song, until that moment. The lyrics reminded her too much of the person Cyrus pretended to be after they split. Shooting Kaz confirmed he needed serious psychological help. Koko wished there was a family member she could contact about his mental health. The more she rejected him, the worse his behavior would become.

According to the GPS, she was five minutes away from her destination. Her nerves kicked in at the thought of seeing Kaz. The chemistry between them was undeniable. Unlike him, she tried to dodge his advances and the way he openly pursued her. If she was honest with herself, she wanted him just as badly, but she couldn't ignore the fact he was a married man.

Pulling into the hotel lot, Koko parked near the entrance. She exited the GPS and texted Kaz, her hands shaking as she typed.

*Koko: I'm in the parking lot*

*Kaz: Come to room 1404*

Stepping out of the car, she tugged her leggings back into place and adjusted her shirt as she headed inside. She scanned the lobby for the elevators when an employee approached.

"Good evening. How may I help you?" he asked politely.

"Can you guide me to the elevators, please?"

"Definitely," he said, turning sideways. "What floor?"

"Fourteenth."

"You'll head down the corridor to the right," he pointed.

"Thank you so much," Koko smiled, taking a step in that direction.

"This is random…" His voice stopped her. "You look familiar. Are you Kameeko Simmons from *School of Chocolate*?"

Koko blinked, surprised. She expected him to mention the news, not the show.

"Yes, that's me. I see you're a fan of the show."

"A fan of the show? Nah, I'm a fan of *you*. I caught it by accident and watched you dominate from episode one. I was your hype man during the pencil challenge. I knew you were going all the way from that point."

"Aww, thank you," Koko said warmly. "What's your name?"

"Jackson," he grinned. "Can I get your autograph?"

He searched for something she could write on as she glanced at him, touched by his excitement. Wanting to do more, an idea sparked.

"Stay right here," Koko said, lifting a finger. "I have something for you in my truck."

She rushed outside and quickly put together her first fan box. Three T-shirts, two hats, a keychain, her business card, and a replica pencil from the show, autographed just for him. When she returned, Jackson was waiting like a kid on Christmas morning.

"These are for you," she said, handing him the box. "The pencil isn't the original, but I hope it's something you can cherish."

"Thank you! This just made my day." he said, nearly speechless. "I just met one of my idols. A real celebrity!"

"I'm not a celebrity yet," Koko said modestly. "One day, though."

"You're humble, and your name is about to shine. I got fifty thousand followers who need to know you."

"That's so kind. Tag me. My socials are on the card. It was a pleasure meeting you, Jackson."

"The pleasure was mine, Miss Simmons."

"Call me Koko. Time will tell if we'll cross paths again. Keep that upbeat, happy attitude because the world needs more of that from people. Enjoy the rest of your evening. I look forward to seeing your content," she said, opening her arms.

Jackson stepped into the hug, and the warmth grounded her in a way she hadn't realized she needed. It felt good to be able to put a smile on the young man's face. Afterward, she waved and headed toward the elevators, leaving him behind to admire his gifts.

***

Kaz paced the floor of his suite, as he checked the time on his watch for the third time, wondering why Koko hadn't arrived. She texted saying she was at the hotel almost thirty minutes prior. Slipping into a pair of slides, Kaz was on a mission; he needed to know Koko's whereabouts. With Cyrus still in the streets, he couldn't take any chances with her safety. The moment he opened the door; his heart skipped a beat.

Koko stood with the biggest smile he'd seen in a while.

"What took you so long to get to me, Koko?" Kaz asked, drawing her in by the waist. "Let me find out you was entertaining a muthafucka in the lobby."

"Actually, I was," Koko smirked.

Kaz stepped back without fully letting her go, his eyebrow raised. He had no right to feel any type of way; she wasn't his woman. That didn't mean he had to congratulate her for the shit either. Koko deserved to move on after Cyrus' old ass, but not with anyone other than him.

"I met a young man who works here," Koko explained. "He said he saw me on TV. He was so excited to meet me, so I left him a few trinkets to remember me by. Now, can I come in, or we gon' talk in this doorway?"

"What's the lil nigga's name?"

"Kaz, move the hell out of my way," Koko chuckled, pushing past him jokingly. "You not about to jeopardize that boy's job."

Koko sat on the sofa, waiting for him to join her. Kaz shook his head, allowing the door close, then sat across from her. He admired her until she got to the reason she came; then the air shifted. It didn't take away from her beauty, though; nothing ever did.

"First, I wanted to make sure you were okay. Thank God you are."

"I told you that on the phone," Kaz replied. "What's the real reason you wanted to see me, Kameeko?"

Koko shifted so she faced him, tucking one foot under her leg. "Kaz, do you know who shot you?"

"Yeah. Do you?" he asked in return.

"I don't know for sure, but I think there was some truth to what I was told."

Koko explained what happened at Cyrus' house and why she went there. Kaz listened in silence. The more she spoke, the more his nostrils flared. He wasn't mad that Cyrus bragged about shooting him; he was furious because the nigga could've hurt her when he invaded her space. It gave Kaz another reason to put him in the ground.

"Did you change the locks on your apartment and the studio?" he asked.

"No. I'm going to get around to it tomorrow. I have time since I learned Cyrus is locked up right now."

"How did you find out that information if you're no longer communicating with him?" Kaz asked.

"One of his homeboys called before I left my apartment," Koko explained. "He said Cyrus asked him to call and tell me to be ready to bail him out. I told him to contact one of his hoes and ended the call. Cyrus can burn in hell if he thought I was going to help him."

Kaz decided to try for more. He didn't know if Koko was going to give him what he was seeking, but it was worth a shot.

"I'll find a locksmith and take care of that for you. In the meantime, I can use your help."

"What can I possibly help you with, Kaz?"

"I want to know about this nigga. What's his full name; first and last? Where does he lay his head? Where does his people stay? What type of car do he drive?"

Koko understood why Kaz wanted information on Cyrus, but she wasn't about to be involved in his demise. Karma didn't play when it came for payback, and she'd worked too hard to throw her life away behind bullshit. She wasn't going to get involved in what they had going on. The most she'd give him was a name; the rest, he could find on his own.

"His name is Cyrus Davis. That's all I'm willing to give. I don't want his blood on my hands. You have every right to retaliate for what he has done to you, but I can't help you take him down." She held Kaz's gaze. "It has nothing to do with me having feelings for Cyrus because I don't. It has everything to do with where I'm going in life. You are already there, and should be thinking the same way. I have a question of my own. How did you and Cyrus end up in the same circle?"

"I was in North Minneapolis on business and just happened to run into him in the process."

"Kaz, cut the shit, okay?" Koko sternly said as she sat up. "This is me you talking to. You may not know me, but I know the man who shot you very well. Cyrus doesn't know shit about business unless it's about drugs and money. Do not talk to me like I'm naïve. As much as I don't want to learn the truth about your dealings, I need to know. So, give it to me straight. Whatever we say in this room stays here."

The way she basically told him not to blow smoke up her ass made Kaz respect her more. In fact, it was sexy. She had to let him know that half-truths were something she wouldn't tolerate. Koko had a come correct or not at all attitude. She also proved loyalty mattered to her. Still, he was wary of allowing her access to that side of his world.

"The less you know, the better."

His response caused her to nod, with her finger to her mouth. Kaz didn't realize not saying anything said a lot. She wasn't new to the lifestyle; she was true to it. Cyrus wasn't the first man she'd been in a relationship with that had dealings in the street. She knew when a nigga had a hand in illegal shit. Kaz had a legit business to cover up his dirt. Which meant he wasn't a corner boy. He had pull. She sat as he studied her from afar. If he thought that was the end of the conversation, he was wrong.

"Do you know what that sound like to me, Kaz?" she asked. "Some drug shit. I'm going to ask you one time to be truthful with me. Are you the plug?"

"Why are you asking me something like that? You know I have a legit business in Chicago."

"And I also know you have illegal business here in Minnesota. Saying *the less I know the better* is basically telling me if I'm ever questioned by the police, I can't tell them shit." Koko didn't blink. "You being the plug is the only thing that explains why you were anywhere near Cyrus."

Koko didn't give a damn how long it took; she had all day for him to tell her what she already knew. Kicking off her shoes, she got comfortable on the sofa. Her stomach growled and Kaz heard it loud and clear.

"Are you hungry?" he asked. "I have some fish in the kitchen I can warm up."

"Please stay on the subject at hand," Koko said. "We can eat after you tell me what I need to know. I promise what you say won't stop me from being your friend. I won't judge you either."

"I'm not worried about any of that, love." Kaz shook his head. "Let's just leave the conversation right here. There's no need to go into detail."

"Why, because I'm right about you being the plug?"

Biting his bottom lip, Kaz leaned forward, elbows on his knees. Koko wasn't backing down. Little did she know, if she kept pushing him, she may end up lying flat on her back with her thighs hugging his head. His dick expanded in his joggers; he shifted to hide it. He wanted to trust her, but he didn't know if she could handle the truth.

"You're not going to allow your mind to stop wandering, are you?" Kaz grinned. "Don't force me to bare my soul to you, Koko. You might have to sell yours to the devil. I don't think you're ready to do that."

"What do you mean?"

"If I tell you what you're inquiring, you'll have to protect it with your life."

"I already told you, whatever we talk about in this room stays in this room."

"I heard you, but how can I be sure you'll hold up your end?" Kaz asked. "Your word isn't enough. You gotta put something up for collateral."

"Well, that's all I have to offer," Koko said with a shrug. "It doesn't matter. Not answering the question outright tells me my thoughts are valid. You don't have to answer. I received what I came for, and I'm sorry my ex shot you. I'm going to let you rest."

Koko reached for her sneakers and Kaz was on his feet in a flash. He kicked both shoes out of her reach standing over her. Even with his arm in a sling, he was sexy as his muscles flexed. The wife beater didn't hide his sculpted abs. She hadn't paid attention to his body when she arrived, but in real time, she saw it clear as day.

"Where you think you going?" Kaz asked. "You want to know about me; I'm going to tell you. First, you have to make a deal with me."

"Nah." Koko's eyes narrowed. "I don't like that twinkle in your eye. You're up to something, and I want no parts. And I already told you; I'm not giving you anything more on Cyrus."

"Fuck Cyrus!" Kaz snapped. "This has nothing to do with his bitch ass.  It has everything to do with you and me."

Kaz used his good hand to caress her face, running his thumb over her lips. His hand traveled to her throat, grasping it gently, forcing a low groan from her. Her eyes closed to slits, but she still had a clear view of the thickness in his joggers. Kaz tightened his hold just enough to make her lift her gaze to his.

"See, this small gesture has your nipples pebbled under your shirt," he murmured. You deserve a man who's gonna love you right. The bullshit you're used to ain't shit compared to life with me. If you let me, I'll love you like no other. I'm ready to show you the world." His voice dropped deeper. "Are you ready for that?"

His baritone almost had her under his spell. Her body responded before her mind could register what was taking place. Her clit throbbed as he controlled her swallow with his thumb. If he had the use of his other hand, he would have palmed her breast without hesitation. Then reality snapped her back to her senses.

"The question is, are *you* ready?" Koko asked, voice sharp. "I'll answer for you. No, you're not because you have a wife and a child back home. I know, you don't love her; it's business." She scoffed. "Bad as I want you to bend me over this sofa, we can't go that route. Long as you're legally married, there can't be anything outside of friendship between us. We have sexual chemistry neither of us can deny, but I will never creep around with a man that don't belong to me."

Kaz loosened his grip and let his hand fall. Koko had a point. Nicolette was in the way; the only thing keeping him and the woman he wanted apart was a divorce. It would create problems, but it had to be done. Kaz refused to stay trapped in a marriage he never wanted from the start. No matter what it took, he was ready to fight for his happiness.

# Chapter 4

It had been a few days since the shit show at Cyrus' house. Jackie hadn't heard anything about what happened on the street, so that told her Koko hadn't opened her mouth about what she'd seen. She even went by her mother's and faked an apology to see if she knew anything, and it turned out to be a good visit. Lowkey had been calling nonstop, but Jackie ignored his calls. She wasn't in the mood to talk to him because all he wanted was to get her in bed. To her, he had to come off some more money before he could ride her wave.

Cyrus must be in his feelings because all her calls to him had gone straight to voicemail. Koko had him in a chokehold, and now he was taking the shit out on Jackie as if she was the reason Koko wanted nothing to do with his ass. They got caught red-handed. What they'd been doing before Koko came into the picture finally came to light. Cyrus couldn't blame nobody but himself because he should've taken the key to his place if he didn't want her to know what was going on.

Jackie wasn't going to sit back while Cyrus ignored her. She got into her truck, heading to his apartment. When she got there, Cyrus' car wasn't parked in his designated spot. It was early afternoon, and he was usually still home at that hour. Tapping her hand on the steering wheel, Jackie left without even trying to knock on his door. She steered her vehicle in the direction of Sheree's house. Jackie didn't want to take the thirty-minute drive, but she had to see Cyrus. There was no other place he could be. The thought of calling

Sheree crossed her mind, but she didn't want to give Cyrus a chance to leave. Plus, the three of them needed to discuss what took place between them.

Replaying the threesome in her mind, Jackie had never experienced a sexual encounter of that magnitude before. She had the best orgasm in the moment and dreamt about the day it would happen again. If the opportunity presented itself again, she would agree in a heartbeat. Sheree was a squirter who could rain down her throat at any given time. Jackie loved the way her clit grew with every suckle of her lips. Sheree rode the hell out of Jackie's face as Cyrus fucked her hard from behind. The encore was when both of them sucked Cyrus' dick together, forcing him to cum all over their faces. That shit was sexy and nasty at the same time.

The ride was shorter than usual due to the story time in her head. Jackie made a right onto the street where Sheree resided. When she pulled up to the house, the only car in the driveway was the Infiniti Cyrus purchased for Sheree. Jackie became extremely worried at that point because something was definitely wrong. Cyrus had never gone missing without anyone knowing his whereabouts. Throwing her car into park, Jackie got out and walked toward the front door. Before she could climb the stairs, it opened abruptly. Sheree stood there with a scowl on her face as she waited for Jackie to get closer.

"Why are you at my house?"

"Have you heard from Cyrus? I've been calling his phone all morning."

Sheree huffed as she folded her arms over her chest. "You should know where he is. That's your man, right?"

"Come on, Sheree. Cyrus is not my man. I'm sorry you had to find out we were sleeping together after all of us fucked. Why does it matter now?"

"It matters because both of y'all bamboozled me!"

"What? You were a willing participant. I don't recall you being against what we were doing. If memory serves correct, you enjoyed the shit," Jackie snapped. "Look, I didn't come here to argue about a good time. I'm just trying to find out what's going on with Cyrus."

"I haven't heard from him since he put me out of his apartment."

"Sheree, that don't sound suspect to you?" Jackie asked. "I don't care what Cyrus does; he never goes anywhere without talking to anyone. Especially me and you."

"I don't know what you want me to say. I haven't heard from Cyrus. Maybe you should try calling Koko. He probably laid up with her ass."

Jackie was getting nowhere with Sheree. She knew Cyrus couldn't be with Koko because there was no way she would take him back after what she walked in on. On top of that, Jackie wasn't ready to contact her former friend to ask about Cyrus. Instead, she was going to hit the block to see if she could find answers there. Waving goodbye to Sheree, Jackie walked back to her car and drove off. She was halted by a red light when her phone rang. Seeing Lowkey's name on the display, Jackie decided to see why he was blowing her up like a madman.

"Hey, Lowkey," she said, putting the call on speaker.

"Don't 'what's up' me," he roared. "I've been blowin' yo' shit up, and you been ignoring me."

"I've been going through some things. What's the emergency?"

"Jackie, I'm not one of these sucka ass niggas you used to dealin' with. What's this I hear about you fuckin' wit' Cyrus?"

"Cyrus? Man, he's like my brother. Why are you listening to muthafuckas in the street? That stupid ass rumor been flowing for years," Jackie retorted immediately.

The last thing she needed was Lowkey believing she was sleeping with Cyrus. Even though she hadn't slept with him, he was shelling out blue faces like she was his main chick. Jackie didn't want her human ATM to run dry. She was ready to lie her way out of the bullshit and was willing to say whatever it took for him to believe her.

“Yeah, I heard that too, but there have been too many muthafuckas saying you fuckin’ that nigga. Everybody can’t be lying on you.”

“Well, they lyin’, and I won’t sit here defending this shit to you. I know where my pussy been, and it ain’t been with Cyrus. You calling me like what you were told is law. It’s not!”

“I’m trying to see how deep you in with the nigga because he has gotten himself in some shit. I don’t know if you heard or not, but he shot the muthafuckin’ plug. Word on the street is he stole a lot of money from the nigga, and they gon’ kill his ass. Along with Jojo and Jerrod.”

“Cyrus don’t have a reason to steal shit from nobody. Jojo and Jerrod, now that’s another story. Them broke ass niggas would steal yo’ shoes off your feet while you’re still in them. I can’t see Cyrus joining forces with them because they are like oil and water. He don’t even like them. Their only connection is his son.”

“Stay away from that nigga. He hot right now. I would hate for something to happen to you behind his bullshit.”

“Since you seem to know so much, where is Cyrus?” Jackie asked.

“He got picked up by the police yesterday. That’s all I know. Aye, I got some shit to take care of. Remember what I said. Stay away from Cyrus. You need anything?”

“Yeah, I’m broke. I need to get a wheel alignment and an oil change. I need gas too.”

“I got you, baby,” Lowkey said. “I’ll send the money through Zelle.”

“Thank you. I’ll talk to you later.”

“Bet.”

“Fuck!” Jackie yelled soon as the call disconnected.

She couldn’t believe Cyrus was locked up. Why would he shoot the man that made it possible for him to make money to take care of his son? Jackie decided to go home and said fuck going on the block. She was bound to get locked up herself if any of them punks said anything to her about Cyrus. Jackie hated when niggas talked about a muthafucka when they weren't around but wanted to chop it up when that same nigga was standing shoulder to shoulder with them. Cyrus must not have been processed into the system yet, which was probably the reason he hadn't reached out. She would be ready when he called to bail him out.

Jackie did the dash all the way to her house and rushed inside the moment she pulled into the driveway. After locking the door, she dropped her purse and keys on the couch, then headed to the basement where Cyrus kept his stash. Entering the code into the wall safe behind a picture of Beyoncé, she began counting out the money she thought would get Cyrus out of jail. If it wasn't enough, there was more to add. It took a little over an hour to get the money ready.

Going upstairs after touching the dirty bills, she washed her hands before going into the kitchen to cook lunch for herself. She took out the chicken breast she'd thawed the night before from the refrigerator along with green, yellow, and red peppers. Fajitas were what she had a taste for. After rinsing the meat, Jackie cut the vegetables to sauté. As soon as she placed the peppers in the preheated pan with a little olive oil, her phone rang. Wiping her hands on a paper towel, she answered the call.

"Don, what happened?" she asked, knowing who was on the other end.

"You already heard; I see."

"Yeah, Lowkey told me Cyrus was locked up, but he didn't go into detail," Jackie said, stirring the vegetables with a spatula.

"Open the door. I just pulled up."

Jackie looked down at the phone, noticing she had a notification from her bank. Lowkey kept his word by sending two thousand dollars. It was more than enough for the things she really didn't need. She smiled, lowering the fire under the pan before going to let Don in. He walked past her the moment he entered. Stress was evident on Don's face, indicating he hadn't been getting much sleep. He and Cyrus were close. Don was going through it just as Cyrus probably was in jail.

Jackie locked the door and rushed back to the kitchen to check on her food. She noticed Don had taken a seat in the living room as she passed.

"Come in here so we can talk," she called out.

"You got it smelling good," Don said, sitting at the table. "My bad for not calling before popping up at yo' crib. I talked to Cyrus earlier. At this point, he has no bond. They're trying to charge him with aggravated assault and resisting arrest. The gun charge was thrown out because he's licensed to carry and he never pulled the weapon. I called his lawyer after getting off the phone with him. He is on top of everything."

"Who did Cyrus assault?"

"Usually, I wouldn't discuss this shit with a female, but Cyrus told me to give it to you straight."

Don dragged his hand over his face, then proceeded to tell Jackie what took place at the trap. The more he spoke, the more it made sense why Cyrus reacted the way he had. One thing she knew about her friend was, he would address bullshit when it was presented to him. That had to be the case in that instance.

"So, the plug is fucking Koko and came to throw it in Cyrus' face; is that what you're saying?"

"On some real shit, I don't even think dude knew who bro was. He didn't mention Koko; Cyrus did. Kaz was at the trap strictly on business. Cyrus brought up the fact he recognized him from being on TV with Koko. Bro wouldn't let it go even after Kaz said he wasn't there for nothing other than his money. Cyrus kept disrespecting the man and Koko. He even disrespected me by pullin' his tool on me. This shit with Koko is making him crazy. Hell, I didn't even know they wasn't together until I called her."

"The fuck you call her for?" Jackie asked, frowning at Don.

"Cyrus had me get in touch with her first. It was useless because she don't want nothing to do with him. At this point, he needs to let it go."

Jackie added the chicken to the pan. She listened to what Don said and knew firsthand Cyrus didn't want Koko. He just didn't want to see her with anyone else. It pissed Jackie off that he was still chasing the bitch when he had his fair share of women who would ride with him, Jackie being at the top of the list.

"Enough about the bullshit with Koko. Who stole the money?"

"Jojo and his cousin Jerrod," Don replied. "Cyrus' name was put in the mix because they are kin to his son."

"Niggas can't be that stupid to think Cyrus would steal money. He don't like them niggas, for one, so why would he plan some shit like that with them? Plus, Cyrus has money on top of money. What did the plug say? Do he think Cyrus has anything to do with what happened?" Jackie asked.

"There wasn't an indication that he did. The only thing he said was for Cyrus to take a couple days off until he decided if Cyrus would work for him or not."

"Regardless of who stole that man's money, Cyrus didn't do the shit. I'm riding with him through it all. If everybody folds on him, he will always have me."

"Even though Cyrus pulled a bitch move with me, I know he was in his feelings at the time. That's my nigga, and I got him."

"Long as you don't let that shit come between y'all, it should be cool. Make sure you keep me updated. I'm going to get him soon as a bond is set."

"You have always held him down like a sister, Jackie. That's what the fuck it's about. Blood don't make you family; loyalty do, and you got a lot of that for Cyrus."

Jackie placed a plate in front of Don, then sat down to eat herself. Little did Don know, loyalty was only part of the reason she had Cyrus' back. It had a lot more to do with the money in her basement and the dick between his legs. Jackie wasn't giving none of it up for nothing in the world. She needed him out so he could give her a dose of the medicine only Cyrus could provide.

***

Don left after filling his belly. He promised to call her if he heard any new information about Cyrus. Jackie cleaned the kitchen, then headed upstairs to take a shower. She laid down thirty minutes later to take a nap. Jackie didn't realize how sleepy she was until her head hit the pillow. Two hours later, Jackie was up and out of the house on her way to the block. Jojo was on her radar. Hopefully, he wasn't hiding out.

Soon as she pulled up to the block in North Minneapolis, Jackie smiled widely. Everybody was out enjoying the last days of summer. The street was lined with cars and motorcycles. Kids ran around with snow cups, chips, and candy. Music blasted from somebody's trunk, causing the ratchet females to throw their ass at whoever was willing to catch it. For once, the environment was peaceful family fun. The sun was beaming, and she wasn't looking forward to getting out of her car and into the heat.

Jackie couldn't find a spot to park, so she pulled her truck into an old lady named Miss Bertha's driveway. She sat on the porch in her rocker, sipping from a bottle of Heineken. Bertha was the neighborhood watcher who had the police on speed dial if anything popped off. When Jackie stepped out of her vehicle, Miss Bertha started snapping on her.

"My driveway is not for public parking! I don't know how many times I have to tell you hard-headed fools this. Every weekend y'all want to disrespect my shit!"

Miss Bertha puffed her Virginia Slim menthol, then coughed. Jackie walked toward the elderly lady but was waved off. Once Bertha caught her breath, she went in on Jackie again.

"Don't bring your narrow ass on my porch! The respectable thing would've been to ask if you could park here. I should make you move!"

"Miss Bertha, I can move my truck; that's not a problem. Disrespect is the last thing I want you to think I'm doing. As a matter of fact, I'll pay you to use your driveway." Jackie searched for her wallet inside her Louis Vuitton purse to give Miss Bertha a few dollars.

"I'm all about the Benjamins, baby," she sang. "Don't pull no chump change out of that expensive pocketbook either. Act like this the parking lot of the club. I won't accept nothing less than thirty dollars."

"This old bitch is about to get slapped," Jackie mumbled. "Who the fuck she think trying to pay thirty dollars to park on the block?"

"What was that?" Miss Bertha asked, holding her hand to her ear.

"Nothing," Jackie said, holding the money out to her.

"Girl, do I look like I'm in any position to walk down those stairs? Don't play with me now."

"I thought you said—never mind." Jackie walked up the steps slowly, handing Miss Bertha the twenty and ten-dollar bills.

"Thanks. You have one hour to move that truck before I have it towed," Bertha smiled as she tucked the bills in her bra.

Bertha was an old hustler. She got money out of Jackie and mocked her quietly afterward. Turning away to survey the scene, Jackie knew she had limited time to find the person she was seeking. Usually, she would be happy to be out and about. That night, not so much.

"Aye, Jackie," a guy named Money called, grabbing her hand as she passed his whip. "How you been?"

Snatching away, Jackie waved without stopping. Money knew she didn't fuck with him, but every time he saw her, he thought it was okay to touch her. Jackie wasn't trying to argue with him. She had to find Jojo.

"Stuck-up bitch!"

"Yo' mama, pussy," she shot back, with her middle finger in the air.

"I should knock yo' head off for saying that shit," Money yelled at her back.

"Nigga, watch how you talk to her!"

The malice in Jojo's voice halted Jackie's steps. It was like music to her ears. When she turned around, Jojo stood nose to nose with Money.

"Gon' with that bullshit, Jojo. Jackie for every muthafuckin' body. I don't know why you trying to take up for a hoe anyway."

"You a lie! Mad niggas always want to talk shit when their game too weak to bag a real bitch."

"I got this, Jackie," Jojo said, holding up his hand to silence her.

She appreciated him taking up for her, but it wouldn't save him from the trap she was setting. Until she acted on her plans, Jackie enjoyed the show taking place in front of her. Money was saying a bunch of nothing, and the shit was funny as hell.

"If she don't want to fuck wit' you, then that's what it is. Niggas nowadays need to know when to back the fuck up when females not interested. There's plenty of other bitches out here. Choose from the litter, muthafucka."

"Man, whatever. I'm sure you still won't get no pussy after trying to save her ass. You better tell her stupid ass to watch her fuckin' mouth."

Money got in his car before Jojo could respond. Jojo reached for the handle to confront him, but Jackie stopped him by grabbing the back of his shirt. He glared at her, but his expression softened when he noticed who was halting his movement.

"See how I get behind you," Jojo said, pulling her into his arms. Money peeled away from the curb, causing Jojo to laugh. "You ready to fuck with a real nigga now?"

"It wasn't necessary to do that to Money. He knows I would never give him any play. Far as dealing with you, you're the one that's not ready."

"I've been ready to make you mine. I guess it's the fact I'm not out here ballin', huh?"

"Stop making it seem like I'm a gold digger or some shit. I have my own bread. A nigga with his own is a bonus," she smirked. "I don't have a problem holding my man down until he gets on his feet."

"That's the type of woman I need in my life. Independent and freaky as fuck," Jojo said, licking his lips. "I don't need you to hold me down financially, baby. I got that covered. Muthafuckas think I'm broke because I don't flaunt my wealth for all to see. I'm like the white millionaires. Dress like you don't have it so a nigga can't rob me. Incognito is the way to be."

Jojo had revealed he was indeed the person behind the robbery of the trap without actually saying it. He assumed Jackie hadn't caught on because she was still smiling. She for sure was aware of the innuendo he had thrown out there. Jojo thought he was saying everything she wanted to hear. In the streets, she was known as a hoe. In his mind, he fantasized about fucking her nightly. He wanted to experience her silky walls for himself because he'd heard how tight and good her pussy was. He had no intentions of turning a hoe into a housewife. All he wanted was to bust a nut that would make her thick ass crazy over him.

"Jojo, I'm going to keep it real with you. I'm not trying to be in a relationship. Keep ya hoes, but be available when I need you to be. And nobody should know about what we do behind closed doors. If you can handle those rules, I'm on what you're on."

"Shid, I'm all for that. You don't have to say shit else. We can get it poppin' tonight if you want. Put my number in your phone and hit me up later."

Doing as he asked, Jackie programmed the number, then texted him so he could do the same. The wheels started to churn in her head, and her plan for revenge was set in motion. Giving Jojo a hug goodbye, Jackie explained she had an appointment, then headed to her truck. When she got closer to Miss Bertha's house, the old lady was still sitting on the porch, but she was on the phone.

"Never mind, the owner of the vehicle just showed up," she said sweetly, then ended the call. "You're right on time. You were really close to walking home. I was just on the phone with the tow company."

"Your old ass is petty. I've barely been parked here fifteen minutes, bitter bitch. You said an hour!"

"You needed me! I should call the police and tell them you're verbally harassing me. In fact, I think I will," Miss Bertha said, writing down Jackie's license plate number.

Taking the stairs two at a time, Jackie snatched the pad from the woman's hand. "Smoke a cigarette or something because fucking with me, you won't see your next birthday!"

Jackie turned to leave the property, then stormed back toward Miss Bertha. The old lady was frightened, believing she would be harmed. It was far from the truth. Jackie reached into the front of Miss Bertha's gown and took her money back.

"Now the joke's on you. Enjoy the rest of your night."

Jackie got into her truck and backed out of the driveway. Miss Bertha was on the phone the moment Jackie was off the block. She didn't appreciate how the woman talked to her, and she was going to have her taken care of in the worst way.

# Chapter 5

Cyrus couldn't believe the pigs were trying to pin bogus charges on him. When they couldn't get him on gun charges, it pissed them off. The assault charges weren't shit, and he would've been able to bail out, but that was too easy. The muthafuckas decided to plant drugs on Cyrus to keep him locked up. Two of the officers discussed their plans in the patrol car openly in front of Cyrus as he sat in the back of the patrol car. He defended himself as much as he could until he was told to shut the fuck up. When he wouldn't, Cyrus was punched in the face. They whooped his ass in the garage of the police station before he was taken inside.

The gash above his eye bled constantly, and Cyrus was in excruciating pain because he'd been kicked repeatedly in the ribs. He wasn't given medical attention even after he asked for it. Cyrus didn't constantly complain about the pain because a nigga like him wasn't built to be pussy. The pigs fucked up by not killing him, though.

Sitting in the holding cell, Cyrus sat by himself while the other inmates chatted amongst themselves. He cradled his side but tried his best to suppress the pain he was enduring. He had been locked up for about two hours and was ready to get back on the street. He hoped like hell his lawyer, Jesse Brooks, came to the rescue before any more bullshit was brought his way. Cyrus leaned against the bars to relieve a little bit of the pain.

"Davis," an officer yelled down the hall toward the holding cell. "It's time to go home," he smirked. "Not the home you're thinking of, though."

"Hahaha, muthafucka," Cyrus sneered. He actually thought Brooks had come through for him. "Take me to the hospital first."

"Not going to happen. There will be a nurse waiting in St. Paul to check you out when you get to the jail."

"And my lawyer will be waiting to sue the shit out of y'all too. Bogus ass charges won't stick. Believe that."

"Shut up and put your hands behind your back, then walk backward toward me. I have a bracelet to fit you for."

"Fuck you!" Cyrus said, struggling to stand upright.

He followed the directions given, and the officer placed the handcuffs around his wrists. The cuffs were tight to the point they cut into his flesh. Cyrus winced in pain.

"Loosen these muthafuckas! You know they're too tight! You lucky we not on the street. I'd fuck you up, nigga."

"It's funny you people don't like anyone outside of your race to use that word, but it's used regularly by the Blacks."

"You muthafuckin' right! I bet not ever hear that shit fall from yo' lips. Stop talkin' to me, fuck boy."

The officer taunted Cyrus to the point of pissing him off even more. Then he'd had enough of his own bullshit. He decided to give his wrists a bit of relief by loosening the cuffs. Opening the bars, the officer grabbed Cyrus roughly by the arm before guiding him through the station. A detective Cyrus knew oh so well blocked their exit, standing directly in front of them.

"Big bad Cyrus. We finally got you, huh?"

"Samson, you ain't got shit! Planting shit won't work on me. Dirty muthafuckas gotta lie to get an arrest. I'm here for it, though."

"We got a warrant to search your car and apartment. There are cops tearing your shit up as we speak."

"Do I look worried? Because I'm not. Make sure you have your money on deck to pay for the damages," Cyrus huffed. "Y'all doing the most because I beat a muthafucka's ass. Preserve that same energy when it's time to work a murder case. That's where your training focus should be."

"Get this dirtbag out of my face!" Samson gritted.

Cyrus laughed as he was escorted out of the station and into a sheriff's van. They were trying to throw the book at him. He had never been locked up for a couple hours before being shipped off. The ride was bumpy, and every bounce made Cyrus think about the beating he'd taken earlier. CJ entered his mind because he never wanted to be behind bars while Sheree struggled to take care of him alone. He needed to be there for his son, not in jail. Debbie's words rang in his ears: *I'll make sure my grandson is well taken care of while you rot in hell.* Brooks had to come through and work Cyrus' case like his life depended on it.

Resting his head against the headrest, Cyrus closed his eyes for the duration of the ride to the jailhouse. He had an hour to reflect on how his life ended up in shambles. It was his fault for the most part. Had he done right by Koko, his life would've been golden. The two of them had so many plans together until she miscarried their child. Cyrus blamed the entire ordeal on her and bottled up his feelings for years. He ignored how the loss of the baby affected Koko and refused to talk about it. Cyrus felt if they didn't discuss what transpired, both of them would forget and go back to how they were before the tragedy occurred. That was wishful thinking.

Life had gone on for the couple, but they were no longer in sync. Koko dove into work to suppress her feelings while Cyrus drowned in pussy. It wasn't the right thing to do, but the shit happened. Producing a baby wasn't in his plans because he didn't want kids with anyone other than Koko. Cyrus didn't regret his son at all. He did regret the way Koko found out about his existence. He hid CJ from Koko, knowing at some point he'd have to come clean. Cyrus just didn't know how to tell her. There was no chance of reconciliation because of the shit she saw taking place at his apartment. But he was going to give Koko time while he was away to get her mind right because he was going to get his woman back.

That nigga Kaz was going to be a distant memory; if he wasn't already dead. Cyrus tried to shoot his ass in the head but ended up finishing Kurt off. He wasn't the intended target, but karma works in mysterious ways. Cyrus heard Don when he said Kaz wasn't one to be fucked with while they raced away from the scene. He wasn't trying to hear that shit. In Cyrus' mind, he wasn't the one to come for either. There wasn't an ounce of pussy in his blood. When he shot Kaz, he knew a war would follow. Like he said to Kaz's face, he lived that street shit. Kaz had some catching up to do in that department. His ass wasn't built to come for a nigga like Cyrus.

"*The muthafucka was in the game because his paper was long. I been in this shit since I was a shorty. We live in two different worlds,*" Cyrus said to himself. "*At the end of the day, I make my guns clap in real life. That nigga probably only know how to shoot at targets.*"

The ride came to an end faster than Cyrus expected. The vehicle came to a halt, and the sliding door was opened from the outside. Three burly guards stood there with menacing expressions as they glared at Cyrus. One of them recognized him from the last time he was locked up at the facility.

"Damn, Cyrus. I thought we agreed you wouldn't come back to this muthafucka."

"Yeah. Shit happens when the system shady as fuck, Terry."

"You not here to make friends. Let's go," the officer said, pushing him toward the building.

"Man, you know what the fuck it is. We take inmates inside. Why you think we out here waiting? I don't know how y'all run shit in the city, but we don't treat inmates like animals. You can learn a lot from an educated Black man who gets paid less than you but is so much smarter."

"I doubt it, but you can deal with his hot-headed ass. You people always stick together whether right or wrong."

"And the cops don't? Man, get yo' ass away from here with that bullshit. Like I said, I got him."

The officer shot Terry a stern look before heading back to the van. Cyrus didn't want him involved in his shit, but there wasn't anything or anyone that put fear in Terry. He always spoke his mind when he felt someone was being treated unfairly. *The least they can do is fire me* were words Terry used often. He looked after his brothers behind the wall as well as talked to them about getting their lives together.

"Terry, you want us to process him?"

"Nah, Henry. I got him. He's one of the good ones and shouldn't even be back here. Y'all go check on the inmates on the yard."

Both officers nodded and left. As Terry and Cyrus headed to the processing desk, Terry's jaw clenched tightly. He had so much he wanted to say, but it would have to wait until Cyrus was alone in his cell. He was going to make sure Cyrus had a space to himself because by the look of his face, he needed it. He also had to put in an order for medical attention. The gash on his head needed more than a few stitches.

Terry did all the talking while Cyrus stared at the woman behind the desk. Her name was Bethany, and he knew her well. She was the person other than Terry, who looked out for him during his six-month bid. Bethany would bring him food from outside, then bent over for him. Their secret was safe because the snow bunny didn't kiss and tell. Bethany glanced up quickly, before going back to typing.

"He should see the nurse," she said loud enough for Terry to hear.

"I know. Put an order in for me."

"It's already done. As a matter of fact, Miracle is waiting. I sent her an instant message through the system. You're welcome."

Cyrus chuckled because she was still looking out for him as if he hadn't left. She was cool with the jailhouse relationship because she didn't appear to be upset that he hadn't hit her up after his release. If she was, she hid the shit well.

"Good looking. Is he good to go?"

"Yeah. he will be in cell nine. There's already an inmate in there. Hopefully, they get along."

Terry shook his head. "Check to see if there's a vacant one available."

Bethany typed and scrolled for a few moments then smiled before glancing up. "Room twenty-three is vacant. It's in the back of the building but I don't think that would matter. Do you?"

"I believe seclusion will be good for him."

"He's logged in. Make sure he sees the nurse because that cut is pretty bad."

Terry nodded as he led Cyrus through the metal detectors. He stopped at the linen room, grabbing an inmate suit, blankets, and a mat. As they walked the corridor, both men were silent. Terry took the initiative to speak once they were out of earshot of others.

"Cyrus, tell me the police didn't do that to your head."

"Yeah. They whooped my ass at the station on Plymouth. The muthafuckas were talking about all the bogus charges they hit me with. I spoke up about the shit and got cracked a couple times. It's all good."

"No, the fuck it's not! Tell your lawyer everything; leave nothing out. Take this to the media. You got a lawsuit," Terry snapped. "Did you have drugs on you?"

"They planted that shit on me. If the drugs are tested for fingerprints; mine won't be on 'em. I was cuffed for whoopin' a nigga's ass with my fists. Nothing more, nothing less. Far as going through all that suing shit, I'm not for it. All I want is to get out of this muthafucka."

"You crazy! You have a police brutality case. You can't let them get away with what they did to you, Cyrus."

"It's called brutality but the pigs never get convicted for the bullshit they do. Nothing will happen to them, Terry. We both know that. They'll get paid leave and be right back on the streets soon as shit die down. I know who did it, and I'm gon' handle it my way."

"Nah, that's not the way to go, fam."

"It's the only way. If I don't protect myself, nobody will. This system was designed to be against us. I'm not a white muthafucka. I didn't get a pitstop to Burger King. I got my ass whooped and was sent straight to the slammer. I'm tired of the police using their badges to put fear in a nigga. I want to see how hard they are when the shoe is on the other foot. I'm done talking. My head hurts."

Leaving the conversation alone, Terry led him to medical. He knocked on the open door, getting Miracle's attention. She looked up then rose from the desk.

"Hello, Mr. Davis, I'm Miracle. Have a seat so I can take a look." She noticed Cyrus favoring his right side as he moved slowly to climb onto the table. "Remove the cuffs. He's badly hurt."

"You know I'm not supposed to uncuff the inmates."

"Where is he going? You're right here. I need to be able to examine him properly. From the looks of things, he may need hospital transport."

"You can stitch him here. Why would he need to go out for treatment?"

"You walked him back here and didn't notice something is wrong with the right side of his body?"

Miracle was upset because she was tired of inmates coming to the jail battered and abused. No matter how many reports she had written, there was never anything done to the officers responsible. There were a couple instances where the inmates ended up dying from their wounds because they weren't taken to the hospital in a timely manner. When would the shit end? Terry closed the door then proceeded to remove the cuffs from Cyrus' wrists. Miracle watched his every move and her eyes turned to slits at the sight of the welts that were left behind from the cuffs being extremely tight.

"This is ridiculous," she said, pulling on gloves. "I'll clean and bandage your wrists, then I'll take a look at your head. From a glance, you'll need six to eight stitches. But I will know for sure shortly."

Miracle retrieved her phone from her purse, taking pictures of his injuries. It was against the rules, but she didn't give a damn. She wanted proof of what she witnessed and planned to hand the evidence over to Cyrus' lawyer with a smile. After recording his injuries, she worked diligently on his wounds. Miracle took extra care closing the gash so there would barely be a scar once it healed. He winced with every stick and pull, but the discomfort never revealed itself on his face. Applying a thin layer of ointment, Miracle stepped back to observe her work.

"Looks pretty good," she smiled. "Now to those ribs of yours. Would you kindly remove your shirt for me?"

Cyrus struggled to take his arm out of the sleeve. Miracle rushed to assist and gasped loudly as more of his skin was revealed. Cyrus' right side was purple and black with a touch of yellow discoloration. The bruises were so severe that tears welled in Miracle's eyes. She'd seen her share of assaults, but the sight before her was heartbreaking. She took pictures of his bruises with shaky hands.

"I'm going to examine you. I'll have to do a little pushing and probing. Are you okay with that?"

"Do what you gotta do. I already know some of them muthafuckas broke."

Miracle barely touched his side, and Cyrus winced again. "Mr. Davis, you may be correct about having broken bones.

The thing is, I don't know how severe the damage is without X-rays. You need to go to the hospital."

Walking across the room, Miracle damn near snatched the phone off the wall. She tapped her foot repeatedly as she waited for someone to answer on the other end of the line. The scowl lines on her face deepened as she shifted her weight.

"Warden Humphrey, I don't want to hear shit about what you can't do," Miracle stated calmly. "I have yet another inmate on my table who has been assaulted by the police. This needs to be taken seriously, and I have yet to see a damn thing being done."

Cyrus sat in shock at the way Miracle spoke to the warden. He hoped she didn't lose her job by speaking up. It was common for people who defended others on a racial level to lose everything they'd worked for. He could tell she was fed up, and honestly, she had every right to be. Cyrus couldn't hear what the warden was saying, but Miracle clearly didn't like it.

"Do you enjoy your job, Miracle?" Warden Humphrey asked.

"Yes, in fact, I love my job. If I didn't, I would be part of the turn a blind eye committee. Since I'm not, you better tread lightly before throwing idle threats about firing me. I'll be the first person to bring this shit to light. The news media will have a field day with this circus of a judicial system. Not to mention, a high-profile lawyer would love to take on my case. I will sue the fuck out of this state while naming you in the indictment."

"Calm down. There's no need to be angry as you are."

"Are you serious?" Miracle yelled. "Warden Humphrey, you will give permission for this inmate to be escorted to the hospital. He has several broken ribs. I've already stitched the gash on his head."

"Miss Watkins, tape him up and have Terry put him in a cell! This conversation is over!"

"Your children are at home with your wife. Don't ever raise your voice at me! If I'm going to lose my job, I may as well take the aiding and abetting charge too. I'm taking this inmate to the hospital myself. I'll allow my attorney to fight this shit on my behalf."

The line went deathly silent, causing Miracle to hang up. Soon as she turned, the phone rang. She sighed heavily before answering.

"I'll allow him to be escorted to the hospital, but you are not to accompany him. You must learn to do your job and stop letting your emotions cloud your judgment about a bunch of thugs."

"Can I ask you a question?" Miracle asked, fighting to stay calm.

"Sure."

"How many Caucasian inmates have come into this facility battered and bloody?"

"Miss Watkins—"

"Dr. Watkins. You will respect my title as I do yours. But continue," Miracle spat.

"There have been a fair percentage of Caucasian inmates who have been roughed up upon entry. Favoritism is not something we do here. Everyone is treated equally because crime is crime, no matter who commits it. Miracle—"

"It's Dr. Watkins from this day forward. You're right; favoritism isn't what's happening. It's racism!"

"You will not bring race into this discussion!"

"Oh, but I am, because it's the truth you refuse to see. In fact, you're part of the problem. African Americans get killed with their hands in the air without a weapon or mysteriously end up dead in a jail cell. Caucasians can crash into patrol cars, swing knives and crowbars, or shoot up a fuckin' school and still live to stand trial! Don't tell me not to bring race into this because it's been in the chat long before me!"

"I'm telling you now, if I see anything on the news about anything happening to Mr. Davis after this conversation, I'm telling everything I know. You and this corrupt ass system can kiss my ass. I quit!"

Miracle slammed the receiver onto the base, tears rolling down her face. As she gathered her belongings, she addressed Terry. "Find out who will be accompanying this gentleman to the hospital. I'd feel better if it were you. I don't trust Warden Humphrey to keep him safe at this point. Keep an eye on him."

Cyrus only heard Miracle's side of the argument, and he appreciated how she stood up for him and every other Black inmate who had been booked into the facility. What didn't sit right with him was her quitting. He could tell she loved what she did as a doctor.

"Thanks for going over and beyond. You really didn't have to," Cyrus said.

"I did because I'm tired of the same shit transpiring with no results or prosecution. Watch yourself in here," Miracle said, slinging her purse over her shoulder. "Give me your lawyer's information. I'll present him with the evidence of your injuries because that's the only proof you'll have of what happened. All evidence will be gone once you heal, but I got you."

Cyrus recited Jesse's information as Miracle scribbled diligently on a notepad. He knew his stay in the facility would be short-lived once Jesse was informed. Miracle walked out with no intention of returning. In the meantime, Cyrus had a feeling life on lock was about to be one for the books. He was going to feel the backlash from the altercation between Miracle and the warden.

# Chapter 6

"Come on, Pax," Kelly whined. "You have to take your medicine."

"I don't have to do shit but stay Black and die."

Pax shot Kelly a menacing glare, but she could see the sorrow and concern in his eyes. He'd been rebelling since Kaz hadn't been around. Pax was on edge. He wasn't sleeping well, barely eating, and was giving Kelly hell at every turn. She was worried about his health because the Pax Kelly knew was nowhere in the building. She tried her best to resist lashing out at him, but it was becoming too hard to contain. All she needed him to do was take his meds.

"Your stubborn ass isn't dying anytime soon, so stop this madness and take the medicine!"

"I'll do so when my son walks through the door! Leave me alone, woman," Pax yelled. "Why are you even here? I don't need anyone to take care of me. Get out of my house!"

"As you stated, I'll leave when your son walks through that door. Until then, take the medicine. You'll feel a sense of normalcy when you do."

Kelly softened her tone in hopes of calming her favorite client. It hurt her heart to see Pax in the state he was in. Kaz had been gone four days, and his grandfather feared something happened to him. Kelly reassured him that Kaz was perfectly fine; he wasn't having it.

Instead of leaving as Pax demanded, Kelly stepped out of the room and pulled her phone from her pocket. She tried to refrain from calling Kaz, but she didn't have much of a choice at that point. The phone barely rang before Kaz answered.

"Kelly, is everything okay?"

"Actually, no. I need you to talk to Pax so he'd know you're okay. He hasn't taken his medicine in two days, and he's been pretty rambunctious."

"Why haven't you contacted me before now?"

"You were away on business, and I didn't want to disturb you."

"I understand, but nothing is more important to me than my grandfather. Never hesitate to call me whenever there's concern about his health. I should be back in about three hours. I'm boarding the plane as we speak. In the meantime, put the stubborn mule on the phone, please."

"I'm sorry, Mr. St. Claire. I should've—"

"You have nothing to be sorry for, Kelly. You've been nothing short of great when it comes to Pax. Thank you for putting up with his bullshit because I know he can be a handful at times."

"I wouldn't be me if I gave up on him. I know he acted the way he did out of concern for your safety."

Kaz didn't reply to what Kelly said. He was shocked to hear he had something to do with Pax's refusal to cooperate and take his meds. He listened while she fought for his grandfather to take the phone. When she told him Kaz was on the line, Pax adjusted himself in the recliner before holding his hand out. Placing the device to his ear, Pax breathed deeply.

"Paw Paw, what's going on with you?" Kaz asked softly.

"When are you coming back? I had a dream you were hurt."

"I'm on my way now. I'll be there in a few hours. Don't worry about me. I need you to take your medicine for Kelly. Paw Paw, you know it's important so you can get better."

"Stop lying to me. That medicine isn't going to make me better. It's only keeping me alive longer. I'll take the shit only because I know you're alright. Hurry up and get here. I have a gut feeling things are about to go wrong."

"Nothing's going to happen to me or anyone else, Paw Paw. You're thinking this way because of the lack of medication in your system. Once you take your dosage for the day, you'll be fine after a nap. I have to get off the phone because the pilot is ready to take off. I'll see you soon, old man. I love you."

"I love you too, son."

Pax held the phone to his chest as Kelly stood by his side. "Why are you still standing there? Get the medicine, woman."

Retrieving the small cup with four pills inside, Kelly held it out to him along with a bottle of water. Pax didn't hesitate, taking the medicine, then turned to her with his tongue lifted to show he had swallowed them all. She couldn't do anything but smile, even though she was upset with him. Kaz proved what Kelly told him all along; his grandson was fine. She tucked the blanket around his body as she set the water on the coffee table.

It didn't take long for Pax to drift off into a deep sleep. Kelly was staying on for the next shift because the caretaker who usually came in after her had called off the night before. She was relieved to know Kazimir was on his way back. Kelly took the time she had to herself to relax; then she would start lunch so it would be ready once Pax woke up.

As she lay back on the couch, her phone chimed with a text message. Groaning, Kelly got up and took her device from Pax's hand. He didn't budge, which made her chuckle softly. The handsome man was sleeping like a baby, and it was much needed.

Kelly opened the text as she sat on the sofa. She didn't recognize the number, but she could hear the venom seeping from every word she read. Her hands trembled as tears fell from her eyes. The sound of her heart beating resounded through her ears.

"How the hell did he find me?" she asked lowly.

Reading the text for the tenth time, Kelly read it once again.

***(327) 555-0319****: I hope you didn't think you could run forever, my sweet Kelis. In due time, you will see me again. Nothing can keep you away from me. I'll be seeing you soon, love.*

Kelly was scared out of her mind. The thought of Jacoby getting hold of her number did something to her mental. She thought she had run far enough for him not to find her, but obviously, she was wrong. It had been two years of peace, and now Kelly was ready to run again.

She got up from the sofa and looked out of the window. She didn't see anything out of the ordinary, so she calmed down a little bit. Her heart was still beating a mile a minute, but she knew long as she was in the St. Claire residence, she would be safe. The relationship she had with Jacoby played in her mind like a movie, causing her to collapse into the nearest chair.

*Jacoby Warfield was a 6'2", dark-skinned nigga who talked Kelly right out of her silk panties. Everything was good between them in the beginning. Jacoby had gone out of his way to win Kelly's heart. He opened doors, pulled out chairs, and kept her smiling. Life was great the first two years they were dating. It wasn't until her grandmother became ill and Kelly had to go on leave from her job to care for her.*

*Kelly was the charge nurse at UAB in Birmingham, Alabama. She made great money and loved what she did at the hospital, but she had to put her career on hold to take care of the woman who had taken care of her since she was thirteen. Kelly spent countless nights at the hospital alongside her grandmother, so that meant less time at home with Jacoby. He wanted her to choose him over her blood. Every day, they argued about how much she was away.*

*Jacoby started drinking heavily because, in his mind, Kelly wasn't always at the hospital. He felt she was cheating, even though her grandmother had suffered a massive heart attack and a stroke simultaneously. She was fighting for her life while Kelly was fighting with the man who was supposed to love her through it all.*

*After a month of being admitted, Kelly's grandmother stopped breathing on her own. The doctors did everything they could to bring her back; they succeeded. She was placed on a ventilator to help her breathe and allow her body to rest. Kelly sat in the room with her for two days with no improvements. The doctors told her to go home and rest for a couple days. Kelly took what they said to heart and left her grandmother in their care.*

*When she arrived at the home she shared with Jacoby, it was eerily quiet. Kelly locked the door and was instantly hit in the jaw, causing her to drop everything she was holding on the floor. Her body hit the wall as she fell to her knees. Jacoby stood over her with his fists balled tightly at his sides. The redness in his eyes told Kelly all she needed to know. He was drunk.*

*"Bitch, where the fuck you been? Lie and say you were at the hospital, and I'm gon' whoop yo' ass!"*

*"I—I was at the hospital, Coby. You know what's going on with Granny. She's on life support," Kelly cried.*

*"I don't give a fuck what she's on! Your obligation is in this house, muthafucka! If your grandmother is unresponsive, why would you be sitting in a room doing nothing? Bitch, you was with a nigga!"*

*Jacoby kicked her in the back, then grabbed her by the hair a top her head. Dragging her across the room, he slung her onto the sofa as she felt her hair being ripped from the roots of her scalp. Kelly screamed loudly, and he quickly punched her in the mouth.*

*"Stop all that shit before these muthafuckas call the law! Clean this damn house from top to bottom. I'm going to*

*handle business. When I get back, this shit better be spotless, with hot food waiting for me to eat."*

*Jacoby left, slamming the door behind him, as Kelly cried silently. She looked around the room and, for the first time, noticed all the garbage scattered about. There were at least five empty bottles of Don Julio on the coffee table, pizza boxes with crust on the floor, and several fast-food bags with half-eaten food still inside. The living room looked like a pigsty.*

*That was the first time Jacoby put his hands on her, but it wouldn't be the last. Throughout the months her grandmother fought to stay alive, the cycle repeated itself often. Kelly suffered broken ribs, black eyes, and he even knocked out several of her teeth. If it wasn't for her dental plan and her good credit, she would've been walking around looking like a jack-o'-lantern.*

*Kelly knew getting her ass whooped on the regular wasn't what she'd signed up for. Getting out was her secondary priority after seeing after her grandmother. She started her exit plan by moving her money into another account. Kelly didn't move all her finances because Jacoby would become suspicious. She left enough for him to buy the alcohol he drank to fuck his liver up worse than it already was.*

*During that time, Jacoby lost his job and expected Kelly to take care of him. She informed the owner of the home she rented that she would be moving. Kelly couldn't give a specific date, but she promised to pay two months in advance to give them time to put the house on the market when the time came.*

*Spending the majority of her time at the hospital, Kelly cried, knowing she would have to make the decision to take her grandmother off life support. She wasn't ready. Instead, she started making the arrangements for her funeral. Kelly and her grandmother talked often about her final days on earth, and Kelly knew exactly what the woman she loved wanted. It took a month for Kelly to pull the plug, and it was the hardest thing she ever had to do.*

*She reached out to family members who never called to check on her grandmother and told them she had passed on. Not only did Kelly have to fight with Jacoby, but she also ended up having it out with family about life insurance money they weren't even entitled to. Kelly was the beneficiary of her grandmother's estate. Everything was left to her. One point two million dollars, and the house all belonged to Kelly. She didn't waste her time arguing with her greedy ass family members.*

*Cremation was what her grandmother paid for because she always said she didn't want to be buried in a box. Of course, her family wanted a funeral, but Kelly had specific orders; her grandmother didn't want people looking down on her with fake tears. It was tough keeping her feelings at bay around Jacoby. She continued to tell him she was going to the hospital to put her plans in motion. If he knew her grandmother was deceased, he was sure to beat the shit out of her.*

*Kelly put her grandmother's house up for sale and donated her clothes and furniture to the Salvation Army. She kept photos, jewelry, and a couple stuffed animals her grandmother loved. After the cremation service, Kelly got in her car and drove off. She stopped at a gas station to fill her tank before hitting the highway with no destination in mind. The weight on her shoulders slowly dissipated the farther she drove. It was only a matter of time before Jacoby realized she was gone for good.*

*Kelly didn't care how he would survive because she had closed the account before leaving the house. She also contacted the owner of the house to let them know she had moved out. Jacoby was about to be a homeless nigga and didn't even know it. Kelly changed her number and wasn't going to look back.*

Now, two years later, the devil was back to turn her life upside down. Kelly had gone over and beyond to stay hidden. She was born Kelis Gray, and she changed her name to Kelly, keeping Gray because it had her granny's blood on it. She didn't have to work; she chose to because she loved taking care of people. Kelly had enough money to last the rest of her life because she invested in a few vending machines at several fitness centers to accumulate a monthly income.

The last thing she wanted to do was bring her problems to the St. Claire residence. She had to leave before Jacoby found out where she lived and followed her. Putting Pax in danger was something she didn't want to happen.

Wiping the tears from her face, Kelly went into the kitchen to start lunch for Pax. She dreaded telling Kaz he had to find another caretaker for his grandfather without exposing her truth.

***

Kaz was exhausted when he stepped out of Steelo's vehicle. He wasn't planning to come over to Pax's home until the following day; until Kelly called. His grandfather needed to lay his sights on Kaz in order to get back to himself. Knowing he'd been shot, Kaz knew he would have a lot of questions to answer. He was going to stretch the truth the same way he had done with Stephan; at least, that was his plan.

"Thanks, bro. I'll get up with you later. See what you can find on the nigga Cyrus."

"I'm already ten steps ahead of you. I'll be sure to keep you posted. For now, I have to ride through the traps to do a massive pickup," Steelo said. "Get some sleep too, nigga. You look like life is whooping yo' ass. Plus, the legit side of business needs your attention."

"The legit runs itself. All I have to do is sit behind a computer and click a few buttons. This illegal shit is what's getting under my fuckin' skin. I'm thinking about just getting out and letting you take over, but not before I bury that nigga for shooting me."

"Kaz, I told you to let me handle that shit," Steelo gritted. "Look, go check on Pops. I'll hit yo' line when I get some concrete shit."

Steelo waited for Kaz to close the passenger door, then drove away heated. As he'd stated before, Steelo didn't want his long-time friend to jeopardize what he'd worked so hard to achieve. That pushed him even more to get all the information he would need to eliminate the enemy before Kaz could.

Kaz walked up the steps of his grandfather's home, then slowly put in the code to unlock the door. Soon as he entered the living room, Pax lit up with pure happiness. The excitement left his face as soon as he noticed the sling on Kaz's arm.

"Boy, I knew something was wrong! What happened to you?"

"I was handling business in Minnesota and got caught in a drive-by shooting," Kaz lied. "The bullet tore a muscle in my shoulder, but it's nothing serious."

"You being shot is bad enough. I told Brown Suga you were hurt. She didn't believe me. Then that other evil-ass woman was here trying to kill me by stuffing pills down my throat. I want you to fire her."

Kelly scowled at Pax and shook her head. "Mr. Pax, that was me, and I didn't shove anything down your throat. If you had taken your medicine, you wouldn't have mistaken me for someone else."

"Ohhh, that was you, Brown Suga? Well, next time listen to me. I may be losing my mind, but I know when my son is hurt."

Kaz took a seat on the sofa next to the recliner Pax was in. Cradling his arm, he closed his eyes and took a deep breath. It was time for him to take the pain meds the doctor prescribed, but Kaz was going to thug it out. He didn't like the way the medication made him sleep. The thought of becoming addicted to the narcotic was also a reason he decided against it. Kelly noticed his discomfort and saw the blood staining his light blue shirt.

She got up to gather a few items from her medical bag before walking over to where Kaz sat. "Mr. St. Claire, you have blood on your shirt. Would it be okay if I check your wound?" Glancing up at her, Kaz nodded but didn't move. "You'll need to take your arm out of the sling and the sleeve of your shirt off so I can get a better look."

Kaz struggled to remove his arm; Kelly assisted. The entire time, Kaz winced in pain. The veins protruded from the side of his head while he gnawed his teeth. The bandage on his shoulder was soaked in blood and stuck to his skin.

"Mr. St. Claire, when were these bandages applied?"

"Thursday. Why?"

"Have you changed them?"

"No. I couldn't do it with one arm. Is something wrong?" he asked with worry.

"Hopefully not. The bandages need to be changed at least once a day. You should also allow the wound to get air while you're inside."

Kelly carefully lifted the first piece of tape from the gauze. She could already tell the dressing was being held by dried blood. Kelly walked away to go back to her bag, then returned with more gauze and saline. She attempted to pull the dressing up, but it didn't budge. As she saturated it with saline, Kelly scolded Kaz.

"The gauze is stuck to your wound. You better pray the stitches stays intact when I'm finished. The dried blood has built up on top, and I have to be very careful trying to remove it." She made sure the dressing was soaked before slowly attempting to remove it.

"Wait! I feel something pulling." Kaz looked up, grabbing her wrist to halt her movements.

Kelly matched his stare until his grip loosened. Pax chortled as he watched the exchange between them. He could see the attraction in both their eyes, and he just had to speak on it.

"Hurry up and change that shit so y'all can go upstairs and get ya rocks off. There's no need to suppress the sexual tension; I can smell the euphoria in the air."

"Knock it off, Paw Paw. It's not that type of party. I would never mix business with pleasure. Kelly, continue, please."

Her cheeks flushed with color at Pax's words. He caught Kelly lusting, and she was embarrassed. After adding more saline, Kelly was able to ease the dressing away from the wound. She cleaned the blood completely, then her brows furrowed. There was a bit of redness around the area, letting her know it wasn't properly cared for.

"Kaz, you can clean around the site with warm water and mild soap. It has been over forty-eight hours since the stitches were placed. Make sure you pat it dry afterward. I'll give you some saline to take with you."

"Thank you, Kelly. That won't be necessary. I'll just come back here and pay you to take care of it for me."

"About that… we'll discuss it when I'm done."

Kelly was silent as she finished tending to him. She knew the time would present itself for her to break the news of her resignation. As she applied the last piece of tape to secure the dressing, Kelly gathered the soiled bandages to throw away. She returned and did the same with her supplies, placing them back into her bag. She went into the kitchen, and tears fell from her eyes.

"I thought you wanted to talk, Kelly," Kaz yelled.

She wiped the tears from her face and blew her nose with a paper towel. The dread of telling Kaz she could no longer care for Pax had her emotional. She hoped both men would understand why she had to step out of her position without getting upset about the short notice. Finally pulling herself together, Kelly made her way back into the room.

"Mr. St. Claire, I need to discuss my position with you," Kelly said as she sat on the loveseat across from Kaz.

"Why are you crying?" he asked, taking in her red eyes.

With her head held low, Kelly played with the paper towel in her hands. She didn't know where to start the conversation. Kaz was the type to ask questions until he was satisfied with the answers. Kelly just wanted to explain that she was leaving, and only God knew what state she would end up in because she didn't have a clue. She just wanted to disappear for the second time and pray Jacoby never found her.

"Are you going to answer?"

Kelly worked up the nerve to give Kaz eye contact. She could feel her anxiety rising with every second that passed. Jacoby had her terrified for her life. Kelly knew he was capable of hurting, or even murdering her.

"Okay," she paused. "I have to quit. I'm sorry for the short notice." A lone tear rolled down her cheek, and she wiped it away swiftly. "I want you to find someone who is going to be as compassionate about Pax's health as I am. Again, I'm sorry, Mr. St. Claire."

"If your decision is because of the way Paw Paw behaved in my absence, I apologize. I assure you it wasn't purposely done. We both know his condition played a major part in his actions."

"No, no. The reason I have to leave has absolutely nothing to do with Pax. I love him as if he's my own grandpa. My past has come to disrupt my life, and I have to do whatever it takes to protect myself."

"Who is the man you're running from, Brown Suga?" Pax asked with his eyes closed. "And don't lie. I can hear the shiver in your voice. Whoever it is has hurt you before, and you escaped the abuse."

Pax spoke as if the dementia he suffered from was long gone. His attention was on full alert as he brought up the subject Kelly wanted to avoid. Kaz waited patiently for her response.

"I'm not running from anyone," Kelly whispered, dropping her head.

"Hold your head up," Kaz said softly. "Whatever you've gone through is behind you now. What I want you to do is grow from it with your head held high."

Squaring her shoulders, Kelly looked up, and the terror was evident on her face. "Listen, I'm going to be truthful with you both. My ex has gotten hold of my number somehow. It will be a matter of time before he gets hold of my address. I took the opportunity to leave him and Alabama behind the day my grandmother was cremated. The planning was intense and took a couple of months to pull together. I kept everything hidden from him, including the fact that she had died, so I could disappear without a trace. Now I have to do it all over again. But this time, there will be no planning. I just have to leave."

"You don't have to say another word. You said a lot, even though you left out key points," Kaz said, holding his hand up to silence her. "My offer for you to move in is still on the table. I'll make sure you're protected at all costs."

"I can't stay here, Mr. St. Claire. If he finds me, it would put Pax in danger. I'd never forgive myself if anything happened to him, or you, for that matter."

Kaz sat silently in deep thought for a few minutes. The silence was killing Kelly because she didn't know whether to wait or leave. Neither man responded. Pax appeared to be sleeping, but Kaz hadn't said a word. Standing to her feet, Kelly decided to lessen the burden she felt she was being to the St. Claire family.

"Sit down, Kelly."

"No, I have to head home to pack." She moved to round the coffee table, but Kaz stopped her by placing his hand gently on her arm.

"Being out there alone with a deranged ex who's searching high and low for you is the wrong thing to do. You're better off staying here. Fuck the clothes and whatever else you plan to load into your car. All that material shit will still be scattered around somewhere on this earth after that nigga kills you! I'll buy whatever you need to start over. Your life isn't worth gambling with, Kelly. Plus, how long do you think you can run?"

"Jacoby is a very wicked man!" Kelly yelled.

"And I'm the big bad muthafuckin' wolf! Give me his full name, last known address, and he'll be gone in no time."

"Kellan! What did I tell you about bringing that street shit in here? Leave that crap outside or get the fuck out!" Pax chastised.

"I'm not my father, Paw Paw. This is Kazimir in the flesh. I'm sorry if I sound like him, but I meant what I said. These niggas are out here harassing females who want nothing to do with them, and I'm tired of reading about the shit. I'd rather protect Kelly than find out later she's dead and gone. We're the only family she has that gives a damn about her."

Kelly cried as she listened to Kaz say she was family. Her biological family didn't give a damn about her because she wouldn't come to their rescue financially. Kelly refused to reward anyone for not giving a fuck about her grandmother. It made her feel good to know she had people in her corner. With no plan in motion, Kelly felt the offer Kaz presented was one she shouldn't pass up.

"I'm not taking no for an answer. You'll stay here with Paw Paw, and that's final. There are plenty of rooms in this big-ass house; choose one. You can make it your own by decorating any way you see fit. Make a list, and I'll pay the cost."

"You are safe, Kelly." Rising from his seat, Kaz walked over and pulled her into a hug. Kelly cried like a baby. "This is the last time I want to see you shed a tear over this shit. I got you. Kelly, you're like the little sister I never had. I'm ready to be the overprotective brother who kicks ass for you."

"Thank you so much," she said, stepping out of his arms. "I really appreciate what you're doing for me. I owe you tremendously."

"You don't owe me anything. Then again, there is one thing I want from you."

"What's that?"

"For you to be happy. Enjoy your life and have fun while doing it."

Nodding, she forced a smile. "I can do that. I have a confession."

"Okay, Usher. I'm listening," Kaz said, trying to lighten the mood.

"My name isn't Kelly. It's actually Kelis. Kelis Gray."

Waving his hand at her, Kaz smirked. "You're forever Kelly to me. Changing who you are to hide was smart, but as you can see, it didn't work. Embrace who you are and never allow anyone to break you down to the point of losing your true self."

"I needed to hear that. Thank you."

Pax cleared his throat, getting both of their attention. Shaking his head, he started laughing. Kaz was confused because nothing funny had been said, but Pax was laughing like a hyena.

"Fill us in on the joke, Paw Paw. We want to laugh too."

"That damn girl ain't trying to be your sister," Pax laughed. "You got twenty-twenty vision and are blinder than a bat. That woman's been following your movements since the first day y'all met; and that was almost a year ago. Your little sister." Pax laughed uncontrollably, shaking his head.

"Pax, it's ironic you can remember things when you want to be messy, but you're not wrong. I did have a crush on Mr. St. Claire for a while; not anymore because he's married. I never stood a chance, and I knew that. So, stop trying to stir up stuff."

"You could've gotten him to leave that white woman had you listened. It's your loss, Brown Suga. Now you'll be around here getting old with me. Get ready to pull out the Bengay and medicated pads for the aches and pains you'll be dealing with soon."

Kelly hugged Kaz once more before heading across the room to go upstairs. She turned briefly to face him. "I need a favor from you. Can you go with me to my apartment so I can get some important papers and a few other things?"

"Yeah, we can do it tomorrow. I'll call my friend Stephan to come with us. You might need help carrying things, and I'm a one-arm bandit."

"Okay. Call me with the time, and I'll be ready. Thanks again, Mr. St. Claire."

"Take his ass upstairs with you, Brown Suga. I bet he won't pass up the invite," Pax chortled.

"I think it's time for you to take a nap. Come on, old man. I have to get home to love on Alessia."

Kaz helped his grandfather to his room. He was pretty exhausted from traveling early and trying to analyze what Kelly was currently going through. Kaz wanted her ex to show up because he was going to beat his ass like the bitch he was. Nothing could convince him the nigga wasn't beating on her. He would bet all the money in his bank account he was right. Kaz mentally added Jacoby to the list in his head. Right under Cyrus' pussy ass.

# Chapter 7

Sheree entered her mother's house with CJ on her hip. She hadn't heard from Cyrus in over two weeks, and he wasn't answering his phone. In fact, it kept going straight to voicemail. Sheree regretted having the threesome with him and Jackie. It put a wedge between them, and she didn't like how he was neglecting his son. Cyrus and CJ had a bond, so when he wasn't around, Sheree had to deal with the whining and temper tantrums. Bringing him to Debbie's would give her a break for a few days.

Sheree had an interview at the post office for a mailroom clerk position. She took what Cyrus said into consideration and started looking for work. Sheree had gotten calls for interviews from Starbucks, Amazon, UPS, and even her previous job at Arby's. The post office was the first interview on the list, and she hoped like hell she landed the job. Working at the post office could damn sure turn into a lucrative career for her.

Depending on Cyrus for money was Sheree's plan in the beginning, but with him being locked up, she couldn't continue to be a stay-at-home mom. The way she pictured having a man who would be there financially wasn't what it was in reality. She had to get back to making her own money again because Cyrus could take away everything she was used to in the drop of an eye; which he had already done.

"Nannie! Nannie!" CJ screamed at the top of his lungs for his grandma.

"Is that my big boy?"

CJ struggled to get down to the floor before Sheree finally lowered him to his feet. He took off running to the kitchen where he believed his grandma was. CJ was correct. Debbie put the dish rag on the counter as she was rushed with a hug to her legs. Outside of his daddy, the little boy loved his Nannie.

"Oh Lord, you are getting heavy," Debbie exclaimed, picking him up and tickling his sides.

CJ giggled in delight as he squealed, "Stop," while squirming around happily. Sheree entered the room, and Debbie's demeanor changed. Rolling her eyes, she turned her attention back to her grandbaby. She kissed his chubby cheeks because she missed CJ so much.

"Go play with your toys while I finish cooking. Uncle Steve is in there too."

CJ took off running to harass his uncle. The smile on Debbie's face faded slowly.

"Where the fuck you been, Sheree? I've been calling you for weeks, and you just pop up at my house like it's nothing."

"It's not even like that, Ma. Cyrus hasn't been to the house, and I've been trying to find him. CJ been acting up because he misses his daddy," Sheree said, sitting at the table.

"Fuck Cyrus! That muthafucka in jail."

"What you talking about? When did he get locked up, and how do you know?" Sheree asked in a defensive tone.

"Daphne called the police on his ass when he went over there and beat the shit out of Jermaine. He brought his disrespectful ass over here first, looking for Jojo, talking about he stole some money from some damn big-time drug dealer. I never liked his ass because he tries to keep you away from us."

"To be honest, Ma, Cyrus has never kept me away from y'all. He just don't agree with y'all smoking around CJ, knowing he has asthma. That's neither here nor there, though. Cyrus shouldn't have come here or to Aunt Daph's house with the mess."

"Cyrus don't have to agree with what I do in *my* house! I pay the bills around here. The only thing he has control over is your ass," Debbie said, lighting a cigarette and taking a long drag. Blowing the smoke from her nose, she stared her daughter down. "You allowed money and material shit to make you forget who would be there when that muthafucka put you out on the street."

"I have his son. Cyrus is not going to put us out of nothing. You talking about I forgot about my family, but that's a lie. I'm always down for blood. You always talking about Cyrus' money as if I haven't helped you several times when things were tight around here. His money is my money, and mine is yours. So you can keep that."

"Sheree, you have been there for me through it all, and from this point on, I won't call you for shit else."

Debbie turned back to her meal on the stove while Sheree sat quietly, wondering why Cyrus hadn't reached out to her since he'd been locked up. She was in the middle of the bullshit between her man and her family. Sheree hated the predicament she was put in. She knew in a matter of time she would have to choose a side.

"Is Jermaine okay?" she asked.

"He is now. He had a mild concussion and a few bumps and bruises. His arm is broken, but other than that, he good. I won't promise your baby daddy will be fine after he gets out of jail. Your cousins and brothers are waiting to fuck him up on sight."

"I don't have anything to do with that. At the end of the day, Cyrus is still CJ's father."

The sound of someone coming into the house caused both Sheree and Debbie to look toward the entrance of the kitchen. Jojo walked in with Jackie behind him. Sheree had the biggest frown on her face as she watched the woman who was fucking on her baby daddy standing next to her brother.

After hearing Cyrus was arrested for assaulting her cousin, Sheree couldn't understand why Jackie would even be in the company of Jojo. Jackie wouldn't turn her back on Cyrus, and that alone had Sheree looking at her funny.

"What y'all in here talking about?" Jojo asked, stepping further into the kitchen.

"First of all, who have you brought into my house?" Debbie asked with her hand on her hip.

"Chill out, Ma. This my girl, Jackie."

"Your girl?" Sheree snickered. "Since when?"

"Since I agreed to be his woman. The fuck," Jackie snarled.

Jojo pulled her to him and kissed her on the cheek. The motion told Jackie he would handle his sister accordingly. She would hate to beat Sheree's ass in her mama's house, but if she had to do it, she would without hesitation. Jackie knew the reason Sheree was acting the way she was, and she hoped like hell the bitch kept her thoughts to herself. Otherwise, her plan wouldn't work.

"Sheree, I don't ask questions about yo' nigga, so stay out of my business."

"Do you even know who you're dealing with is the question," Sheree shot back.

"And you know the nigga you fuckin' with? I think not! His ass is good as dead soon as I catch up with him. He's lucky the law made it to Aunt Daph's house before I did. The muthafucka would be casket ready by now."

"Like I told Ma, Cyrus is still CJ's daddy at the end of the day. I have nothing to do with whatever beef y'all have with him. All this talk about killing him because he whooped Jermaine's ass is fucked up. Fight that shit out like men and leave it at that. Without Cyrus, all you muthafuckas would be homeless. Let's keep it a buck."

Sheree got up to leave, but Debbie's words hit her in the chest.

"Bitch, there you go taking up for that piece of shit again. Since you all about your man, I hope you stand beside him when he whoops your ass. Keep that same energy because you better not come to my damn house for help. I'm gon' show you how it feels to not have a mother's love when you need it most. A nigga come and go, but this family stick together forever. You outta your damn mind talking about without that stupid muthafucka I'd be homeless."

Debbie scoffed. "Long as I got a pussy, Mama will never be broke. I still get mine. I just tucked that shit away to spend your baby daddy's money. I hope your smart, stupid ass been doing the same. Cyrus is going to turn his back on your goofy ass."

"CJ, come on!" Sheree yelled. "It's time to go."

Debbie was talking as if she never needed her daughter, and it hurt Sheree to the core. At that point, she realized blood doesn't make one family. Her mother basically used her for the help she obviously didn't really need. They hated Cyrus so much but never turned down the money he was hustling hard for in order to support Sheree and his son. If Cyrus knew how much money she handed over to her mother willingly, he would cut Sheree off without thought. But for Debbie to openly admit she was saving her money was a low blow. Whether her family liked it or not, Sheree was going to stand by Cyrus no matter what they thought.

"You can leave, but CJ stays. Isn't that why you brought him over? I'll bring him home in a few days."

Sheree agreed with her mother and didn't want to put her son in the middle of their mess. Debbie loved CJ and wouldn't do anything to harm him because she hated his father. Without arguing further, Sheree grabbed her purse to leave her mother's home. Jackie stood with a wicked smile, and Sheree's senses were tingling to knock her head clean the fuck off. Instead, she turned to Jojo, leaning in to whisper in his ear.

"She's going to be your downfall. Jackie ain't shit, and she will be the death of you. There is no reason for me to go further because the scent on your top lip got you in a trance. Remember, I am my brother's keeper and will always have your back."

With that, Sheree left her mother's home without her son. As soon as she sat in her car, the phone rang. An unfamiliar number appeared on the screen, and Sheree answered, then put the call on speaker, knowing it was probably another job opportunity for her. Shifting the gear into drive, she pulled off.

"Hello."

"Aye, Ree," Cyrus' voice came through the speaker. "How you doing?"

"How you think I'm doing, Cyrus? I haven't talked to you in weeks, then I find out you are in jail. Why are you calling me now? Wait, are you out?"

"Nah, I had my homie call on three-way. Look, I don't have too much time on here. I wanted to make sure you and CJ is straight."

"Cyrus, why didn't you tell me you and my family was into it? This shit is going to get ugly."

"What me and yo' people got going on has nothing to do with you. I'll never want you to choose between me and yo' family. I'm sure you know what went down, and I'll understand if you move on from me. There's only so much I can say to you, but I'm sure you know what I'm talking about."

"Actually, I don't, but I'm not going to turn my back on you. Do you have a bond?"

"I don't have one as of yet. My court hearing is next Tuesday, and I'll find out what will happen then. Sheree, all I want you to do is take care of my son. This is my situation, and I don't want you to stress about it. I will continue to take care of y'all even though I'm not on the street physically."

Sheree continued to drive silently as she listened to Cyrus. She fought back the tears that threatened to fall from her eyes. Sheree missed Cyrus so much. Even though the last time they communicated was after the incident at his apartment, she still loved him and didn't want him to be in jail. A car merged in front of her without using its signal. Sheree pressed the horn repeatedly while stepping on the brake to avoid rear-ending the vehicle.

"Stupid ass!" she yelled.

"Where are you?" Cyrus asked.

"I'm on my way to an interview at the post office."

"Oh shit, you about to be a working woman," Cyrus laughed. Sheree didn't. "Where is my son?"

"He's at my mama's house. Before you start talking crazy, I didn't have a choice. You not here to keep him for me, so I took him over there."

"You could've called Jackie. She would've watched him. I don't want him around them muthafuckas."

"Jackie wouldn't have done nothing. She's too busy fucking my brother. Yeah, your sneaky link is sucking on your opp. Now maybe you will knock her ass off the pedestal you have her on. For Jackie to be your best friend, her loyalty isn't with you."

*You have sixty seconds left for this call.*

The automated voice cut into the conversation. Cyrus didn't say another word for the entire minute remaining. Sheree kept driving, but the three beeps indicated the call ended. She didn't feel bad about telling Cyrus who Jackie was dealing with. He needed to know, and it just so happened she was the one to let the cat out the bag. It was up to Cyrus to decide what he would do with the information.

Sheree pulled into the parking lot of the post office on Elm Street and parked close to the door. She sat for a few minutes to gather her thoughts before getting out to complete her interview. Sheree entered the building and informed the clerk why she was there. An hour later, Sheree exited the building as a new employee of the United States Postal Service. She was set to start orientation the following Wednesday because she wanted to be front and center at Cyrus' court hearing. Since she was child-free, Sheree headed home to get some much-needed sleep.

# Chapter 8

Koko watched as the delivery truck pulled away from her studio. She and Horace had just finished a major project for Warner Brothers. The life-size cake of Beetlejuice was on its way to California. It took a week to complete, and Koko was finally able to relax after doing her best to perfect the job. She pulled it off because the piece was phenomenal; and it tasted good, too. Koko made miniature cakes and handed them out to passersby outside of the studio, and they loved every morsel. That alone gave her the confidence she needed, knowing how the production would love the taste of her creation. Soon as she entered the studio, Horace was giving her the flowers she deserved for the work they had put in.

"You did that, friend!" he clapped as he walked over to give her a hug. "The cake is going to give Michael Keaton a run for his money because it looked just like my favorite character."

"Thank you, but you put in just as much work as I did. I appreciate all you do for our business."

"Girl, that's what I'm here for." Horace stepped back, folding his arms over his chest. "Why we not in Cali for this reveal? I wanted to wait until the project was complete before I asked."

"Warner Brothers is the big league. With all the shit going on with these celebrities, I'm not too eager to be in the same room with them. Back in the day, I would've been in groupie mode. My work will speak for itself."

Koko made her way to the back of the studio to change her shoes and grab her purse. She was so ready to go home after all the work she put into her latest projects. Going to the post office was the first thing she had to do in the morning because there were a lot of orders she needed to mail out for same-day delivery. Tired was an understatement when referring to how she felt. Koko was overly exhausted.

"What are you doing this weekend?"

Horace startled her when he walked into the office while Koko was tying her shoe. Rising up, she sat down in the nearest chair as she prayed for her heart to stop beating erratically. For the last couple of nights, she'd been having dreams of Cyrus hurting her in the studio. Knowing he was in jail helped, but it didn't stop her from feeling a sense of uneasiness. She was afraid of what he could possibly do to her after she chose herself and not him. Koko hoped it didn't get to that point, but she was not going to ignore the dreams because there was most likely a warning in the message.

"Why are you shaking?" Horace asked, kneeling in front of his friend.

"I'm just tired. What's going on this weekend?"

Koko changed the subject as she reached for her other shoe. Going into what she was worried about with Horace would only rile him up. She felt a headache coming on and didn't want it to surface from him hollering about how he would fuck Cyrus up.

"I see what you did there, and I'm going to leave it alone for now. Anyway, you want to take a trip to Chicago with me?"

Looking up with a questionable stare, Koko tilted her head to the side. "Why are you going there?"

"Well… my lil boo thang invited me to come out on Thursday. I figured I'd invite you because you need to relax."

"Whoa, go back to your boo thang. Who is it? Because you haven't mentioned meeting anyone in Chicago."

"Malcolm and I have been talking since Stephan's event."

"Oh, Malcolm, huh? You've been holding out. That's what we're doing now? Keeping secrets," Koko smirked.

Horace blushed, smiling from ear to ear. "Don't do that. I wanted to make sure things progressed more because I didn't want to jinx it. We've been getting to know one another on many levels, and I love his vibe."

"Tell me more about the man that has my friend so smitten. You didn't mention meeting anyone at the event."

"I know," he sang. "I'm sorry, friend. But he is the owner of a jerk chicken spot called Jamaican Spice Café. He's from Falmouth, Jamaica, and the man is beyond fine. He's dark-skinned, about six-three, with dreads. Malcolm gives hood nigga vibes, and you know how I like 'em. I think those Jamaicans are up there with the O'Block niggas. The difference is this one has legal money."

"Okay! I'm so glad someone got your mind off that O'Block shit," Koko laughed as she leaned back in the chair she was sitting in. "Why would you want me to come along when you're about to be doing the nasty? I don't want to be the third wheel."

"I've already told Malcolm I would talk to you about coming with me. He understands and said he will be there whenever I'm done hanging with you."

"Nah, go ahead and have your fun. I'm going to sit this one out. You deserve to spend time with Malcolm because he has you glowing."

"I'm not taking no for an answer, Koko. I know your schedule because I'm your right-hand man. We already fulfilled all the orders we had, and you will be getting on the plane with me on Thursday. Your flight information is in your email, and I sent everything Jackson would need to upload to social media and the website. So, I don't want to hear any more excuses. We are about to enjoy this fall weather in Chitown."

Horace picked up his man purse and walked out before Koko could protest. He covered all bases because he knew Koko would find something work related to stay in Minnesota. She picked up her phone to make sure Jackson had indeed received what Horace sent to him. The young man had done exactly what he told Koko he would, and it landed him a job as her media manager. Jackson failed to mention he held a degree in graphic design, so when Koko ran into a problem with her website, it was Jackson who came to the rescue. He even updated the site and had been doing excellent work from that day forth.

Once she had that squared away, there was nothing more to be done in the studio. Turning off the lights as she moved toward the exit, Koko activated the alarm and left the building. She got into her vehicle and made a beeline for her apartment. Walking into her place, the smell of gravy covered oxtails, carrots, green beans, potatoes, and onions hit her nostrils. She put them in the crockpot before getting herself together to head to the shop. The only thing she needed to cook was a pot of jasmine rice.

Koko filled a pot and put it on top of the stove with medium heat. She peeled her clothes off as she moved toward her bedroom. A nice hot shower was what she needed before she could relax. In times like that in the past, a good dick massage would've gotten her right. Too bad it wasn't an option for her. The quick shower she took was a source of relief, but she couldn't stay in any longer because her stomach was in her back.

Rushing to the kitchen, Koko had to add more water to the pot for her rice. It had evaporated quickly. Soon as the water came to a boil, she added the rice and waited. Scrolling through her phone, Koko noticed she had an inbox message on her business account. As she read the message, Koko converted back to the invoices she kept of previous orders. The customer's order was back at the studio for the next day's deliveries. Going back to the inbox, Koko read the message once more.

*Kathy Woods:*

*Good evening. I'm reaching out about the order I placed a few weeks ago. It is a shame that I've been waiting so long for two dozen chocolate cookies, and buttercream cupcakes. I'm requesting a full refund immediately. Thank you.*

Koko thought about what Miss Woods stated and knew there was a disclaimer of delays on the website at the time she placed the order. Not wanting to argue, Koko decided then and there she would just refund the money and leave the matter alone. The loss of one customer would bring five more in her place, so she wasn't worried about the money she would return. Keeping it professional was her motto when running Koko Kakes & More.

*I'm sorry for the delay of your order, and I will definitely have no problem sending your money back. I already have your package ready for shipping tomorrow, but that's neither here nor there. Your money will be refunded and available to you within the hour. Thanks for considering Koko Kakes & More.*

Putting the phone on the counter, Koko checked the rice with a smile. It was time to eat. She plated a nice amount of food, then sat down to enjoy her meal. The oxtails were falling from the bone, and the gravy was thick just the way she liked it. With every forkful, she moaned lowly. She was going to sleep good after eating, for sure. Before she knew it, the food was gone, causing her to get up for a second serving. Her phone rang as soon as her butt touched the seat. Grabbing the device, Koko answered quickly so she could get back to eating.

"Hello."

"Miss Simmons, how are you?"

Kaz's baritone automatically hit one of the ten thousand nerves in her clitoris, causing it to harden in the boy shorts she wore. Her nipples followed suit, sending a shiver down her spine. Koko hadn't spoken to him since she left the hotel when he was in town. She tried her best to deviate her mind away from the man she wanted to get the kinks out of her back. The only thing standing between them was his marital status. Koko masturbated while thinking about his lips taking the place of her toy on many occasions.

"You tuned all the way out on me. What do you have going on over there?" Kaz asked, cutting into her thoughts.

"Oh, sorry. I'm in the middle of dinner. I'm fine, though."

"Other than pastries, I didn't think you could cook," he laughed.

"You got jokes. How are you in Chicago assuming I can't cook? Everybody can't afford to have a chef like you, Mr. St. Claire."

"In due time, you will have the best of both worlds. You just have to allow me into your life. I don't understand why you're fighting what is meant to be."

Koko forked food into her mouth before responding. She needed a moment to get her thoughts together. The last thing Koko wanted to do was come off as rude when she stated her truth.

"We both know the reason we cannot be. Once you take care of your situation, we can come back to address this conversation. For now, can we just be friends?"

"I've explained why I'm with Nicolette several times. Our marriage is a business deal; nothing more. Kameeko, you are the woman I want to explore, get to know on all levels, become your best friend, and possibly start a family with. The life I've been living for years is fictitious. There has never been any physical contact between Nicolette and me. So, what do you say about that?"

"Divorce over everything," Koko replied as she continued to eat.

When Kaz didn't say anything after her response, neither did she. The silence grew as time ticked away. Koko could hear the sounds of computer keys clicking rapidly. It seemed

Kaz was in the middle of conducting business, and she didn't want to interfere with what he had going on. Their conversation seemed to have come to an end anyway once she didn't give him the response he was clearly seeking.

"You're working, so call me when you finish."

"No need. I'm wrapping up a conversation with my lawyer. Divorce is what you want; divorce you will get. I'll have a meeting with him Soon as the sun rises to put this shit in motion. I've been married on paper far too long. I want to love on one woman and one woman only."

"Wait, you set a date to resolve your marriage because I said divorce over everything?" Koko asked.

"Hell yeah, I did! My name is Kazimir St. Claire. I don't play with the feelings of anyone I care about. You stated what needed to be done, and I listened, then made it happen. There will be trials and tribulations behind my actions, but that has nothing to do with you. I'm going to handle the shit hands down. For the one I care about, I'll move mountains. Whether it's physically, mentally, emotionally, or financially. T.I. is not the only muthafucka who can say you can have whatever you like."

Kaz was laying it on thick, and Koko loved every bit of what he said. That's all it was for her, though… talk. Being with Cyrus taught her a valuable lesson; never listen to the words coming from one's mouth and pay attention to actions. Koko hated the fact that she was allowing her past relationship to interfere with what could be between her and Kaz, but it wasn't something she could ignore. Kaz was ending his marriage to be with her. It was too soon for both of them to jump into something new.

"You're saying the right things, and I appreciate you taking the steps to dissolve your marriage to be with me. However, the divorce should've taken place long before now if you didn't want to be a husband anymore. In fact, the wedding shouldn't have taken place if you weren't in love with the woman you vowed to love and cherish. That's just my opinion, though. Kaz, you're doing this for me; not for yourself."

"You're right about going through with the wedding. Again, I gave you the backstory. I never wanted to marry Nicolette. I stayed married because of Alessia. Getting a divorce wasn't necessary at the time. I lived my life as a single man the entire marriage. For years, I fucked whoever I wanted without an ounce of remorse. All that shit came to a halt when I met you. Damn near two months passed before I attempted to have sex to get the edge off. My dick wouldn't even get hard. Why? Because I wasn't lying down with you."

Koko listened while Kaz told her about his experience. Still, she didn't budge. She called bullshit, but who was she to battle him about it? By his own admission, Kaz had slept with many women without a hint of being with them long-term or without love. How would she be any different? That was her thought. In her mind, it would be a setup for failure and disappointment. She wasn't going for that. Instead of piggybacking off what he said, she decided to deflect the conversation altogether.

"Um, I have a long day tomorrow. It was good hearing from you. We'll catch up soon. Goodnight, Kaz."

Koko felt bad because she ended the call before he could say anything else. Kaz was persistent with the way he expressed how much he wanted her in his life. The thing about that was the fact they didn't know each other well enough for him to come to that conclusion so easily. Koko contemplated entertaining the notion of seeing where things might transpire between them, but she shook the thought away immediately.

Standing to her feet with plate in hand, Koko headed to the sink to wash the dishes and put away the remaining food she had cooked. She spent the next thirty minutes in the kitchen, then turned the lights off after checking the alarm and front door. Koko settled into her bed as she turned on the TV. *Bad Boys: Ride or Die* had been added to Netflix, and she really wanted to see what Mike and Marcus had in store for their fans. The opening scene started at the same time her phone chimed. She reached for the device, and there was a text from Kaz.

Kaz: *Be in Chicago this weekend. I'm not asking. Don't play with me.*

Another text came through soon after.

Kaz: *You bring the beast out of me, and I'm done playing nice. Now I'm staking claim. You're mine. See you soon, beautiful.*

Koko was conflicted like a muthafucka. She didn't bother to respond; instead, she put the phone beside the remote. With a smile plastered on her face, Koko was excited about the trip to Chicago with Horace. The devil perched on her shoulder like shoulder pads, whispering in her ear. *Allow him to fuck you for the one time, bitch. I mean, I can see the cobwebs coming out of that thang while you're sleep. A roll in the hay has never hurt anyone.*

Turning on her side, Koko squeezed her legs together because her kitty developed a heartbeat, which had her horny as hell. The sound of a text took her attention away from her sexual desires briefly. There was a notification from her bank on the screen. She didn't have to go to the app because the context was there for her to see.

Notification: *Kazimir S sent $5,000.00*

Memo: *This trip is on me. Do something nice for yourself.*

Koko smiled wickedly. "Maybe I could give him some pussy."

She didn't need his money by any means. Koko was impressed because he was making shit happen to see her. The devil was leading her to the dark side, and Koko was prepared to fall down the rabbit hole for the upcoming weekend. She had to make sure to cut the strings after their tryst. Picking up the remote, Koko got comfortable as she started the movie over. She was asleep the moment Marcus collapsed at Mike's reception.

# Chapter 9

Jackie entered her mother's home after a long night with Jojo. What he lacked in funds was made up in dick. The man was hung like a horse with a strong back to match. The positions she was placed in during the duration of their sexcapade prepared her for yoga. Jackie planned to ride that bull until Cyrus touched down. There wasn't shit wrong with a lil bump and grind before killing a nigga.

After they left his mother's house, Jojo questioned her about how his sister was throwing silent shade. Jackie simply told him she had slept with quite a few men, but she was grown. He came back with, *shid, I've had my share of bitches, so that ain't nothing.* If he knew the truth about her fucking his sister, Jojo wouldn't be in tune with the bullshit.

"Ma, where you at?"

Peeking in the kitchen after not seeing Stella in the living room, Jackie checked the rest of the house without finding her mama. She knew she was around somewhere because her car was parked in the driveway. There was one other place she could be, and that was outside on the patio. Noticing the blinds were open, Jackie knew her mother was chilling, probably with a drink in hand. Fall season was Stella's favorite time of the year.

"I've searched this entire house for you. I was about to call the police and file a report."

Jackie stepped out of the door and paused. She locked eyes with Koko, then turned to leave the same way she entered. If looks could kill, Stella would be heading to jail for the murder of her daughter.

"Bring your ass back here," her mother scolded as if she were a child. "Y'all are about to hash this shit out right now. Both of you are my daughters, and I don't like the way y'all are behaving toward one another. It stops today."

"Nah, you only have one daughter, and that's me. She was my best friend. Without me, you wouldn't even know her."

Koko scoffed. "If that's what you call yourself, who needs enemies? My best friend would never do the things you have done behind my back."

Jackie glared at Koko. "You're mad because my loyalty is with Cyrus. It wasn't my place to tell you about Sheree and CJ. That was something he should've told you himself. You seem to forget he was around before you were. How many times did I tell you to leave him alone? You didn't listen, and it's my fault. Get the fuck outta here."

"Watch your mouth, Jackie," Stella warned. "Take a seat."

"I'm good standing." Never breaking eye contact with Koko, Jackie took her silence for weakness and decided to twist the knife deeper. "Had you listened, maybe you wouldn't have lost the baby you wanted so badly by Cyrus. Now you're mad because somebody else brought a healthy baby into the world and he is the daddy."

"Now, Jackie, you're wrong."

"It's okay, Stella. Let her get whatever she's been holding inside off her chest. This may be the only opportunity she has to speak her mind openly to me. Looking back on the day I lost my baby, I realize now it was the best thing to happen to me. I grieved far too long for something I had no control over. Being a baby mama was never part of my life's plan. For you to bring up a moment which almost broke me shows what type of person you are, Jackie."

"Koko—"

"I'm talking," Koko sneered, cutting her off before she could say anything further. "Cyrus will continue to be an ain't shit nigga. Excuse my language, Mama Stella. I'm glad he has his loyal friend and baby mama to keep him busy so he can leave me alone."

"Koko, you want to be relevant in that man's life so bad. He's not thinking about you," Jackie laughed.

"Is that why he left you and Sheree butt naked in his bedroom, then ran after me talking about it's not what I think?" Jackie's eyes bulged. "You know exactly what I'm talking about."

Jackie wanted to tell her version of what Cyrus does, but Koko was about to knock her off the high horse she believed she was on. Glancing at her mother to see if she caught on to what the bitch said, Jackie took a step toward Koko, causing Stella to rise from her seat and stand between the two of them. There wasn't going to be any fighting on her watch.

"Jackie, do not take another step."

"I'm about to swell this hoe up. Her mouth just wrote a check her ass can't cash."

"No, you're not! Now, what is she talking about?" Stella asked.

"She ain't talking about shit!"

Koko smirked. "My so-called friend has been sleeping with Cyrus and his baby mama. This isn't speculation either. I saw them in the act myself. Maybe that is the reason she wanted me to leave him so bad."

Jackie pushed away her mother's arm and charged at Koko. Backing away from Jackie, Koko didn't want to disrespect Stella's home. The truth hurts, but Jackie didn't want her treacherous ways to be known. It would've been less painful if she had just lived in her truth because when she swung and missed, it was game over for Jackie. Koko grabbed her by the front of her shirt, beating her in the face.

"You gon' swell who up? You must've forgotten who the fuck I am. I've told you about running up on me, Jackie!"

Koko screamed as she continued to lump up her face. "You ain't shit and will never be shit! Cyrus got yo' ass dick dumb like he had me, but I'm done with both of y'all. This ass whooping will remind you to steer in the opposite direction whenever you see me."

Jackie fell to the ground and balled up like a fetus. That didn't stop Koko from fighting her, though. She sat on Jackie's chest and hit her until she saw blood. Stella pulled Koko off of her daughter with all the strength she could muster, leaving Jackie lying there with her arms protecting her face.

"Koko, you have to go."

"I'm sorry it came to this, but I'm tired of your daughter coming for me. You were the reason I came over here. Nothing changes between us, Mama. I'll still call you and send you treats via mail. I need you to do one thing for me; keep your daughter away from me. I won't promise not to kick her ass again."

Koko grabbed her purse from the table and left. Stella looked down at her daughter while shaking her head. Jackie sat up, wiping blood from her mouth. The corner of her eye had a small cut, and her cheeks were red. The tears flowed down Jackie's face as she touched the wounds Koko left behind.

"Why are you crying? What you and Cyrus did was wrong. You were supposed to be that girl's friend. You don't do no shit like that to somebody who looked out for you! If I was in her shoes, I would've beat your ass too. Get your life together, Jackie. Stay away from Koko. I told you once; you didn't listen. Now I'm saying it again because next time you may not come out with a few bruises. Cyrus is no good for you either. I won't tell you who to sleep with; that's on you. Any man who needs two women at the same time isn't trying to be committed to one. Remember that shit."

Stella left Jackie where she sat and went into the house. Jackie, on the other hand, was thinking of a way to get back at Koko. She didn't want her mother to know she had lied about sleeping with Cyrus. For one, what she did with her pussy wasn't her business, and two, Jackie never wanted her mother to look at Cyrus differently. Koko put her business out there, and now her mother was disgusted with her. It was cool because she may have gotten her ass beat again, but Koko was going to die behind the shit she pulled.

Her phone rang, and Jackie got up to get her purse. She grabbed the phone as it stopped ringing and saw Lowkey's missed call. While unlocking it, he called back. Not wanting to talk to him, Jackie accepted the call anyway.

"Hello."

"What you doing?" he asked.

"I'm spending time with my mama. What's up?"

"I want to see you. It's been a minute, and a nigga miss you."

"Look, I'm going through some things right now. I need time to get my life together, and entertaining is not one of my interests right now. It was good while it lasted, but I'm focusing on me now."

Lowkey was silent before he hung up the phone. Chasing females was something he didn't do, and it wouldn't start with Jackie. He knew she was lying because he heard she was dealing with that nigga Jojo. None of his workers could find him, but Jackie would know exactly where Jojo laid his head. In due time, Lowkey would find him, and hopefully the bitch with the good pussy wasn't with him when shit went down.

Jackie left her mother's house through the back gate and got in her car. Pulling off, she called Stella to let her know to lock up, then headed home. Soon as she entered her home, Jackie went to the bathroom and grabbed a bottle of witch hazel along with a few cotton balls. The entire right side of her face was swollen, the blood on her bottom lip was caked up, and her eye was starting to turn purple. Koko had done a number on her face. Seeing the results pissed her off even more.

Once she cleaned herself up, Jackie entered her room and sat on the bed. She thought about everything she knew about Koko and what could be done to turn her world upside down. The only thing Koko cared about was Cyrus at one point, but her business was the light of her life. Jackie knew exactly what would make her ex best friend fall to her knees. She would hit her pockets.

A loud knock at the door brought her back to reality because she wasn't expecting anyone to show up at her place.

The knocks became louder, pissing her off. Jackie jumped off the bed, stalking toward the front of her apartment. She was so mad that she didn't even ask who it was before yanking the door open. That was a mistake on her part. Lowkey grabbed her by the throat while pushing her inside, slamming the door behind him. His movements shocked the hell out of her because Jackie wasn't expecting it.

"You thought blowing me off was gon' be sweet?" he snarled. "Yo' hoe ass accepts my money to take care of a bum ass nigga you fuckin'!"

Lowkey's thumb dug deep into her neck, cutting off her air supply. Jackie opened her mouth to speak, but nothing came out. She attempted to defend herself to no avail. The fire in his eyes matched the venom of his words. Jackie didn't know if she would be able to talk her way out of whatever he had heard, but she was damn sure going to try. As she pried his hands from her throat, Lowkey slapped the fuck out of her.

"Jojo is the muthafucka you want to stop fuckin' with me for? That nigga will be dead soon, and hopefully you're nowhere near him when it happens. I told you to stay away from Cyrus, now I'm telling you to stay away from his ass too! Jackie, I will kill you, bitch! Do you think I give my money away freely to just anybody? No, the fuck I don't!"

"You come to my shit jumping to conclusions you know nothing about, Lowkey. Yeah, folks have seen me with him, but it's not on no dating type shit. I'm trying to find out where he stashed the money he and his cousin stole. Jojo can't do nothing for me. Why would I even think about being with him?"

"Muthafuckas seen you kissing this nigga in the mouth. You can't lie to me. If you swapping slob, you suckin' his dick!"

"Wrong! I have not slept with Jojo. You are assuming like everybody else, and it has you out here looking like an ass! Why didn't you just ask instead of putting your hands on me? I've never had a man beat me, and it won't start with you. There is no way we can pursue anything further because you can't control your anger. If you want your money back, I'll give you every fuckin' penny of it."

Lowkey looked down at her before walking out of the apartment. It wasn't about the money he gave her; it was the fact that Jackie was playing in his face. She could say she wasn't fuckin' Jojo, but he knew better. They were, and he was going to catch her lying ass in the act. It was cool, though. Jackie involved herself in some deep shit she wasn't ready for.

Inside, Jackie sat on the floor looking at the blood on her fingers. The hit to the mouth caused the cut Koko had given her to bleed once again. Lowkey put his hands on the wrong woman. Her list of enemies was growing by the hour, turning her into a woman no one would recognize. She eyed the lockbox she kept on the bottom shelf of her entertainment center and smiled wickedly. Cyrus fucked up when he bought her the .38 Ruger handgun and taught her how to use it. She never had to defend herself; therefore, she never carried it on her person. It was time for her to show folks she wasn't a scary bitch.

Going back into her bedroom, Jackie's phone chimed, and she noticed a text from Lowkey. She didn't bother reading it because he violated her in the worst way, and there was nothing more to say. Instead, she took her clothes off as she prepared to shower. The entire time, she pictured herself holding the gun to someone's head and pulling the trigger.

# Chapter 10

Nicolette sat in her chaise by the window while listening to her daughter squeal in delight. Kaz showed up with his arm in a sling and had been home since. It had been some time since he stayed at the house for days and his actions alone had Nicolette wondering what was going on with him. When she asked what happened to his arm, he ignored her. Instead, he spent most of his time with Alessia. Kazimir removed his belongings to the guest room down the hall and that's where he slept. The only time she saw him was when it was time for them to sit down as a family to eat.

The night before, Nicolette was heading to the kitchen when she heard her husband on the phone in his office. She stopped to listen but Kazimir was speaking lowly so she couldn't make out the words. As she turned to walk away his voice elevated a little louder causing her to pause. He was telling someone the reason he was with her was on the account of Alessia. She never witnessed Kazimir explaining their marriage to anyone. He must've been talking to a woman because the conversation wouldn't have been relevant to another man. Nicolette went upstairs before she could hear anything further.

Getting up to take care of her hygiene, Nicolette had plans to ask her husband about what she overheard. The talk with her father didn't put fear in him and she didn't like that. Kazimir was still going to push forward to end their marriage. The woman he was with at the black-tie event disappeared from his life and that was a plus for Nicolette.

She was glad because it meant he wasn't serious about her either.

Nicolette's mind worked nonstop as she stood under the water preparing to wash her hair. She thought about the conversation she had with friend Shelly. She'd finally told her the truth about her marriage to Kazimir. Which she wasn't surprised at all. In fact, Shelly said she figured something was up at the wedding because love was not in the building.

*"How could you tell he wasn't in love with me?" Nicolette asked.*

*"A blind man could see the shit was forced, Nikki. Kazimir didn't even look at you most of the ceremony. And when the preacher said he can kiss the bride, the man kissed you on the cheek as if you were his little sister. I didn't say anything about it because it was your life to live. Now, damn near three years later, the truth comes out. I have one question for you though. Is he Alessia's father?"*

*"No. Kazimir is not her father. I was raped and she is a product of that. My father wasn't enthused about me being pregnant without being married. He demanded to know who knocked me up and I had to tell him about what happened to me. Of course, he found the man that violated me and killed him."*

*Tears rolled down her face as she sat ripping a napkin to shreds. Shelly handed her a cloth napkin to clean up because they were sitting in the middle of a restaurant. She hated to see Nicolette in the position she was in but it was what she signed up for.*

*"Kazimir was forced to marry me because his grandfather owed daddy money," Nicolette paused. "He wants a divorce, Shelly. What am I supposed to do?"*

*"Let his ass go. There's no love in that house, Nikki. You are holding yourself back from receiving the love you deserve. When God made man, he didn't stop at Kazimir St. Claire."*

*"What about Alessia? He has been her father all her life. If I walk away from the marriage, he will not be there for her."*

*"I'm going to stop you there. One thing I do know is, Kazimir loves the hell out of that little girl. He will not leave her out here alone. They have a bond that can't be broken. You cannot use her as a pawn to hold on to the man who was forced to be with you in the first place."*

*"So, I'm supposed to give my husband a divorce to be with another woman?"*

*"No, you're going to sign those papers so you can be free to live a life of love. Not one of convenience."*

*Nicolette thought about what Shelly said and she was right. Being married to Kazimir had been nothing short of a nightmare. She honored her vows by being loyal to him throughout the marriage while he'd gone out to get pussy elsewhere instead of making love to her. Nicolette was tired of getting herself off with toys when she had a husband. Divorcing Kazimir wouldn't be easy for her though. A lot of drama was sure to arise once she told her father about it.*

*"You are right, but daddy will not see things that way. He told Kazimir the only way he would agree to the divorce is if he paid six million dollars."*

*"Guess what? That's between Anthony and Kazimir. You have lived under your father's rules all your life. It's time for you to do what's best for Nicolette now. He will probably try to take you out of his will and may even disown you, but you have been married to a rich man for years; you will be alright. If push comes to shove, you can move in with me until you find a place of your own."*

*"That won't be necessary. Kazimir isn't the type of man to put a child out on the street with nowhere to go. Especially not Alessia. My daughter and I will always have a place to call home."*

Nicolette promised Shelly not to fight Kazimir if the subject presented itself again. She told a bold-faced lie because she wasn't giving up on her marriage that easily. The only reason he was even entertaining the thought was another woman. Nicolette would be the only woman who would live the life of Mrs. St. Claire.

Stepping out of the shower, Nicolette towel dried her brown hair with blonde highlights while staring at herself in the mirror. She took in her appearance and thought, why wouldn't a man like her husband not be attracted to a woman of her caliber? She stood five feet eight inches with skin the color of almond milk, and full kissable lips. Her breast stood at attention with the help of enhancements after giving birth. Her hourglass figure turned heads any time she walked down the street with a nice butt to match. Nicolette was beautiful.

After blow drying her hair, she applied a light coat of makeup before walking back into the bedroom to dress. Entering the closet, Nicolette chose a pair of jeans, a long-sleeved t-shirt, and a pair of black red bottom sneakers. The moment she was dressed, she left the bedroom making her way downstairs. The aroma of pancakes evaded her nostrils. Every morning, she smelled the breakfast her daughter loved since she started eating solid foods. It also was a dead giveaway that Kazimir was in the house.

Rounding the corner, Nicolette witnessed a smile on her daughter's face that she never saw when they were alone together. The scene before her brought out a lot of envy toward the relationship Alessia had with Kazimir. Nicolette forced a smile as she entered the kitchen. Leaning down to show her daughter some love, she planted a kiss on her forehead. Alessia wiped it off in disgust.

"Ewwww! No kisses," she shrieked. "Only daddy."

"Stop that, baby girl," Kaz scolded. "Mommy needs your hugs and kisses too. Okay?"

"No. Mommy is a meanie. She not my friend anymore."

Nicolette sat in the chair across from her husband with a frown. Alessia held her fork out for him to eat some of her pancakes. He accepted without hesitation and it angered

Nicolette even more. Marisol placed a plate containing a bagel, egg whites, and a bowl of fruit in front of her. Slowly eating a piece of cantaloupe, Nicolette grilled Kaz as she watched him interact with her daughter as if she wasn't in the room. Choosing that moment to question Kazimir about what she overheard outside his office door. Nicolette was about to get the answers she craved by hook or crook. Her husband showed her time again that he didn't give a damn about her feelings. So, it should be a very informative conversation and she would know exactly how to move from that day forth.

"Kazimir, is there something you want to talk about?" she asked between bites.

Glancing up, Kazimir cut his eyes at her silently letting her know to choose her words wisely in front of Alessia. "What do you mean?"

"I heard you on the phone last night. Are you making plans to leave me for another woman?"

"We're not going to discuss this in the presence of Alessia." Kazimir took a sip from his coffee mug. "If you don't have anything planned later, we can talk about you listening outside of my office before I head to my meeting."

"I guess you're going to miss the meeting because what I have to say is going to take a while. I won't wait either. I've waited three years already. Now, we can discuss this like adults then come to an agreement on this marriage." Nicolette turned her head. "Marisol, take Alessia into the playroom to finish her breakfast."

Marisol didn't move until Kazimir nodded. She gathered Alessia and her food as Nicolette grilled her from afar. Not able to hold her frustrations in any longer, she jumped up.

"Marisol, when I tell you to do something, you do it! I'm your boss!"

"Nicolette, you are no one's boss. Marisol did what she was supposed to do; wait for me to give her the okay. Mind how you speak to her."

Marisol left the kitchen in a hurry before she could hear what Nicolette would say to hurt her feelings any further. She knew what happened in the kitchen was only the beginning of Nicolette's rage. Marisol hoped Mr. St. Claire would stay in the home longer to save her from the wrath of his wife. After getting Alessia settled, she sat in a chair when Nicolette's yells filled the room. Marisol immediately got up to shut the door.

Back in the kitchen, Nicolette was screaming in Kazimir's face like a madwoman. "Don't ever undermine what I say to her ass! You are the reason she feels she needs to mother my child."

"Get yo' ass out of my face before we have a problem," Kazimir stated calmly. "Marisol is only doing what she's being paid to do. It's not her fault Alessia gravitates to her more than you. That should be a reason for you to mother your child better. Now, I will talk to you when I come back from my meeting."

"No, we are going to talk now. Cancel the meeting, Kazimir."

"Canceling what I have to do isn't an option. You are coming at me as if I killed your dog. What did I do?" he asked.

"It's not what you've done. What you haven't done is more like it. I'm ready to be treated like a wife!"

Shaking his head, Kazimir already knew where the conversation was heading. He thought about what conversation Nicolette wanted to talk about and the only one that could have set her off was the one he had with Koko. He wasn't worried about what she heard because shit was going to hit the fan eventually and Nicolette was going to be upset either way. Sitting back, Kazimir folded his arms over his chest then sat up in the chair.

"Nicolette, for the last time, this marriage happened by default. I'm sorry to say this repeatedly but you aren't getting with the program. I will never love you the way you want. In fact, loving you at all is farfetched."

"Kazimir, you have never even tried to love me. No matter what I've said or done, you overlook the woman you married for a piece of ass outside of this house! Signing papers to save your grandfather shouldn't have been the reason to make me believe you would love me for better or for worse!"

"That was the *only* reason I did it and that's the truth. I never agreed to marry you for love. How many times must we go over this? As my wife, you have been taken care of the entire time. My grandfather's decisions were the main reason I agreed to walk down the aisle. Being the father Alessia needed in her life was the strong follow up. I never expressed any type of love towards you, Nicolette.

"But you loved my daughter from the start. Make it make sense, Kazimir."

"Alessia shouldn't even be part of this conversation. Regardless of what may happen between us, she won't be affected at all. She is my daughter. I've told you that already."

"Are you planning to leave me for another woman?" Nicolette asked.

"To be honest, it won't be for another woman. I am filing for divorce because I deserve to be happy. The woman I choose to marry next time around will know for sure that we're getting married for the love we have for one another."

"We are not getting a divorce! My father would not allow me to sign the papers. There will also be dire consequences if it's even brought up to him!"

"Dire for whom, you? "Fuck yo' daddy!"

Kaz's street side emerged instantly when Nicolette mentioned her father. The shit Anthony presented to him weeks back came to mind and he knew it was all about money with him. There was no way Kaz was coming off six million dollars to end a marriage he never wanted to begin with. He would leave his ass somewhere stankin' before he would continue living in a dead-end ass marriage. So, whatever consequences Nicolette was speaking of wasn't a concern for him.

"You are the one who has to deal with the tantrum your father is going to throw because of my decision about my life. The divorce will happen…soon. Believe that."

"You won't live happily ever after with the next bitch! You promised 'til death at the altar. I'm willing to honor those vows if that means going to jail for my actions!"

Rising to his feet, "Is that a threat?" he asked. "As a matter of fact, don't answer that. Be ready to sign the papers."

Kaz snatched his suit jacket from the back of the chair and walked out of the kitchen. He was tired of listening to Nicolette and her bullshit. He had the urge to choke her the fuck out for threatening him but her day will come sooner than later. As he grasped the knob to leave the house, Nicolette's words stopped him in his tracks.

"My father will be here upon your return."

"If that muthafucka is anywhere near my home you better have 9-1-1 on speed dial," he said without turning around to face her. "And that's not a threat."

Kaz opened the door and left. Getting into his vehicle, he pulled up the live footage from inside his house and activated the split screen option before backing out of the driveway. He increased the volume so he could hear every word Nicolette or anyone else spoke inside. When Kaz stopped at a red light, he glanced at the screen because he could hear Nicolette's voice clearly. She paced back and forth with the phone to her ear.

*"Daddy, Kaz is going to file for divorce. You need to talk to him," she cried. "I can't lose my husband."*

Kaz chortled because it was impossible for Nicolette to be hurt as she portrayed to be in that moment. There was no way a woman who hasn't received an ounce of love from the man she had been married to for three years, could cry about a divorce. Any other woman would feel neglected to the point she would want to be free to date and get away from the man who wasn't showing any affection toward her. Not Nicolette. Why was she trying to hold on so badly was now the question Kaz had to figure out. Driving through the intersection, he focused on the road with his eyes as he continued to listen in on Nicolette's conversation.

*"What do you mean I need to get as much money as I can from him? We don't need his money, daddy. You have always been the breadwinner in our family. I still have the trust fund you've built since I was a baby."*

Nicolette stopped pacing as she listened to whatever her father was saying to her. Kaz glanced down to see what was happening and it appeared as if the woman he married had seen a ghost. The color drained from her face rapidly. She placed her hand over her mouth as she slumped against the nearest wall. Nicolette's actions caused Kaz to pull over and park so he could focus.

*"Daddy, I haven't touched that money! How is it gone?" she cried. "There was seven million dollars in that account. You promised to take your name off once I was old enough to manage it myself. You lied to me!"*

Sliding down the wall, Nicolette sobbed into the phone as she continued listening to Anthony spew more lies to her. The conversation Kaz had with him about the six million dollars came to mind. He had to be going through financial difficulties because the amount he was seeking was absurd. Now, Kaz knew why. He tuned back in on the screen once he heard Nicolette's voice again.

*"I can't believe you made me marry Kazimir just so I would have access to his money. News flash, daddy, I've never had control over any of his finances. I don't even know who he banks with. Kazimir takes care of all the bills and he is the person who puts money in my account. Your plan was foiled from the start. Had you told me what I was getting*

*into, maybe this would have turned out differently. I'm about to lose my husband and everything I have and you can't even help me!"*

*"No! No! Don't you dare bring my daughter into this!"*

The mention of Alessia peaked Kaz's interest.

*"You have a what on her? An insurance policy? Why are you telling me this?"*

Kaz didn't wait to hear the rest because he heard all he needed to hear. Picking up his phone, he dialed Marisol's number. It took her a minute to answer but she eventually did.

"Marisol, where are you?" he asked calmly.

"I'm in the backyard watching Alessia play on the slide. What do you need?"

"Take Alessia, get in your car, and go to the penthouse. Do not say anything to Nicolette. Go now!"

Kaz kept his sights on Nicolette. She was still on the phone with Anthony. He needed Marisol to get Alessia far away from the house. The one-sided conversation told him, Anthony was desperate for money and he was willing to kill his granddaughter to get it. Nicolette wasn't agreeing with him and didn't want anything to do with his sick antics, but he had a way of convincing her to do whatever he told her to do.

"Marisol, are you in the car?" He asked.

"Yes, I just buckled Alessia in her car seat. What is going on?"

"I'll explain it to you when I finish up with this meeting. You are not to answer any of Nicolette's calls under no circumstances. Do you understand me?"

"I understand," Marisol replied as she started the car.

Nicolette got up from the position she was in and ran to the door when she saw Marisol's car. With the phone still to her ear, she tried to catch up to her but was too late. Nicolette only wanted to know where she was taking her daughter but assumed they would be back. It wasn't unusual for Alessia to tag along when Marisol had errands to run. Going back into the house, Nicolette finished her conversation with her father agreeing to get rid of Alessia.

Hearing Nicolette saying the words *I will make sure she dies,* Kaz logged out of the footage. He would be able to log in to find out what else was said later. With a father like Anthony, Kaz couldn't put anything pass what he would do. He was glad Marisol was able to get Alessia out of the house and away from her mother. As Kaz pulled back in traffic to get on the highway, he made a much-needed call.

"Mr. St. Claire. Long time no see. What can I do for you?"

"Judge Eisenhower, it's time to make good on that favor you owe."

"Long as it's not unreasonable, I think we can get it handled. Talk to me."

"I need you to add my name to my stepdaughter's birth certificate. It needs to be dated two weeks after her birth."

"No. That is something I can't get involved in. Falsifying paperwork of that magnitude could jeopardize my seat as a Judge. I won't do it."

Kaz laughed lowly as he signaled to change lanes. "See, that's where you're wrong. Remember Stew, I hold your livelihood in the palm of my hand. You wouldn't want your wife to know about all the times you had inmates bent over the desk in your chamber just to get back home to their families, would you? Not to mention all the bribes you accepted to sweep shit under the rug, and last but definitely not least, the drug habit you worked so hard to keep a secret. Don't fuck with me, Eisenhower! I will leak all that shit to the media and have it run as a breaking story at ten o'clock tonight."

"Okay! You win. What do you need me to do?"

"I thought you would get with the program. Alessia Bella St. Claire born November 22, 2021 at Northwestern Prentice Women's hospital. Her mother is Nicolette Alessandra Santoro-St. Claire. I need that information in the next hour and you will fax a copy to Lamont Mitchell. Write this down," Kaz paused. "The fax number is (312) 555-0731. I would hate the world to see what could happen if I don't have what I need in my possession pronto."

Ending the call, Kaz pressed his foot down on the gas pedal and rushed to his meeting. He arrived to his destination in record time as he parked in the garage of Mitchell's Family Law. Lamont was Kaz's right hand in the street but he was too smart for the drug shit. He was needed on the right side of the law so Kaz paid his way through school then helped him open his own law firm. Lamont wasn't the only one out of his crew that he helped throughout the years.

Kaz rode the elevator to the twelfth floor and stepped into the lobby of Lamont office space. Soon as he entered, Vanessa the secretary picked up the phone to announce his arrival. She displayed the biggest smile whenever Kaz came by to see his friend. Usually, they would sneak off to the bathroom for a quickie, but Kaz wasn't on that anymore. The moment Vanessa stood, he shook his head no and walked away toward Lamont's office.

"Kaz, my man, you late." Lamont rounded his desk giving his friend a brotherly half hug.

"Man, shit done hit the fan. Not only do I need you to get this divorce going, I want full custody of Alessia too."

Lamont's right eyebrow rose slightly. He couldn't have heard him correctly. Kaz didn't have any children and for the last three years Alessia had grown on him. Lamont didn't think he loved the little girl enough to fight her birth mother in court for custody. Last time he checked, Kaz wasn't even listed as the father on the birth certificate so that in itself was going to be a problem.

"Fam, that's going to be hard to pull off. First you need to be deemed the biological father of the child in order to even be considered for full custody. Then, there is this thing called probable cause. Physical proof of the child being at risk of harm will be needed as well. It will be wise to concentrate on the divorce first and foremost."

"That's automatic. The divorce is going to happen no matter what. My baby girl is my focal point right now after the shit I just heard. Evidence will not be a problem because I put cameras in the house and there's footage. Going through it all to find what I need will be a task I'm willing to attack."

"Tell me what's going on, Kaz."

"You know the marriage was arranged from the start. I offered to pay Santoro the money he loaned Paw Paw to end the shit but the muthafucka talking 'bout he's not taking anything less than six mil. Who the fuck he thought he was talking to? If he thinks I'm coming off that type of money to divorce his daughter, he dead wrong. Then this morning, I had Marisol take Alessia out of the house because Nicolette and her father plans to kill her for insurance money. I definitely have that conversation recorded."

Kaz removed his phone from his pocket to see what Nicolette was doing. He checked every camera in the house until he found her lying in bed in the master bedroom. *No wonder she hadn't called asking about Alessia's whereabouts. Her ass was sleeping.* There was no doubt his phone would ring once she realized Marisol hadn't returned. Kaz had just the story for her when she did decide to contact him.

"Well, I drew up the paperwork and listed irreconcilable differences as the reason for divorce. You stated you have never loved Nicolette and it hadn't changed in three years. There's also the lack of intimacy, and the continued arguments between the two of you. I already know there will be no fault on your end against her, but she is going to find fault in you for sure."

"The only thing Nicolette can say is, I didn't touch her sexually. I took care of all of the bills and all of Alessia's wants and needs. I have her admitting that to her stupid ass daddy. Nicolette is getting nothing other than the house from me. I'm not giving her a dime so don't ask."

"I don't blame you," Lamont replied as he added the information about the house to the document. "We have to discuss Alessia. If you don't get custody, what is your plans far as her care? Are you willing to pay support for her?"

"Paying Nicolette for Alessia won't happen because she will be with me. I have a judge working on it as we speak." At that moment, the fax machine started up. "I think that's the birth certificate. If this backfires, I'm going to do everything I need to do until I kill her grandfather and mother. I will also set it up to kill the fuckin' judge who thought it was okay to send a little girl back to the very people who wants her dead."

"Kaz, I don't want you putting hits on anyone. Your success speaks for itself," Lamont said as he looked the birth certificate over. He then stood to make a copy of it to put in his file. "Tonight, I need you to go through the footage so you will have it ready to present to the judge. Now, where do you want her served?"

"Nicolette will be at the house or her father's."

Giving the address to Anthony's home, Kaz thought about all the ways to kill Nicolette. No matter the outcome. She was a dead bitch walking along with her punk ass daddy. They fucked up conspiring to kill an innocent child who didn't ask to be born. Not only did Kaz have to deal with the bullshit from his wife and in laws, he still needed to get on top of finding the muthafucka that took his money. Not to mention Cyrus shoot and run ass.

"How long will it be until you have Nicolette served?" Kaz asked pinching the bridge of his nose.

"Don't worry. I'm going to update the document and hand deliver it myself. I want to make sure it gets directly in the hands of your soon to be ex-wife. Kaz, stay away from the house. Your emotions will cause you to do something irrational and we can't have that at this pivotal time. As you say, Alessia is in danger and she needs you there to take care of her."

"Overstood," Kaz said as he glanced down at the vibrating phone in his hand. Nicolette's name was on full display and he knew she was going to ask about her daughter. He put the phone on speaker soon as the call connected.

"Hello."

"Kazimir, have you heard from Marisol? She's still not here with Alessia!"

"Nicolette, calm down. I sent Marisol home for the day. Alessia is with me. You were sleeping soundly and I didn't want Alessia to disturb you."

"Bring her home. I miss my baby," Nicolette lied through her teeth.

"We'll be back Monday. She mentioned Disneyland so we are on our way to California for a father daughter trip."

Lamont was amused because the lies rolled off Kaz's tongue with ease. As a lawyer, he had never witnessed anyone, including himself lie so effortlessly. It was rather impressive. He knew Kaz was in street mode and he needed to make sure he had his boy's back at every turn.

"Why would you take her on such a trip without me being there to experience the moment with her?"

"Did you not hear me say this is her time with her daddy? Nicolette, you have to get used to not being involved when Alessia is with me. It's called co-parenting."

"We will not be co-parenting, Kazimir! I've told you several times she needs both of her parents under the same roof."

"And I've also told you to go…"

Kaz stopped himself from telling her to go find her baby daddy but he bit the side of his cheek. Lamont tapped the desk lightly until his friend looked up. Mouthing the words *hang up*. Kaz knew he should've listened but he had to finish what he had to say.

"The reality of what's happening between us is something you need to come to grips with. We learned to live together without love and you will have to do the same when it comes to co-parenting. I'm sure we can come up with a reasonable schedule that will benefit both of us."

Nicolette sniffled. "If you file for divorce, you will never see Alessia again. I put that on my mother's grave."

She ended the call and Lamont heard the idle threat clear as day. Veins protruded from Kaz's temple indicating how angry he was. The way his hand tightened into a fist on top of the desk was another sign that he chose violence. Still, Lamont didn't want him to fall into Nicolette's trap and end up in prison for murder.

"Kaz, book the trip to Disneyland. I think it would be great for you to get away for a few days to regain your composure and also show your daughter a good time."

"Sounds good. I'll do just that. Get those papers to Nicolette pronto. The faster I end this bullshit of a marriage, the better. Thanks for your help."

"No problem. I'll always do what I can for you. Trust me, I'm going to make sure you win this case and custody of Alessia. Watch yourself out there, Kaz. Nicolette is about to play dirty and I would hate to hear that she was able to reel you in for the kill."

"That won't happen. If anything, you will receive a call about me being locked up for leaving her body on display for the world to see. It will be a gruesome scene if the bitch keeps playing with the life of the little girl, I call my own."

# Chapter 11

Koko was up early cleaning her apartment. It was much needed since she had been busy at the studio. She spent majority of the night thinking about the altercation at Stella's. The ass whooping she gave Jackie for the second time still wasn't enough for her liking. Koko allowed Stella to pull her away out of respect. Nothing would be able to stop her the third time over.

Moving throughout the living room while vacuuming the carpet, the music blared GloRilla's *Glorious* album through the speakers. Koko bopped to the track "Procedure," and she loved everything about it.

*What's the procedure when a bad bitch walks in the room?*
*Huh, bitch ass nigga?*
*What's the fuckin' procedure?*
*I told that nigga I need the world, the sun, and the moon*
*What's the procedure when a bad bitch walks in the room?*
*The type of bitch that makes a nigga wanna jump the broom*
*He hit it once and got to tweakin' he on some shrooms*

The music stopped and was replaced by an incoming call. Her phone was on the coffee table, and she didn't take time to look at her watch beforehand to see who was calling. Koko tapped her earbud to accept as she turned the vacuum off.

"Hello."

"Miss Simmons, it's Kaz. I need you right now."

She could immediately hear the sadness in his voice. "What's going on? I'm due to get on the plane to Chicago in two days."

"I know. Cancel that flight or see if you can have it rerouted to LAX instead. For today."

"Um, Kaz, why California?"

"I'll explain it to you once I pick you up. Make sure you send the flight information soon as you make the changes. There's a lot to discuss, and I'd rather wait until you arrive. Oh, I also have Alessia with me. So, this is not about me."

"Okay. I have to call Horace because I was going to Chicago with him. I'm sure he will understand. I'll call you back shortly."

"Text me, and I'll get back with you once we land. We're on the plane and it's about time to take off. Talk to you soon, Chocolate drop."

Koko held the phone, wondering what could've possibly happened. She wanted to go to his aid, but something was telling her not to get involved. That was too much like right though. Finding Horace's number in her call log didn't take much time. Koko sat on one of the bar stools at her island, waiting for him to answer.

"Friend, I know you don't have a project you need help with. We have a trip to prepare for."

"That's what I'm calling about. There has been a change of plans."

"See, Koko! Why are you bailing out on me?"

"It's not like that, Horace. Kaz called asking me to change my flight to California for today. Something is going on because he wouldn't say why he wanted me to come over the phone. I have to take a rain check. I'm going. I'll pay for the ticket you purchased for me."

"Hunni, that's all you had to say. Kaz summoned that ass across the country. All I ask is for you to relax between the dick massages," Horace laughed.

"Honestly, the way he sounded, it won't be that type of party. Not like I was planning to have sex with him anyway. Plus, Alessia will be present. Maybe he had a fallout with the wife." Koko paused, then gasped once realization kicked in.

"What?"

"Oh my God! The man filed for divorce while we were on the phone last night. Could he have served her already?" Koko didn't realize she spoke her thoughts aloud until Horace responded.

"Shit, Mr. St. Claire is not playing, huh? Save the story time until you return. I'm going to need all the tea at once," Horace cheered. "Get off this phone so you can book your flight. Text or call me the time you have to be at the airport because I'm dropping you off."

"You're reading my mind. I was surely going to ask, but you beat me to it."

"Now you know I'm not about to have you paying to park. Hell, the man may not even allow you to come back. I'm here for your happiness, though. I love you, boo. Talk to you later."

"I love you back, and thank you."

The call ended, and Koko went to her travel app and booked the flight to California. She had two hours to pack, shower, and get to the airport. The Minneapolis airport isn't hard to get through the security checkpoint. Koko wasn't taking any chances because she booked priority check-in so there wouldn't be any delays in her travel. She had to contact Kaz to determine the time for her departure flight. He responded for her to do a one-way ticket; he would make sure she got back home. She was kind of leery, but Koko went with the flow because if she decided to leave, she had the finances to do so.

As she packed her luggage, Koko thought about the weekend getaway she planned with Horace and the switch to traveling with Kaz. The butterflies in her stomach were fluttering. She just about wanted to cancel. On the other hand, she couldn't pass up the opportunity of being there for the man who had gotten shot for being kind to her. Koko wasn't blind to the fact that Kaz wanted her in the worst way. She just didn't know if she wanted to put herself in the middle of a failing marriage. After taking a shower and getting dressed, Koko was ready to head to the airport.

"Fuck! I forgot to call Horace back."

Koko would have to drive herself because it was going to take Horace half an hour to get to her, and she didn't have time for that. The phone rang through her earbud as she shuffled around, putting last minute things in her purse. Horace answered on the third ring.

"What time is your flight?" he asked without saying hello.

"At two. I'll drive myself because you won't get here in time."

"Good thing I left the house to go shopping. I'm five minutes away. Be downstairs. You will not drive yourself. See you soon."

Koko smiled as she placed her phone in her purse. She didn't know how Horace always knew what she was thinking without even being in her presence. It was the same when Koko would silently doubt herself when she didn't think a cake was good enough. He had been her saving grace since the day she met him at the club.

As she walked toward the door, her phone rang again. Koko caught the call from her watch before it was forwarded to voicemail. The number on display was one she didn't recognize.

"Hello," she answered as she pulled her luggage out the door.

"Koko, it's Cyrus. Don't hang up."

"What do you want? I have a plane to catch."

"Where you going?"

"That's none of your business. Again, what do you want?"

Cyrus sat on the steel stool, clenching his fist. Koko was acting as if he never meant anything to her, and it didn't sit right with him. If she was on her way to the airport, he wondered if she was going to see that nigga Kaz. Cyrus didn't want to put her on alert to his feelings, so he sucked that shit up.

"I called because I wanted you to know I will be getting out of jail in a few weeks. My lawyer is working to have all the charges dropped because they don't have nothing on me. On top of that, I have a lawsuit against the police department, and they are going to settle without a fight."

Koko locked the door and made her way down the stairs. She didn't care about anything Cyrus was saying. If he thought she was happy about his news, he was sadly mistaken because she couldn't care less. Horace was parked in front of the building waiting patiently. Koko couldn't get in the car with Cyrus on the phone, so it was time to end the call.

"Are you still there?" Cyrus asked.

"I'm here, but I think you are explaining your problems to the wrong woman. We are done, and that was established a long time ago. Congratulations on your freedom and the lawsuit. I hope you invest in something meaningful, Cyrus. You have a son to take care of. Raise him to never be the type of man you are."

"Koko, I miss and love you so much."

She didn't hear the end of the conversation because she hung up after she spoke her truth. Horace got out of the car to get Koko's luggage. He had many questions but decided not to voice them. Getting her to the airport was his main objective. All that other shit would still be relevant once Koko was ready to talk about it.

As they traveled on the highway, Koko didn't allow the call to live rent free in her head. She wasn't worried about Cyrus or the bullshit he was talking. He made his choice, and he had to live with the decision he chose. It was time for him to move on with his life and forget about Koko altogether. Horace kept glancing over at her, but he never said anything. If she had to guess, he was wondering who or what had her sitting quietly in the passenger seat when they were usually chatting it up whenever they were in the car together.

"What's on your mind, Horace?"

"You don't seem too excited about this trip. Did Kaz tell you what was going on?"

"Actually, no. I haven't talked to him since earlier. Cyrus called as I was coming downstairs. He thought it was okay to call me about what was going on in his jailbird life. I hung up after telling him for the hundredth time to stop calling me. He will be released soon."

"He knows you're done. It won't stop him from contacting you again. I won't be surprised if he calls several more times while you're away. Don't entertain his ass, though. Enjoy your time away. On another note, there's a few bags in the back for you. Add them to your luggage when you get out. You can thank me later."

The look on his face let Koko know her friend was on good bullshit. She would have to wait to see what he purchased. It didn't make sense to ask because he would only say wait and see. Instead, she sat back and enjoyed the ride until she realized she stopped cleaning her apartment to jump into action when Kaz called.

"Horace, I need a favor. I'm paying too."

"What you need me to do?" he asked.

"Would you go back to my apartment and wash the dishes I left in the sink, take out the garbage, and finish vacuuming the carpet? I stopped what I was doing and never finished when Kaz called."

"I sure will. That's what friends are for. Plus, I would hate for you to go back home and walk into your apartment thinking there's a dead body in there. Your place will smell like shit," he laughed. "We can't have that."

"Thank you so much. How much should I send for your service?"

He thought about it for a moment, then turned to Koko briefly. "A monetary payment isn't necessary. I want you to give this trip your all and have a lot of orgasms. That would square away your fee."

"I'm not fucking that man! I'll send you a generous payment soon as I get checked in. You ain't shit, Horace."

"You are not wrong. I have never been shit when it comes to giving up the goods. You should do the same. It will get the kinks out ya spine and save you a trip to the chiropractor. Trust me, sex is way cheaper long as you use the condoms I stored in your bag."

"I thought I told you I didn't need those!"

"Stop yelling in my ride, girl. Better safe than sorry. We have too much business to handle, and little Kazimir St. Claire would hold us up. So, we are trying to prevent pregnancy at all costs. Now, what terminal are you going to?"

"Terminal 1, troublemaker. I'm flying out with American Airlines."

They were minutes away from the airport. Traffic was moving, so Koko was going to actually get to the airport on time with a few minutes to spare. She was glad she followed her first mind to book priority check-in. Horace exited the highway, then maneuvered through traffic to pull into the arrival line outside of the airport. He turned to Koko after putting the car in park.

"Koko, I'm a phone call away if you need to talk. Enjoy yourself to the fullest."

"I will. Thank you for always being there when I need you."

"No problem," he said, getting out of the car.

Unfastening the seatbelt, Koko opened the door to get out as well. Horace was already taking her luggage from the backseat. He held two bags out to her with a smile. Koko took the items from the first bag and gasped. Inside was a sexy green dress with matching shoes and silver accessories. The other bag held a black and green two-piece bikini with matching cover-up and a pair of black water shoes.

"These are so cute! I'm not going to wear any of these things during this trip, but it's the thought that counts." Koko unzipped her luggage to place the items inside.

"How much you wanna bet?" Horace challenged. "When you put on either one, I want pics."

"Whatever," she laughed. "I gotta go."

They hugged before Koko made her way into the airport. Horace waited until she was safely inside before getting back into the car and driving off. Koko walked through the airport and straight to TSA. She showed her pass on her phone after handing over her identification, then she was allowed to beat the line. Waiting for her belongings to come through screening, she was ready to board the plane so she could sleep. The flight was going to be four hours too long. When she arrived at the gate, the boarding process had begun. Koko was on the plane in no time, seated with earbuds in her ears. She was sleeping soundly before the flight took off.

***

The wheels hit the pavement with a thud, causing Koko to wake up from the much-needed rest. Her seat was in the third row from the front, and she was ready to stretch her limbs after sitting too long. She removed her earbuds and turned airplane mode off on her phone. Going to her contacts, she sent Kaz a message to inform him of her arrival. He immediately texted her back, assuring her he would be waiting patiently for her outside. Koko was glad she didn't have to retrieve her luggage from baggage claim because it would've taken much longer for her to get out of the airport. Being that she had never traveled to California before, she hoped like hell she was able to find Kaz in record time.

Standing to her feet soon as the aircraft stopped, a nice man helped by retrieving her bag from the overhead. Thanking him, Koko waited patiently for the doors to open. Like herself, the passengers in front of her were eager to get off as well. Her phone vibrated in her pocket nonstop, but she couldn't check to see what was going on because it was time to get off the plane. She moved behind the others and thanked the attendants as she exited.

Koko walked through the tunnel with her luggage rolling behind her. She looked up at the signs, following them to the exit. Her stomach growled as the aroma of food filled her nostrils while she made her way through the concourse. Hopefully, Kaz had something prepared once they arrived at the hotel. Soon as she walked out of the automatic doors, her eyes locked in on Kaz as he leaned against an all-black G-Wagon. Pushing off the vehicle, he smiled when he looked up and noticed her.

"Chocolate drop, thank you for coming," he said, pulling her into a hug. "You are so beautiful. How was the flight?"

"I made it here. To be truthful, I slept the entire time."

Kaz grabbed the handle of her luggage and popped the trunk before opening the passenger door for her. Koko looked in the backseat and noticed Kaz's daughter wasn't in attendance. The thought of him lying about having her with him almost caused an instant attitude. She took a deep breath so she wouldn't snap when he got into the vehicle. Kaz noticed her mood change the moment he closed the door.

"What's wrong?"

"I thought you had Alessia with you. Where is she?" Koko asked as she fastened her seatbelt.

"She's at the hotel with Marisol; the nanny. I snuck out to come pick you up while she was watching the *Trolls* movie in the theater."

"Oh, okay. So tell me why you needed me here today."

Kaz started the truck and pulled out into traffic. They had about a forty-minute drive back to the villa, so there was plenty of time to fill Koko in on what was going on in his life. Not wanting to scare her with his bullshit, he thought for a few about what he wanted to share. A part of him believed it would be wise not to hide anything, seeing Koko was the woman he wanted to build forever with.

"As you know, I filed for divorce. Nicolette isn't happy about it at all. I had to get Alessia away because her mother and grandfather are planning to kill her for insurance money."

"What the fuck! Kaz, please tell me you're joking."

"Nah, I'm dead ass," Kaz said as he handed her his phone after pulling up the video from his home. "You can connect your earbuds because I don't want to hear that shit again."

Koko's hands shook as she connected to his device. She pressed the play button nervously. Watching as Nicolette displayed every emotion throughout the footage, she went from a hurt wife wanting her husband to love her, to a little girl who thought the love from her parent was unconditional, into a scared woman who would do anything to please her father. Koko didn't have children, but there was no way she would ever think about harming her child; any child for that matter.

Koko was on the verge of crying once she finished the video. Alessia deserved a better mother than the one she was given. Kaz was not wrong for taking his daughter out of harm's way and putting her on a plane out of Chicago and away from evil. Wiping the wetness from her cheek, Koko turned her head toward the window and cried so he wouldn't notice. Somehow, he knew exactly what she was doing.

"Don't get weak on me, Chocolate drop. I'm doing enough of that on my own. The video was hard to stomach; I know. I'm sorry for springing this on you."

"It's okay. I can't imagine how this situation has you feeling. I've met Alessia once and fell in love with her soon as she came out of her shell. She is the sweetest little girl, and I believe you have a lot to do with that. What is your plan, Kaz? You can't hide her forever."

"I'm not hiding my daughter. Yes, my daughter. I made a vow the moment I laid eyes on that little girl to love her with all my heart and soul. Protecting her is what I'm doing right now. The two of us have never gone on a trip alone. It's a perfect time to shower her with love she will remember for the rest of her life."

"If being here is about the two of you, why am I here?" Koko asked.

Kaz kept his attention on the highway as he thought about an easy way to explain the invite he extended to her.

"Speak freely. I'm all ears," Koko said, turning in her seat. He was thinking too hard for an answer to the simple question she asked.

"To be honest, you were the only woman I thought to call. Alessia is going to need a good woman to give her motherly love. Chocolate drop, you are that woman. I know you don't have any children and you're doubtful about carrying on a relationship with me; I understand. What I want you to overstand is, I won't pressure you into anything you don't want to do. But I can promise to get to know you, help you through whatever you may need assistance with, and in the process, I'm going to love you like no other, Koko."

"I want to be the man who lifts you up, not put you down. You have my word; I will not cheat on you. If things don't work out between us, I will still be there to elevate you to the top. For now, I just want to be able to relax and make Alessia smile for a week. Are you alright with that?"

"Of course, I'm going to help make baby girl's trip memorable. Everything else you said is going to be a work in progress. You already know I need to see the paperwork for your divorce before I can even attempt to take things further. I was unknowingly sharing a man with my best friend and others for years. I'm not about to set myself up by getting involved with a man I know has a wife. An ain't shit wife, but nonetheless."

Kaz nodded his head, acknowledging what she'd said. He reached to turn the radio on, and Anthony Hamilton's "Float" filled the interior of the car. The words alone calmed Kaz, and he rocked to the beat.

*Could it be your nice silky tone*
*Oh, that makes me want you, girl?*
*Distant nights and love on the phone as I touch myself*
*How I want you more*
*The mood evokes incense smoke*
*And I'm burnin' up in temperature*
*Ready to explode, yeah*
*Come take a toke, let's float*
*Baby, on higher ground, oh*
*Baby come float with me*
*(Let me take you to a place on higher, honey)*

Taking his right hand from the steering wheel, Kaz automatically locked his fingers with Koko's. He expected her to pull away, but she did the complete opposite and caressed the back of his hand with her thumb. The song came on in the car, but it had to be a sign because he played that song every night until he fell asleep thinking about the woman sitting next to him. Kaz couldn't wait for his life to go back to normalcy. He knew it would get worse before it got better. The rest of the ride was pretty intimate for Kaz, but Koko had a lot on her mind.

The things she had going on in her life were hectic for a while, but she walked away from the drama because there were other things she wanted to focus on. Cyrus, his love child, Jackie, and anything else were no longer her concern. Koko was going to enjoy herself for the time being and maybe, just maybe, her problems would be long gone once she returned to Minnesota. She didn't know what would happen being in the same space as Kaz. She would just have to allow the cards to play out as they may.

Kaz pulled into the Grand Californian Hotel, and Koko was impressed. She had never been to Disneyland during her childhood. Being there as an adult made her feel like a kid again. She couldn't suppress her excitement and couldn't wait to have fun with Alessia. Koko reached for the handle of the door to get out, but her movements were halted when Kaz gently grabbed her arm.

"I will open the door for you. Sit tight, Chocolate drop."

Sitting back in the seat, Koko waited until he finished conducting business with the valet attendant. Kaz headed to the back of the truck before popping the trunk. After retrieving her luggage, he made his way to the passenger side of the vehicle. The door opened, and he reached out to take her hand. Koko placed her hand inside of his, and for a brief second, an electric current traveled up her arm. His grip tightened, and it was that moment she knew Kaz had felt it too.

Koko stared at the side of his dark chocolate face as he led her into the hotel entrance. Kaz's skin appeared to be sun-kissed as he strolled beside her. Lance Gross had been her celebrity crush since she first saw him in the TV series *House of Payne*. Now, she had the chance to have the closest replica of the man within arm's length. It seemed the harder she tried to fight the sexual attraction she had for Kaz, the more she craved him. Koko put up a fight, but she was ready to dive deep to test the waters.

They entered the hotel, making their way to the elevators. The different characters invited them into the building from the time they stepped out of the vehicle. Every character Koko grew up loving was present everywhere. The atmosphere was a child's dream come true, and it was hers too. The doors opened, and Kaz ushered her inside first. Mickey and friends sang while the car rose higher by the second. She kept her eyes on the numbers until it stopped on the eleventh floor. There were only twelve floors in the building. Kaz paused at the door, then turned to Koko.

"Alessia may not remember you, but I know she will come around in a day or two. Be patient with her."

"Kaz, I'm here for her. I will do any and everything I can to put a smile on Alessia's face. You should be worried about your daughter ignoring you for the duration of our stay," she smirked. "I got this."

"That won't happen. My baby will never put anyone before me."

"We'll see. Now open the door. I gotta pee."

Pulling the keycard from his pocket, Kaz unlocked the door. He entered first and guided Koko to the bathroom. Soon as she closed the door, she heard Alessia squeal with delight when she realized her daddy was back. Taking care of her business, Koko took the opportunity to text Horace to let him know she arrived safely to the hotel.

*Koko: Hey, friend, I'm at the hotel with Kaz. Thanks again for the ride to the airport.*

*Horace: No problem. I'm glad you got there safely. Enjoy yourself and don't forget to bust it open! It's time to clean out the cobwebs, sis.*

*Koko: There's more serious shit to worry about than sex. When I tell you what the fuck is going on, your mouth is going to hit the floor. I'll fill you in soon as I return.*

*Horace: Lawwwwd! Do what you have to do but I need you to fuck on something.*

*Koko: Your ass isn't reading to comprehend, are you? It's is not going to happen on this trip. Plus, we are in a hotel suite that's decorated with a Princess and the Frog theme. Who can think about sex in that type of environment?*

*Horace: Turn off the lights...in my Teddy P voice. LOL*

*Koko: You stupid. I'll talk to you later. I love you, friend.*

*Horace: I love you back.*

Koko placed her phone on the counter to wipe herself. After washing and drying her hands, she gathered her belongings, then left the bathroom. Kaz was sitting on the sofa with Alessia on his lap. She turned to see who was coming into the room and damn near jumped out of his arms when she laid eyes on Koko.

"Koko!"

Alessia ran the short distance across the room, wrapping her little arms around Koko's legs. She hadn't forgotten about her like Kaz thought. Alessia knew exactly who she was, and it made Koko smile.

"Hey, big girl. How you been?"

"Good! Daddy didn't tell me you was coming to Disneyland," she said as Koko scooped her up to hug her tightly. "You see Tiana? She pretty."

"She sure is! Just like you."

Alessia said more words in the few minutes they were talking than she did the first time they met. It surprised Koko, but she was impressed. Kaz sat watching the interaction while thinking on the same wavelength as Koko. Alessia was being very vocal, which was surprising because he was the only person outside of Marisol who witnessed that side of her. At the tender age of two, Alessia was more advanced than the average toddler. She knew how to spell her name, numbers up to one hundred, all of her colors, and she could speak Italian fluently; all thanks to Kaz.

"I'm not pretty, I'm beautiful. Daddy tells me every day."

"As he should. Your daddy is right. You are beautiful."

Looking over Koko's shoulder, Alessia leaned back slightly, palming her face. "Is Uncle H here too?"

"No, he didn't come this time. I can't believe you remember us."

"I do. I missed y'all. We had so much fun eating ice cream. Can I call Uncle H?"

"We sure can."

Retrieving her phone, Koko called Horace on FaceTime. When he answered, she made sure Alessia was the person he saw first. If she hadn't, there was no telling what would've come out of his mouth. Koko knew him oh so well because it worked.

"Alessia! Hey, cutie!"

"Uncle H! I miss you," Alessia shrieked.

"I miss you too, sweetie. Are you having fun yet?"

"Not yet. We had to wait on Daddy. Will you come here?"

"No, not this time. I'll see you soon, okay?"

"At my birthday?"

Koko looked over at Kaz for clarification. He stood and came over to where they were. Alessia was waiting for Horace to tell her he was coming to spend time with her for her birthday. Neither Koko nor Horace knew the date. That's where Kaz came in.

"Her birthday is November 23rd. She will have a party, and both of you are welcome to come celebrate with us."

"I will be there with lots of gifts. And I will stay for the Thanksgiving feast too," Horace replied. "Alessia, I need you to get a list together so I can get everything you may want. But I have to go. Have fun, and I'll talk to you soon."

"Okay, Uncle H. Bye-bye."

Horace ended the call, but Koko was still stuck on Kaz inviting them to her party. She didn't think that was a good idea, being Alessia's mother would be in attendance. They were already going through a lot with Kaz filing for divorce. Alessia's birthday was a month and a half away, and things were bound to still be heated between her parents. Koko didn't want to cause any unnecessary drama at a child's birthday party. She didn't voice her concerns, but once she and Kaz were alone, she would.

"Daddy, are we going to the pool? I wanna swim."

"We can go," he said, never taking his eyes off Koko. "Marisol," he called out.

An older Hispanic woman entered the room moments later. She looked at Koko, and her face lit up like a Christmas tree. Marisol was glad to see her boss with a woman other than Nicolette. She prayed for the day Kaz would find his forever woman. The sadness in Kaz's eyes was always present when he was around the woman he married. The only time she ever saw him smile was when he was in the presence of Alessia. He deserved to be happy, and Marisol wanted to witness it right along with him.

"Hello, I'm Marisol. Alessia's nanny," she said, holding her hand out to Koko.

"Kameeko, but you can call me Koko. Nice to meet you."

Kaz took Alessia from Koko's arms, placing her on the floor. "Can you help prepare her for the pool? She wants to swim."

"Of course. I can take her down if you want."

"No. We're all going to go together. You are not the nanny this week, Marisol. We are in California as a family, so we will enjoy this trip as such. So make sure you dress for the outing as well."

"Oh, thank you so much. I didn't know I wasn't here to work."

"You will still get paid for the week though," Kaz made it clear. "Take Alessia to put on her swimsuit, please."

Marisol nodded as she led Alessia to one of the bedrooms. Koko walked to the sofa and sat down. She was going to take the time they had alone to ask Kaz about the birthday thing. He could feel the energy change in her, so he followed, sitting next to her.

"What's on your mind, Chocolate drop?"

Every time Kaz called her by the pet name he'd come up with, it made Koko blush. She never had a man call her anything other than Kameeko or Koko. Other than Cyrus calling her Ko, that was far as nicknames had gone for her. For years, she was self-conscious about her complexion because of the things her mother said to her growing up. It took years for Koko to realize her black was beautiful, and Kaz only added to what she already felt.

"With everything going on, how are you going to pull off having me and Horace at Alessia's birthday party? I mean, isn't it going to cause more problems with her mother?"

"Koko, all I want you to do is show up. I'll handle Nicolette. You don't have to worry about any of that. By the time Alessia's party takes place, my marriage will be dissolved and hopefully you and I will be in a full-blown relationship. I meant what I said earlier. I want to make things work between us. As you can see, Alessia loves you. Truthfully, I didn't think she would remember you, but I was wrong. The way my baby lit up when she saw you was everything to me. She doesn't react that way toward her own mother. So that says a lot."

"I don't ever want to take the place of her mother. I think being here now is a bad idea."

"You being here is exactly how it's supposed to be. If you want to leave, I won't stop you. The choice will always be yours to make. Would I like for you to stay? Of course. But it's not my decision, Koko. You already know I would rather have you here with us. If I didn't, you wouldn't have gotten a call to come."

Marisol's shaky voice interrupted their conversation, causing both of them to turn in her direction. Kaz could see the terror in her eyes, and he didn't like it one bit. Standing to his feet as Marisol walked slowly into the room, the tears rolling down her face told him something was wrong.

"What is it?" he asked.

"I need you to come see something, Mr. St. Claire. Please try not to be angry in front of Alessia." Kaz's jaw clenched tightly as he waited for Marisol to tell him what she was afraid to reveal. "Um, there are bruises on her back."

Kaz pushed past her, but Marisol grabbed his arm to stop him. Snatching away, Kaz entered the bedroom and found Alessia sitting on the bed with her head down. Examining her back, he saw red. There were a few bruises that were fading, but they were there nonetheless.

"What happened to your back, baby girl?"

"Mommy hit me." Alessia sniffed. "She said not to tell you because you would hit me too. So I didn't tell you, Daddy."

"Have I ever hit you before?" She shook her head no. "And I never will. Do Mommy hurt you a lot?"

Alessia nodded yes. "She hit me when you are gone, Daddy. Mommy says you not my daddy."

Hearing that Nicolette was telling her he wasn't her father pissed Kaz off even more. The truth was told, but he was sure it was out of spite. Nicolette was speaking on their marriage ending, but behind the scenes she was beating on his daughter and trying to hurt her by telling Alessia he wasn't her daddy. Taking a few deep breaths, Kaz fought the tears that threatened to fall. He was the only father she would ever know if he had anything to do with it.

"I'm your father, Alessia. I don't care what your mama says. Are you ready to go swimming now?" Kaz asked as he stood behind her, taking pictures of her back.

"No, I'll just watch *Princess and the Frog*," she replied sadly.

"Well, let's order food and I'll get the movie started while you put on a shirt."

"Okay. I want pizza and ice cream. I love you, Daddy."

"I love you too, beautiful. Come to the living room when you're ready."

Kaz kissed the top of her head and walked out of the room. Koko heard every word, and her heart ached for both Kaz and Alessia. The fury in his eyes would have scared any man that came into contact with him. His fists clenched tightly at his sides as he blindly walked into the room Koko was in. She met him in the middle of the space and wrapped her arms around his waist, resting her head on his stomach. Instantly, the muscles in Kaz's body relaxed.

"The bitch hurt my baby," he whispered. "She doesn't even want to go swimming anymore."

"It's going to be okay."

"I know it is. The evidence is on the cameras. Nicolette is so stupid. She has no clue I've been monitoring her ass for over a month. When I see her abusing my daughter in 4K, I'm gonna kill her."

"No, please go to the police," Koko pled.

"See, there's a method to my madness, Chocolate drop. Kazimir would allow the police to handle this situation. But Kaz is going to take care of this shit on his own."

"I think—"

Before Koko could continue her thought, Kaz bent down, kissing her passionately. The thought of him killing Nicolette vanished with the quickness. It was at that moment Koko knew she wouldn't be able to resist him much longer.

# Chapter 12

Horace stopped at his home to eat after dropping Koko off. He took care of a few things, including sending pictures to Jackson so he could upload them to the internet. When he was ready to head to Koko's, Horace received a FaceTime call from his friend. Taking a seat in the kitchen, he was ready to say something about sex to piss Koko off, but the person in front of the screen made him keep it PG. Alessia made him smile big as she told him how much she missed him. Hearing her call him Uncle H meant so much to him because Horace hadn't seen his two nieces much.

He was raised in a home with three women. His mother and two sisters. He was the only male in the home after his father left. Horace and his father bumped heads throughout his teen years because he wouldn't accept the fact his son was gay. Patrick, his father, was disgusted that he birthed a son who wanted to live his life dating other boys. He felt if the man upstairs wanted him to have three daughters, that's what HE would've provided.

The day before his high school graduation, Horace and his father got into a heated altercation to the point of it getting physical. His mother stepped in, defending Horace, and Patrick didn't like that his wife had gone against him. It was the last time Horace ever laid eyes on his father, and it had been well over seven years. Stopping himself from going down memory lane, Horace left his home, and headed to Koko's.

When he arrived, Horace started cleaning immediately after locking the door. Turning on the surround sound speaker, he connected his phone. *Let Her Cook* by GloRilla had him rapping the lyrics with his chest. He was doing the Memphis jook when he felt a presence behind him. Turning around slowly, his breath caught in his throat as he made eye contact with Cyrus. Horace was surprised to see him standing in the entryway of the kitchen because Koko said the nigga was still locked up.

"What are you doing in here?" Horace asked once the initial shock wore off and he was able to speak.

"This my bitch crib. Where is she?"

"Last I heard, Koko wanted nothing to do with you. Also, how the fuck did you get in her apartment if she took the key from you?"

Cyrus swiped his thumb across his nose as he approached Horace. Taking a few steps back, Horace observed every move he made. The crazed look in his eyes prepared Horace to defend himself when the time presented itself. One thing was for certain; he had never run from a fist fight; no matter who was bringing the smoke.

"You know, sweet nigga, I've never liked yo' ass. I bet all the money in my bank account you are the reason Koko call herself leaving me."

"Cyrus, you thought what you said would hurt my feelings because I'm gay, huh?" he laughed. "It's nothing new. I don't give a fuck about you not liking me. Get in line, muthafucka. Koko left because you ain't shit. Once you realize your actions played a major part in losing her, the better off you'll be. Blaming others for your fuck-ups is diabolical. Own up to that shit."

The truth was spoken, and Cyrus didn't like that shit. The way Horace rolled his neck and eyes had him feeling as if he was being punked by a female. There was only one way for him to react, and that was with violence. Depending on how his questions were answered would determine how badly Cyrus would whoop his ass.

"Where is Koko?"

"Minding her business," Horace responded smartly.

Cyrus took three steps and grasped him by the throat. Clawing at his hands, Horace tried his best to breathe through his nose. It wouldn't be the first time he was choked and wouldn't be the last. He knew how to handle that freaky shit.

"Where the fuck is she?" Cyrus snarled.

Horace smirked because he had gotten under his skin. Koko would have to forgive him for the damage that was bound to be done to her apartment. The muthafucka was going to learn Horace loved men, but he was far from being a punk.

"Hopefully, she's poppin' her pussy for a real nigga. Now, let me the fuck go!"

Using his elbow, Horace hit Cyrus in the temple, forcing him to loosen the grip he had on his throat. Throwing a right jab, the blow stunned Cyrus momentarily, making him even angrier. Horace stood in a boxing stance to see what his next move would be. It was a major mistake on his part because Cyrus commenced to punching him anywhere he could. What Cyrus wasn't expecting was for Horace to hang with him blow for blow.

The two fought from the kitchen; knocking over the table and chairs, to the living room, breaking anything in their path. Cyrus fell to the floor after he tripped over the leg of Koko's glass table. Horace took advantage and sat on top of Cyrus' chest as he punched him in the face repeatedly. Blood poured from Cyrus' mouth and nose as he tried defending himself to no avail.

"I asked you nicely to leave me the fuck alone and you didn't listen. Now you getting whooped by a LGBTQ member. Go to the street and brag about that shit, bitch!"

Horace got up and kicked Cyrus in the head before turning his back to call the police. That was a mistake he would wish he never made. The 9-1-1 operator came on the line when a single shot sounded.

"9-1-1, what is your emergency?" the dispatcher asked. "Are you there? Do you need the police, ambulance, or the fire department?"

Horace couldn't respond because Cyrus shot him in the back. He was knocked unconscious when his head hit the floor after he fell. Cyrus kicked him in the side, then walked out of the apartment as if nothing happened, closing the door behind him.

***

"Nigga, what the fuck you do?" Jacoby asked as Cyrus jumped into the driver seat of the vehicle.

"Nothing."

"I heard a gunshot. Tell me you didn't go in there and kill that girl. We just got out of jail and you making shit hot already."

"Sit back and chill! I didn't kill her," Cyrus shot back.

"So, who whooped yo' ass then? You come out of the apartment leaking and I'm supposed to just sit back. Hell nawl! Start talking."

"When we get to my crib, I'll fill you in. Until then, shut the fuck up and let me drive. I have to make sure we don't get pulled over because I know Koko's nosy ass neighbor got the pigs on speed dial."

Jacoby watched as Cyrus wiped at his mouth with the sleeve of his shirt aggressively. The man sitting next to him was different from the kid who left Alabama back in the day. Cyrus wasn't like most of the cats he went to school with. While most were trying to make a name for themselves in the streets, Cyrus was adamant about getting an education so he would be able to move his mother away from the man she was madly in love with.

Miss Landa and Jerome's relationship turned Cyrus into his mother's protector. There were plenty times Jacoby saw him bruised up from a beating he had taken for his mother. At the time, the fights were getting worse as the days would go by. The intensity of the altercations always sounded like a bunch of men brawling for their lives. In reality, it was either Cyrus or his mother getting the shit beat out of them by Jerome.

No matter how many times Jacoby's mama called the police, Jerome was never arrested and stayed in the apartment. Living next door to the chaos was traumatizing for Jacoby too, but he was always there to walk the streets with his friend so he could clear his mind. Cyrus never wanted to go home. He would rather sleep outside or make up a story to stay at his uncle Sila's house. He stressed often how he would kill Jerome so his mother would be safe. Jacoby always wondered why Cyrus didn't tell his uncle what was going on in the household. Silas would've taken care of the situation with no questions asked. There was no doubt about that.

Jacoby would still hear the assaults in Miss Landa's apartment, but he didn't see Cyrus anymore. Thinking something bad happened to his friend, he knocked on the door to check on him. Jerome answered, telling him the lil nigga was gone and wouldn't be back, before slamming the door in his face. Jacoby thought Cyrus was dead until he heard there was a bounty on his head. Word on the street was he stabbed, robbed, and killed Huncho; a big-time drug dealer. Jacoby knew his friend didn't have it in him to kill anyone. Unless it was Jerome's bitch ass.

The day Miss Landa was killed, Cyrus didn't show up in the neighborhood. Jacoby knew wherever he was, he received word that his mother didn't survive the wrath of Jerome. The entire neighborhood was out looking for that nigga who disappeared like a thief in the night; including Jacoby. He wanted to seek revenge on Cyrus' behalf. Waiting for the information of Landa's funeral arrangements, Jacoby couldn't wait to see his friend, but they were never announced. In the back of his mind, he figured Cyrus' mother was taken wherever her son was so he could say his final goodbyes without having to worry about getting killed in Birmingham.

It surprised Jacoby to see his childhood friend in jail at the St. Cloud facility. The first couple times he saw the man who paced back and forth in the eating area of the building, Jacoby thought he was crazy. The nigga looked like a battered woman in that muthafucka, but the deranged look in his eyes told every inmate not to fuck with him. Still, Jacoby watched him like a hawk in case he had to lay hands on the nigga. One day he came in from the yard and Cyrus stormed down the hall in his direction as if he was about to beat somebody's ass. The guard, Terry, wasn't too far behind.

*"Davis! Stop and talk to me," Terry yelled out, but the nigga kept moving. "Cyrus!"*

*The name paused my steps because there was no way another muthafucka on earth would have the name Cyrus Davis. The shit was not a coincidence. When Terry said his government, the cat Jacoby now knew was, in fact, Cyrus, spun around with his chest heaving. He allowed Terry to approach him and they talked until he was calm enough for them to shake up. Terry patted Cyrus on the shoulder and walked back in the direction he had come from. Looking up, Cyrus saw Jacoby eyeballing him and became angry all over again.*

*"The fuck you lookin' at me like that fo', nigga?" he asked aggressively.*

*"Cyrus? Five Point South Cyrus?"*

*Defenses went up the moment Cyrus heard the muthafucka mention his old neighborhood. He hadn't been back to Birmingham since he left thirteen years prior. The shit that had gone down was detrimental to his life because he knew revenge didn't have a date. Cyrus killed a man and never looked back. Now, the shit was coming back full circle and he was prepared to kill again if needed.*

*"Who the fuck is you? And what you know about Five Point?"*

*Jacoby folded his arms over his chest and spread his legs apart. He smirked at Cyrus because his stance indicated he was ready to tear some shit up. Bad as he wanted to prolong who he was, Jacoby didn't want to rile Cyrus up for nothing. Instead, he revealed himself with a smile.*

*"Southtown Court. We used to walk for hours while you cleared your head about the shit going on at the crib. By the way, I want to send sincere condolences to the loss of Miss Landa."*

*Recognition flashed on Cyrus' face, but he wasn't sure. Nobody knew what was going on in his home other than one muthafucka. The man standing before him was nothing like the scrawny kid that used to live next door to him. The muscles in his arms were bigger than the size of his legs back in the day. And the nigga was always on nerdy shit when they were growing up. It couldn't be who Cyrus thought.*

*"Jacoby?"*

*"The one and only, nigga."*

*The tension dissipated, and the two men bear hugged each other as if they were long lost brothers. Cyrus always wondered what Coby, as he called him back then, was up to. He wanted to contact him when he left for Minnesota, but his uncle told him it was best to leave everybody behind. Cyrus still regretted leaving his mama because he would never see nor hear her voice again.*

*For the rest of the day, Cyrus and Jacoby chopped it up, getting to know one another as grown men. They listened to each other's stories and the reason they were locked up. It was a shock to both of them when they walked out of the facility together two weeks later.*

"Get out the car, nigga. Where yo' mind at?" Cyrus asked as he turned the car off.

Jacoby didn't answer as he got out of the vehicle. He waited for Cyrus' move before he followed. When they entered the apartment, Jacoby looked around in astonishment because the place wasn't what he expected. The spot was in the hood and didn't measure up to the status Cyrus claimed he possessed. That was neither here nor there because he wanted to know what happened back at the apartment they'd just left. Taking a seat on the couch, Jacoby rubbed his hands together before addressing Cyrus.

"You want to tell me what happened now?"

Sitting across from Jacoby, Cyrus sighed. "I told you what I was going to do. Koko wasn't there, but her gay ass friend was. His punk ass got juicy at the lips and I had to yoke his ass up. In the end, I shot his ass. Case closed."

Jacoby laughed heartily to the point tears ran down his face. Cyrus grilled him hard because he didn't find shit funny about what he had gone through at Koko's spot. Jacoby wiped the tears while clearing his throat.

"You mean to tell me you got yo' ass whooped by RuPaul's lil brother and you had to shoot the nigga! What happened to throwing them haymakers?" Jacoby laughed. "Don't tell nobody else that shit, my guy. You lost a lot of street cred behind that one. If anybody asks what happened to yo' face, tell 'em you got jumped by three niggas on a dark street. Make sure you say they stole hella stacks and some jewelry too."

Cyrus slapped him in the back of the head when he started laughing again.

"Fuck you, muthafucka!"

Cyrus walked away to the kitchen, grabbing a bottle of yak from the counter along with two glasses. He made his way back to the living room, hoping Jacoby was done with his comedy session. Cyrus wasn't proud that he had to pump some hot shit into a faggot, but it had to be done in his mind. Fighting Horace for a long period of time was something he wasn't there to do. When Cyrus shot him, he knew his actions would probably cause Koko to come home quickly. The moment he walked into the room, Jacoby looked up and started laughing hysterically. Cyrus slammed one of the glasses on the coffee table.

"It's over, nigga. When you leaving to head back to Alabama?"

"Damn. You putting me out already?" Jacoby asked, sipping the drink he poured.

"Nah, it's not like that. I don't want you just hanging around doing nothing. You don't know shit about the Sota."

"You right. I was coming through this muthafucka trying to reup and got caught. These pigs was on bullshit because I didn't have shit on me but bread. It's cool though. To answer yo' question, I'm heading out in the morning. I got some business to take care of. I've been gone a month too long and time is tickin'."

"I hear you, but if you need me to front you some shit, I got you. We go way back to the trenches and I'm just glad we reconnected."

"Thanks, man. I'm good though. My lawyer will be back to this bitch to get my bread sometime this week. I already got what I need on the streets of Birmingham. All I gotta do is hit the connect with what is owed. He knows I'm good for it."

"Who you cop from?"

Cyrus wanted to make sure his nigga wasn't fuckin' around with Kaz's bitch ass. He and Jacoby already talked about having each other's back in the streets. Cyrus would hate to fuck up his money by killing the plug then his well runs dry. Soon as he dealt with Koko and got her back into his life, Cyrus was going to get rid of Kaz. If he couldn't have the woman he molded for himself, no one else would have the opportunity to show her a different type of love either.

"Fatman. You may know him. He's out in Duluth."

"Nah, I don't know none of them niggas that way."

Cyrus took a sip of his drink before leaning forward to roll a blunt. He was in deep thought, and Jacoby allowed him to do that without interruption because he knew the homie was fucked up about his girl. Cyrus was on the verge of crashing out. The signs were in plain sight for all to see. What he did earlier spoke volumes.

"I need to find this bitch!" Cyrus screamed, beating on the table. "She claimed to be out of town, but Koko would never leave a muthafucka in her crib like that. Her hot pussy ass is somewhere in this state. Wherever she is, that nigga with her hoe ass!"

"Cyrus, let me ask you something. Is Koko yo' woman, or you just want her back?"

"The bitch will forever be my woman! The fuck you thought? Ain't no leaving me! I don't give a fuck what I've done!"

Jacoby understood Cyrus' mindset because he once had the same feelings toward his ex, Kelis, when she left him without notice. Those emotions turned into hate when he learned what she had done behind his back. The bitch was clever as hell with her shit too. It had been a little over two years since she'd been gone, and Jacoby searched everywhere he possibly could to find her without any luck; until one of her cousins decided to drop a dime on her ass.

The saying *money is the root of all evil* is true. Skylar asked Kelis for money and was flat-out told no. According to her, Kelis was sitting on bank and wouldn't help out the family. In return, Skylar called Jacoby and gave up her number. He texted once. Knowing Kelis, she was probably on the run once again. For the time being, he was going to scare the fuck out of her until he pulled up on her deceitful ass.

"Why you always zoning out?" Cyrus asked. "Yo' ass got demons you not sharing, huh?"

"Nah, I'm thinking about my next move. It will be the best one yet." Jacoby downed the shot as if it was water and poured another. "If Koko hasn't done nothing wrong to you, why not leave her alone to live her life happily? Now, don't get me wrong, if she is an ain't shit bitch, find her and whoop her ass!"

"I like the way you think with the last statement. That's fact!"

Saluting their glasses, they passed a blunt back and forth, chopping it up while watching the Vikings versus the Texans game. Both men pretended to enjoy themselves, but in reality, they were anticipating seeing the women who still made their dicks hard whenever the thought of them occurred.

# Chapter 13

Three days passed since Kazimir told Nicolette he was taking Alessia to Disneyland. The trip was sporadic and didn't sit well with her. He had never taken her daughter anywhere without consulting with her before. Marisol hadn't returned to clean, cook, or even call to see if there was anything needed in the home. That alone told Nicolette she was in cahoots with her husband and was in California with them.

Nicolette called Kazimir countless times and he hadn't answered. She sat drinking wine for hours as she waited for a different result. It was taking everything in her not to report Alessia missing since he wanted to play with her intelligence. Nicolette knew Kazimir was up to something, but his threat of divorce wasn't it. She was sure he was bluffing when he made the threat because the consequences he would face were something Kazimir wasn't built for. He was a businessman, and Nicolette's father was a killer. She didn't want anything to happen to him, but it seemed that was the direction the scene was going to play out.

There was no hope for a happily ever after because Kazimir stated from day one he wasn't marrying Nicolette for love. He made it very clear his grandfather's debt was all he cared about until he laid eyes on Alessia. Kazimir fell in love at first sight and made a vow to be the best father he could to the little bundle of joy. Nicolette never received the affection she craved no matter how persistent she was with the man she married. She thought over time he would learn to love her as his wife. The day never presented itself.

Standing to her feet, Nicolette picked up her phone, attempting to call her husband for the hundredth time. Anger built up rapidly within her the longer it took him to answer. When she was about to hang up, the call connected, prompting her to put it on speaker.

"Hey, Mommy."

"Hi, sweetie." Nicolette was ready to go off but stopped herself the moment she heard her daughter's voice. "Where's Daddy?"

"Right here. He said you calling for me," Alessia replied. "Mommy, I'm going to see Tiana today! Daddy bought me a princess dress and shoes just like in the movie!"

The excitement coming from the little girl would've caused the average mother to smile. Not Nicolette. She was waiting for the almost three-year-old to indulge more about what her father was doing. She could care less about her daughter going to see her favorite Disney princess. As Alessia talked about everything she had done the past couple of days, Nicolette was focused on what was going on in the background. She snapped back to reality when she heard her daughter squeal and the phone falling to the floor.

"Koko! Your hair pretty! Right, Daddy?"

Nicolette's nose flared as she listened to the interaction between her child, husband, and the mystery woman. Kazimir swore he wasn't demanding a divorce because he wanted to move on with someone else, and there he was, in California playing the role of a happy family with a child that didn't belong to either one of them. Kazimir must've forgotten Nicolette was on the phone because Alessia didn't come back to the line. She couldn't hear what was being said, as if they had left the room.

She hung up to call back but was interrupted by the doorbell. Walking across the room, Nicolette wondered who would come to her home unannounced. She could see a male figure through the glass but didn't recognize who he was. Opening the door, Nicolette took in the man's appearance, from his fresh haircut to the leather loafers on his feet. Her gaze found its way to the envelope he held tightly in his right hand.

"May I help you?" she asked.

"Yes, is Nicolette Santoro-St. Claire available?"

"I'm her. What is this pertaining to?"

"This is for you," the man said with a smile. He held the envelope out, causing Nicolette to receive it with caution.

"What is this?" she questioned.

"You've been served. Have a nice day," he said, walking away.

"Oh no, motherfucker!" Nicolette screamed. "Come get this shit!"

Lamont laughed as he got inside his car. Nicolette ran along the walkway barefoot, trying to catch him, but he drove off before she approached. As she watched the back end of the vehicle round the corner, the envelope trembled in her hand. Walking slowly back toward the house, Nicolette tapped the envelope against her leg.

"I know this bastard did not follow through with filing those papers."

Shutting the door behind her, Nicolette locked it, then proceeded to open the envelope. She pulled the contents out, and the top page confirmed her suspicions. Her eyes were stuck on the opening statement.

*Nicolette Santoro-St. Claire*
*Vs,*
*Kazmir St. Claire*
*Decree of Divorce*

That was as far as she read before throwing the papers across the room. She stormed into the living room and sat down on the sofa. Kazimir was playing with her emotions, and Nicolette wasn't going down without a fight. She pushed her husband's contact, calling him for the second time within the hour.

"What is it, Nicolette?"

"Kazimir, how could you file for divorce? I just got served! That shit is embarrassing because the man laughed in my face!"

"You embarrassed for what? People get divorced every day; this isn't new. I don't know why you're surprised you received the papers. This union was fraudulent from the start, and you knew my plans to end this shit a long time ago. It shouldn't have been an element of surprise that it happened because I forewarned you, Nicolette. The only thing you have to do is sign on the dotted line and walk away. It's that simple. But I want you to read everything so you won't think I'm trying to backdoor you on anything. Then drop the shit in the mail."

"I don't care what's in those papers! I'm not signing my marriage away. You may have stood before God and lied to love me for better or for worse; I didn't. My plans were for us to come together to make it work. You never gave love a chance because all you wanted to do was stand up for your grandfather. What about me?"

Nicolette cried as she fought for Kazimir to hear how much she wanted to work things out. Knowing her father basically fucked her over by spending her nest egg, she needed him to lean on to survive. Plus, deep down inside, she didn't want her daughter to lose her life behind a dollar.

"What about you? My decision is final. I refuse to be stuck in a relationship I never wanted to be part of. Repeating this shit over and over is becoming very annoying. Love is something I would never have for you. Take this for what it is and go out there and find your Mr. Right because I'm not him."

"What we have isn't just a relationship, it's a marriage! Kazimir, you and that bitch will die fuckin' with me! I've allowed you to play in my face for years just for you to choose someone else to lay under!" Nicolette was so mad she was spitting with every word.

"What bitch are you referring to?" Kazimir asked casually.

"The one you have in that hotel room playing mommy to my child! You don't think I heard Alessia when she greeted the bitch, leaving me on the phone as if I don't matter to her. She said her name as if she's comfortable with her. That shit isn't cool for me. I've told you not to have any of your women around my daughter, and you said there was no one worthy of being around her. You lied!"

"All that doesn't matter. I brought Alessia here to enjoy herself." Kaz must've left the hotel room because Nicolette heard a door close before he started speaking again. "You can keep the house, your car, and I will deposit two hundred thousand dollars into your account for you to live your life comfortably. I advise you to read the papers because I am fighting you for one thing and one thing only, and that is gaining full custody of Alessia."

Nicolette thought she heard him wrong because he couldn't have said what she thought he had. "Come again."

"You heard me the first time. Don't fight me on this. Alessia is better off with me. You don't truly love her the way I do. On top of that, you don't spend much time with her either. Majority of the time she is with Marisol. You deal with her on a need-to basis, and you can't deny that, Nicolette."

"Just because I don't spoil my child and allow her to whine her way into whatever she wants does not make me a bad mother! How the hell can you part your lips to say I don't love a child I carried for nine months? You sound stupid. I'm not worried about you trying to take my daughter because you have no rights to do so. I'm her mother, and she will forever be with me. Kazimir, you better enjoy the time you have with her because it will be the last time you see her. As a matter of fact, bring her home now! If she's not back in Chicago tonight, I will be making a report for kidnapping."

"That's where you're wrong. I will get custody without a doubt. Alessia isn't safe being alone with you. I have solid proof. Don't make this worse than it already is. My daughter has old and new bruises on her body, and I have pictures. She may be young, but I believe her when she says you hit her. One thing I won't tolerate is you harming the only thing I give a fuck about in this so-called marriage. If I had my way, I would come back to Chicago and beat yo' ass the same way you did my daughter."

"She is not your daughter! I am her legal guardian, Kazimir! No matter how much money you have, there isn't enough money in the world that would help you take my child from me! Let me enlighten you. The section on her birth certificate, where the father's name should be, says—"

"Kazimir Keonte St. Clair. Play with it if you want to. Alessia is legally my fuckin' daughter. You said all that shit for what? Any mother being accused of abusing their child would've mentioned the allegations presented to them before all the other bullshit you spoke on. Address the fuckin' bruises Marisol found on my daughter's body!"

"I don't know what you are talking about. Ask Marisol since she is the one that's always with her. While you're interrogating me, the person who is laying hands on Alessia is with you in California! Don't blame me for something I haven't done!"

Nicolette had to keep up the tough persona in order for Kazimir to believe her. There was no way she would admit to hitting her daughter. She knew her husband didn't play with anything that meant something to him, and that included Alessia. She knew it was wrong to harm her, but at times the crying and whining when Kazimir wasn't home was too much for her to bear. For the most part, he was right. Nicolette didn't like her daughter some days. She felt getting pregnant by force had ruined her life. Then, the man she wanted to love her only loved the same child Nicolette didn't want. Jealousy was part of the reason she spazzed out on Alessia, but it wasn't intentional. It was more instinctive.

"You definitely did it, and I will prove it. Bow out gracefully and sign over your rights. Nicolette, you are lucky I'm taking the legal route on this. The man you have known for the past three years is only a fraction of who I am. There has never been a reason for me to bring the demon to the horizon, but the shit you have done to Alessia would truly get you hurt. I want you to call your bitch ass daddy and tell him everything I have planned. Hopefully, you've been paying on his insurance policy because I'm ready to beat his ass to death, and I'm ready for the battle he thinks he will bring."

Nicolette listened to Kazimir, and as he spoke, she could hear the malice falling from his tongue. He even sounded different than the man he portrayed himself to be. Since she met him, Kazimir was mild-mannered and came across as a little nerdy businessman to her. The person she was going back and forth with on the phone sounded like a stone-cold killer. Obviously, her father didn't do his homework because there was a side of her soon-to-be ex-husband neither of them knew about. She would have to do some digging into his background to find out who the hell she was married to.

"Far as bringing Alessia home tonight; it's not going to happen. We're going to enjoy our time here. I will be back in a few days, but I'm telling you now, Alessia isn't coming back to that house until the judge tells me I have to return her, which I highly doubt. On that note, I'm being rude standing in this hall while my daughter is waiting to be the most beautiful princess in the castle. Enjoy the rest of your day, Nicolette. Oh, do me a favor and refrain from calling my phone. There's no reason for you to contact me. Alessia is with me already."

"So, you're still going to spend time with the woman that you're with?"

"Nicolette, don't ask questions if you're not ready for the answers. The woman that's here with me isn't your concern. Okay?"

"Fuck you, Kazimir! I'm going to kill you, motherfucker! You better watch your back when you land in Chicago because I have something for you!"

Nicolette was foaming at the mouth as she threw threats left and right. She was sweating as if she was in hell and had to fan herself. When Kazimir didn't respond, she looked down at the phone to discover he had hung up. Nicolette didn't know how much he heard, and at that moment she didn't care.

Running up the stairs two at a time, she went straight to her closet so she could get dressed. The mission she was on wouldn't require her to dress fancy. Nicolette snatched a jogging suit from her closet along with a pair of sneakers. Once she was ready, she snatched her keys and phone, damn near running out of the house.

"I tried to love you, Kazimir, but you wouldn't allow me to do that," she said out loud as she started her vehicle. "You fucked with the wrong woman this time. I'm not one of the bitches you want to ignore. It's time for me to show you how I get down like my daddy. I'll make you bring your ass back to Illinois one way or another."

She backed out of the driveway and headed straight for the gas station to get some gas. The alcohol she consumed had worked its way through her bloodstream, causing her vision to blur a little bit. Nicolette pushed the button to lower the window, hoping the cool air would help her out. Driving was the last thing she should've been doing, but Kazimir pissed her off to the max.

She stopped at the first gas station she saw, pulled alongside pump three, and hopped out of her vehicle. She walked inside searching for a gas can. May as well call her the Firestarter because she was about to torch some shit. Nicolette found what she was looking for, then headed to the counter. There was one person in line before her, but she was impatient. Nicolette pushed her way to the front, knocking the woman to the side.

"Excuse you! I'm trying to find my card," the woman hissed.

"Well, move your ass to the side because I have shit to do. This is not the day to fuck with me, bitch," Nicolette snapped. "Let me have twenty on pump three."

"Ma'am, I have to assist the customers that were in line before you," the cashier said.

"No, you are going to give me twenty dollars on pump three so I can get the fuck out of here. Her ass is still looking for her damn card. That means she still isn't ready. Now ring me up…please."

Doing as she was told, the cashier hurriedly checked Nicolette out. Snatching the receipt, she left the store after bumping the woman a second time. She heard the woman call her a fuckin' cunt and immediately turned back to smack her ass but thought better of it. Nicolette had something more important to deal with. Melody the meth head wasn't one of them, so she allowed her to think she won that battle. If she ever saw her again, she was for sure going to knock the rest of her teeth out of her mouth.

It didn't take long for her to fill the five-gallon can. After tossing it on the floor in the back, Nicolette merged into traffic like a madwoman. She slowed down because getting pulled over by the Plainfield police was something she didn't want to deal with. The only thing she wanted was to pull up and hurt Kazimir worse than he had hurt her. It took ten minutes for her to arrive at the destination she was focused on. The moment Paxton's house came into view; Nicolette was happier than a sissy with a bag full of dicks.

She was surprised the gate was open because Kazimir made sure his grandfather's house was locked down like Fort Knox. It worked in her favor because Nicolette didn't have to buzz for someone to allow her entry. She drove up to the door, retrieved her nine-millimeter and stuck it in the front of her hoodie, got out of her vehicle, then walked up to the door. Ringing the doorbell, Nicolette waited patiently for one of the aides to open the door. She hoped it wasn't the Kelly chick. That one was devoted to Kazimir, and she would have to call him to get permission to enter the house.

The door opened, and his uncle David stood there, licking his lips while sizing her up as if she were a neck bone. She didn't like that man because something wasn't right with him. He truly creeped her out, and Nicolette was ready for his ass if he tried anything with her.

"You are Kaz's wife, right?"

Nicolette never called her husband by the name his family used. Once she realized, she nodded. "Yeah. Kazimir is out of town, so I came to check on Mr. Paxton. Do I have to stand here at the door, or can I come in?"

"Oh, my bad," David said, stepping aside. "You can have a seat in the living room."

Sitting on the sofa, Nicolette looked around the room, wondering why all the lights were off. The house was eerily quiet, and she felt uncomfortable as fuck. She looked over her shoulder to see where David was, then jumped when she felt his hand on her shoulders.

"What are you doing? Don't touch me," Nicolette said, moving out of his reach. "Where is Mr. Paxton?"

"He went on an outing with Kelly. They will be back in a little bit. I'll keep you company until then. Why are you acting like you don't know me?"

"I don't. I'm married to your nephew, and touching me is very disrespectful. I would appreciate if you wouldn't do that."

David laughed as he walked around to sit next to her. Nicolette pushed off the sofa and was yanked by the arm almost into his lap. The night she was taken advantage of flashed before her eyes. The way she fought to get away from the man who was ripping her clothes off in public,

Nicolette could hear her cries from years prior. When David put his tongue in her ear, she started trembling.

*"Not again."*

Tears welled in her eyes as she tried to get away from her. Nicolette regretted coming to the house. She came to harm Paxton to hurt Kazimir and found herself in a situation she would have to kill or be killed to get out of. Karma didn't waste any time spinning the block, and she hadn't even done anything. David started groping her breasts as he kissed her neck. The entire time, he still held a strong grip on her arm, causing pain to shoot through her body. She reached into her hoodie, wrapping her hand around her gun. Nicolette was glad the silencer was in place because she was about to turn David into Swiss cheese.

"You may as well let me fuck you good. I know my nephew ain't hitting that pussy because he never wanted it. I've always wanted you, Nikki. You should've been my wife instead of his. If you allow me to have my way with you, I'll give you fifty thousand and Kaz won't know a thing."

"Give me the money first," she said, squeezing the gun tighter.

"Shid, you ain't said nothing but a word. I have to go downstairs to get it out of the basement. Lay back and get comfortable for me. I'll be right back."

Nicolette knew he was lying. Kazimir wouldn't dare leave money in the house his uncle had access to. She knew all about his gambling addiction, and David didn't have a dime to his name. He was probably at the house waiting for Mr. Paxton to come back so he could take money from him. She waited until he released her arm, but he jumped on top of her while tugging at her pants. Nicolette was able to free her hand, producing the gun. David thought he was about to have a good time, but it would be his final day breathing. He was going to die with pussy on the brain.

"Damn, you smell good as fuck," he murmured in her ear.

Releasing the safety with her thumb, Nicolette placed the barrel of the gun against his ribcage and pulled the trigger twice. David's eyes bulged as he looked down at her while he struggled to catch his breath. She pumped another bullet into him, and he slumped against her chest. Pushing his body off her, David hit his head on the corner of the coffee table. That gave her the opportunity to spring to her feet. He was still breathing, and that wasn't a good sign to her.

"Forgive me, Lord, for I have sinned," she said aloud before shooting David in the head three times, making sure he was dead.

Nicolette ran to the kitchen and grabbed a few paper towels to wipe her hands. She then went to the door, peeked out to make sure no one was lurking, then dashed to the car to get the gas can. Once she reentered the home, she started throwing gasoline everywhere; even upstairs. Nicolette took another look at David as she backpedaled toward the door. She opened it, and before stepping outside, she had some parting words for his corpse.

"I bet you won't try to fuck nobody else. Tell the devil I said save me a spot, sick bitch," she snarled, then struck a match, throwing it into the pool of gasoline.

The fire spread throughout the home fast as she closed the door. Hurrying to her car, Nicolette drove in the opposite direction of the home she shared with Kazimir. There was no way she would be around when he returned to find out his grandfather was homeless and David was dead. Stopping at the bank, Nicolette withdrew all the money she had in her account because she was going to a hotel until further notice. Using a card was out of the question. It would be dumb to leave a paper trail that would lead to her death.

# Chapter 14

"Barkhado! Barkhado, where yo' ass at?" Jojo yelled as he looked around the property of the Cedar High Apartments.

He was meeting up with the Somalian to conduct business, and Barkhado was fifteen minutes late. Jojo didn't like when a muthafucka wanted in on money but couldn't be on time. He turned to head back to his whip when he saw movement out of his peripheral vision. Barkhado was walking from the side of the building, buckling his pants, then a woman followed, swiping her hand across her mouth. Jojo shook his head as he watched in disbelief.

"My bad, homie. I had something to take care of real quick," Barkhado said in a heavy accent as he watched ol' girl walk down the street.

"I thought shit like that was against your Muslim beliefs."

"It only applies to our women. American women are free game. They don't have respect for themselves. Plus, my daddy ain't here no more to tell me what I can and cannot do. I'm my own man," Barkhado smirked.

"Nawl, nigga. Crackheads don't have respect for themselves. Don't put my sistas in the same category. So get yo' facts straight because disrespect won't be tolerated while talking to me. Save that shit for your immediate Somalian folks. As a matter of fact, I don't even want to do business with yo' ass no mo'."

Jojo walked to his whip and put a leg inside before Barkhado called out to him.

"Aye, Jojo. Come on, man. I apologized. I'll cut the price down for you. We gotta get this money together. I'll give you the bricks for five thousand less."

"How about eight?" Jojo pressed.

"That's highway robbery!"

"Nigga, you disrespected my people. Get the fuck outta here or deal. Ain't no in between."

"Stay right here. I'll be right back. Have my money ready," Barkhado said, heading toward the entrance of the building.

"Aye, Bark. Don't try no funny shit. I got eyes on you, nigga. I would hate for your people to see you out here with yo' noodles out."

Waving him off, Barkhado disappeared around the building. It took ten minutes for him and one of his homies to come back carrying the cargo. Jojo got out of the car, rubbing his hands together because he was about to take over the drug game on the north side. The money he took from the trap was going to have him eating good. Jojo popped the trunk. He removed the amount they agreed on and put the rest in the hidden compartment before zipping the bag back up.

The air was crisp in Minnesota, and it wouldn't be long before it looked like Christmas with tons of snow. Barkhado dropped the bags inside the trunk, then Jojo handed him a duffle full of cash.

"Go count that shit. I'll wait here until you call or text stating I'm good."

"Jojo, you seem like a stand-up dude. This is business, and I don't think you would fuck up with me like that. I allowed you to check me about American women, but you will get no passes if my money not right."

"Correction, I checked yo' ass about Black women. For the record, you didn't allow me to do shit; I did that on my own accord and will check yo' ass again. I'm out. Be up, nigga. Be ready when it's time to reup."

Soon as he was far enough away from Cedar's, Jojo hit up Jerrod. They had been practically begging that nigga Cyrus to put them on since he started fucking with Sheree. He wanted the shine for himself and wouldn't let them eat with him. So Jojo and his cousin decided to fuck up his spot and take what they needed to come up on their own. Word on the street was the plug was looking for them along with Cyrus. Jojo wasn't too much worried about his punk ass because he was locked the fuck up. Hell, he wasn't bent out of shape about the plug either. It had been weeks since they took his shit and there hadn't been any fire behind it. Jojo thought the money they stole wasn't shit to a rich nigga.

"What up, cuz?" Jerrod smacked in his ear. Whatever the fuck he was eating sounded like it was good.

"Damn, nigga, what you eating? Shit, you got my stomach growling."

"Shid, my lil yea-yea cooked like a muthafucka ova here. I'm gon' have to fuck her good for this shit and make her my main. I ain't never had a bitch cook on the level of my mama."

"I want you to finish eating, but the fuckin' gotta wait. We out here. I need you to meet me at the spot. I'm on my way there now."

"You got the work?" Jerrod wanted to make sure he was on the same page as his cousin.

"Hell yeah, I did! Make sure you have yo' half when you pull up. I paid for this shit out of pocket."

"How much was it?"

"Fuck you mean? It's the price he told us it would be. Pay me or I'll do this shit dolo."

"I got you. No need for the hostility. Usually, yo' ass can talk a nigga down to the low on some shit. I guess that shit don't work in the drug game. Let me talk to this girl and tell her I gotta bounce. I'll be there within the hour."

Jojo hung up without replying because he felt some type of way that Jerrod questioned him on the sale. He got a deal, but that wasn't his muthafuckin' business. Jojo didn't give a damn about nobody but himself. Getting a couple thousand out of his cousin actually put money back in his pockets. All profit is better than half any day. If it ain't about money from that day forward, it wasn't about shit, was Jojo's thought process.

As he drove the speed limit to his crib, Jojo smiled. He copped him a spot in Apple Valley to get out of his mama's crib, but he hadn't told anybody other than Jerrod. Knowing what they had done, Jojo didn't want nobody to know where he laid his head in case he had to go in hiding. Not even Jackie. His plan was to keep pretending to live with his mama. It was just a cover, though.

His thoughts switched to Jackie, and the way she sucked his dick from the back the other night played vividly in his mind. One thing he could say was Jackie was a freak. She did any and everything in the bedroom without question; even allowed him to hit that booty shoot. Jojo didn't trust her far as he could throw, though. He had a feeling she was up to something. Jojo asked her if she was fucking around with Cyrus, and she denied it. Niggas on the street kept telling him how close they were, but Jackie insisted she and Cyrus had no dealings. Time would tell, and when it presented itself, Jojo had no problem shooting a bitch in the head. In the meantime, he was enjoying the orgasms they shared.

Stopping at a red light, Jojo called Sheree. It went straight to voicemail. Every time he tried to holla at his sister, he received the same result. That only meant she blocked his number. It was something else Jojo thought about on the regular.

Sheree turned her back on family for a man. It was something she had never done. Cyrus had her stupid ass eating out the palm of his hand, and she was the side chick. According to Jackie, Cyrus had a bitch and she recently found out about CJ and left his ass. Sheree thought she won, but in reality, her ass lost like a muthafucka. How could a woman stand by a man who kept her and their son a secret? When he breaks her heart, she bet not remember she has a big brother.

Turning onto Redwood Drive, Jojo hit the button to let up the garage door before pulling into the driveway. He made sure the door was secure before he got out of his car. Retrieving the bags from the trunk, Jojo entered his home, kicking his shoes off. There was carpet throughout the crib, and he had furnished the entire house. The money Jojo stole had him living the way he always dreamed. He headed straight for the basement—the lab, is what Jojo called it because that was the only place in the house where anything drug-related would be conducted.

The lower level was the first area Jojo set up when he moved in. There were scales, a table with chairs, money counters, as well as a complete kitchen. It was actually a small apartment with one bedroom along with a sitting room. Tossing the bags on the table, Jojo got to work.

Forty-five minutes later, there was loud knocking on the security door. He knew the person banging like the police was Jerrod.

"Nigga, you late," Jojo stated as he allowed his cousin inside.

"Alexis wouldn't let me out the crib," he explained, draping his jacket on the back of a chair. "When I told her I had moves to make, the crazy bitch gon' say, 'You ain't leaving with my dick.'"

"What type of chick would say some shit like that?" Jojo asked, laughing.

"You ain't heard the worse part, though!" Jerrod exclaimed. "She went into the kitchen, then came out with a big ass butcher knife in her hand! Nigga, I wanted to knock her muthafuckin' head off, but I was scared she would chop me up like a fish."

The way Jerrod recounted the story was hilarious because Jojo could see the entire scene taking place as if he was in the room witnessing the encounter. Alexis was a big boned cutie who was soft as cotton; until she couldn't fuck. Jerrod needed to make their relationship official before things got out of hand. The day Alexis wilds out when she sees him with another chick, which is bound to happen. Murder will be the case the judge gives her.

"Yo! What did you do after she pulled the knife?"

"Man, we tussled for a few minutes before I took possession of the it. I tossed that shit across the room, then yoked her ass up. Any other woman would've been throwing punches; not Alexis. The shit turned her on. So I gave her what she wanted, putting her ass to sleep. When I leave here, I'm going to my mama's house. Ain't no way I'm going to lay down next to her and sleep with one eye open."

"That's the most toxic shit I've ever heard in my life. There is no way I'd be able to fuck after a female threatened to cut off my most prized possession. Alexis may be crazy, but you right there with her. I blame you for her actions, nigga. Make a choice about what you want to do with this one. Alexis is a firecracker. The last thing you want to do is ignite her fuse. It's going to be explosive. Be careful with how you handle her."

Jojo expressed the way he saw his cousin's relationship. Therefore, he hoped like hell Jerrod took heed to the critique. Time was ticking, and Jojo had money on the brain, so there was work to be done.

"Enough about your bullshit. We gotta bag up this shit. My plan is to have this work on the street pronto. We've been starving too long out here. The hunger pains end right now. Barkhado hooked us up. I mostly copped meth and pills," Jojo explained.

"What about the coke and weed?"

"Ain't nobody really fucking with the white girl no mo'. I got a little bit, but you can deal with that. Far as weed, there's a few pounds of that too. Feel free to do what you do with it. My focus is on the meth and pills. That's where the money is right now. High demand, too. Half of this shit will be off my hands, and I just bought the product. You feel me? We'll see how shit move on the street, then go from there. It will be me and you for now. Moving this shit quickly is the goal so we can show Barkhado we getting this shit off in no time. You ready?" Jojo questioned.

"Hell yeah, I'm ready. I got folks on standby for weed, and I have a few old heads looking for coke along with crack. Nigga, an addiction is an addiction. At the end of the day, muthafuckas just want to get high. The product really don't matter; to some. We gon' be good regardless. All we have to do is deliver while staying under the radar. I got yo' back long as you got mine."

"With that being said, where's my money?" Jojo quipped.

"I got you. Come by the crib to pick it up. The shit with Alexis prevented me from taking the ride across town. I came straight to you."

"Aight, bet."

Jojo and Jerrod spent hours bagging and reminiscing back to when the struggle was real for them. Neither one of them spoke on the war against them because they felt talking about it would produce an omen around them. In other words, they thought it was safe and nothing was going to interfere in their come-up. For the moment, it was. But for how long?

# Chapter 15

As she stepped out of the shower, Koko was dead tired from the day's events. She was ready for the hotel mattress to hug her body. Running around the park with Alessia was fun she never thought was needed. Koko's mom couldn't afford to take her kids out of Chicago when they were younger. Her experience of an amusement park was the metal merry-go-round at the playground down the street from where they lived. To actually ride the carousel was a delight, and Koko enjoyed it just as much as Alessia.

The entire day played in her mind. Koko could see the smile on Alessia's face, and the shit warmed her heart. She couldn't fathom how a mother could harm her child in any way. The little girl was the sweetest child who hadn't done anything to upset any of the adults around her. She whined a bit when she couldn't get her way, but it was nothing a look from Kaz couldn't fix without opening his mouth nor raising his hand. Alessia gravitated to Koko, and it was fine with her. With a mother like the one she had, Koko didn't mind being in California to be a stand-in.

Her body was relaxed, the fatigue was setting in, but Koko had to make sure her skincare was taken care of before she could crawl under the linen. Oiling her thighs, a sudden euphoric surge traveled to her honey pot. Koko knew exactly where the feeling generated from. Throughout the day, she found herself lusting over Kaz. It wasn't his features alone. The way he handled fatherhood was sexy in itself. He licked his lips one too many times for Koko, and the action was embedded in her head.

She scurried out of the bathroom, making a beeline for the bedroom. Closing the door, Koko opened the drawer where she stashed her trusty vibrator. Kaz had her clit poking out, and she needed to release. Placing a dry towel on the bed, Koko laid on top of it, closing her eyes. She bit her lip as the vibrations shook her core, getting her into a sexy groove. Kaz invaded her mind, causing the intensity to rise within her. A moan escaped from her mouth just as the door opened quietly.

Kaz heard when Koko came out of the bathroom. He couldn't sleep with so much invading his mind; he thought talking about it with her would relax him a little bit. What he didn't expect to see was her spread eagle while rubbing a vibrator along her clit. The sight caused a tent to rise in his pajama pants. He decided to ease out the door, closing it behind him. Kaz knocked then entered without waiting for her to invite him in, causing Koko to lock the toy between her legs.

"Um… keep playing with it," he stammered, licking his lips. "I came in to talk, but I like what you're doing better."

Throwing the cover over her body, Koko's cheeks heated up as Kaz fucked her with his eyes. "I don't think that would be wise. What did you want to talk about?"

"Actually, I don't know anymore. The sound of that vibrator is music to my ears. Fuckin' my thought process all the way up."

"Well, when you remember, come back, and I'll be ready to have that conversation with you. Until then, I would like to get some sleep."

Kaz smirked as he closed the door. "You were wide awake playing in your box a few seconds ago. Come from under the covers and spread your legs. This time for me. Anything that battery-operated tool can do; I can do better."

"Kaz, we can't—"

"Can't isn't in my vocabulary, Koko. Now show me that pretty snatch I got a glimpse of by mistake." Koko's hesitation only made Kaz want her more. "You've been sneaking peeks at me all day, in lieu of me doing the same with you. I kept shit on the low out of respect for my daughter. She's sleeping now. It's time for both of us to act on our feelings."

Strolling to the bed, Kaz grabbed the corner of the linen, removing it from her body. Koko had her legs closed tightly, with the toy humming near her ass. Her body was stiff, but he could see the moisture of her kitty traveling between her cheeks. His dick was on brick, and that shit didn't feel good at all. Kaz needed to release immediately. Koko didn't know her fantasy of him making her cum would turn into a reality when she decided to play with herself. Every nerve in her body was activated when his hand touched her skin. Caressing her ankles as he made his way up to her calf, Kaz never took his eyes off the beauty lying in front of him in all her glory.

Koko started to relax. She wanted the intimacy between them to happen. The moment presented itself; now she was going to stop fighting. Therefore, she was going with the flow. His touch was sensual, sending shivers down her spine. Kaz kissed her knee as he reached for the vibrator. Turning it off, he tossed that muthafucka on a nearby chair, then positioned himself between her legs.

"From this day forth, you won't be needing that bullshit. I promise," Kaz muttered lowly. "If you want me to stop, the time to make it known is now. Once we cross this line, there is no turning back. I'm going to mold this pussy to respond only to me. Is that understood?"

Koko bit her bottom lip, trying to suppress the moan that was forcing its way out of her mouth from the way Kaz strummed her clit with his thumb. She pushed her kitty into his hand, causing him to chuckle lowly. Koko was aroused, and the scent of her sweet nectar lingered in the air. She wanted him to put out the fire between her legs, but he was going to make her beg for more.

"Tell me what you want, Chocolate drop. You do know a closed mouth don't get fed, right?" She nodded. "Tell me what you want."

Kaz slipped a finger into her wet center. Koko's walls tightened around his digit at the same time his meat hardened more. Inserting another finger, she moaned lowly. Her head fell back onto the pillow, and her eyes rolled to the back of her head. Kaz took the moment to give her a reason to moan. He knew she wanted him in every way imaginable, and he wasn't going to deprive her from getting it. To be frank, Kaz was prepared to send her soul to the king and catch that muthafucka before it had a chance to cross over.

With his fingers still inside of her, Kaz replaced his thumb with his mouth. Koko came immediately, coating his tongue with her sweetness. The shit tasted like pineapples; his favorite fruit. She palmed his head, then ground into his face. Her actions made Kaz go all in on her pussy. She tried to run, but he pulled her ass right back into his mouth. Drenched beard and all, he was still thirsty for her juices.

"Mmmmm, Kaz. Suck it," Koko moaned. Therefore, he obliged.

The oral assault he gave her was one for the books. Kaz was determined to go the entire ten yards to score with Koko. What he wanted, he always got in the end. She'd been running from him too long; now her legs were weak with no more energy to escape. Koko held on to the fact of Kaz being married; he fixed that. There was only one thing left to do, and it was for Kameeko to submit to being his and only his.

"Oh shit, I'm cummin'," she moaned as her clit hardened.

Koko was a squirter, and that was a plus for Kaz. She wet his ass up, damn near choking him to death. His mouth, beard, and chest were drenched along with the bed. Kaz smiled at his handiwork. Giving her kitty one last kiss, Kaz had already eased out of his pajama pants, so his dick was ready to act out. He climbed to the head of the bed, lying on his back. Koko was still trying to catch her breath from the tidal wave she'd hand delivered.

"This is just the beginning, Chocolate drop. Come take a ride with me," he said, rubbing his hand up and down her leg.

"Do you have protection?" was Koko's reply.

"We are both grown. We've come too far to quit now. Plus, my pull-out game is strong as fuck!"

"That's what he said, and I ended up pregnant."

Koko rolled out of the bed, going to her luggage. She thanked Horace silently for putting the condoms in the inside pocket. When he thought she wasn't paying attention; she was. Kaz couldn't take his eyes off her plump ass and thick thighs. Koko was shapely, good enough to eat. He couldn't wait to devour her again. Waiting patiently for her to return back to the bed, it wasn't long before she sauntered slowly over with something in her hand. Koko tossed two gold wrappers on the bed, then her eyes bulged. Kaz was stroking his wood to keep him hard in between the delay of game.

"You came prepared, I see," he smirked. "Now slide one of them on so you can ride this muthafucka. He's ready to throw up."

"Who you think about to ride that?" Koko exclaimed. "I'm going to tell you now; I have never had one that big before."

"There's a first time for everything, Chocolate drop. You're wasting time. Don't make me come to you. It will only be worse. Come ride this dick, ma."

Koko was hesitant because Kaz was three times larger than Cyrus. She was sure he would fuck up her uterus with that thing. There was nothing to do except bail out on the mission. Her yoni had dried up at that point, and Koko wanted him to leave.

"I can't handle that. I'm sorry. It would be best if you leave now."

"Speak your mind, Chocolate drop. I won't know what's for you if you stay silent. Be vocal with that shit."

He climbed out of the bed, picking up one of the condoms along the way. Koko backed up against the wall with a frightened expression. With every step he took, Kaz prepared himself to get inside her silky walls. He knew her shit was slick because his tongue explored every crevice when he was devouring it. Tossing the wrapper onto the floor, he gave his muscle a hard tug before rolling the latex over his member. Koko willed herself to calm down because she had never backed down from a challenge. Kaz was approaching her as if she was prey, but she was going to show him she was the last woman he would try intimidating with sex.

Kaz secured the protection as he neared her. Koko opened her mouth to say something but was silenced when he kissed her passionately. She could taste herself on his tongue. A few minutes prior, Koko's essence had dried completely. The kiss caused her juices to flow again. In a swift movement, she was picked up and pinned against the wall. Before she could protest, Kaz entered her slowly without breaking the kiss.

"Mmmmm," she moaned into his mouth.

"Shit feels good, don't it," he whispered in her ear. "Never say what you can't do. This pussy is about to be redesigned just for me."

Her yoni opened wider with every thrust Kaz delivered. Her walls constricted around his meat like a glove, hence causing Kaz to dig deeper. In his mind, she was it for him. There was no way he could let her go to find the next nigga to give that good pussy to. The tip of his dick hit the same spot repeatedly. Koko buried her face into his neck, clenching her teeth into his skin. At the same time, she was scratching the fuck out of his back. The pain was coming from both directions, but the only sensation Kaz focused on was the one in his lower region.

With his mouth gaped open, a little spittle escaped from the corner. Kaz gripped her cheeks tightly as he growled like a bear because his kids were rushing to the finish line. Koko pushed up on the wall while spreading her knees further apart. Her action gave him more access to her core, and he took flight. Kaz's knees were weakening as he bounced her onto his manhood. The squishy sounds coming from her tunnel bricked his shit up more. Her moans were the song he didn't know he needed to hear.

"Fuck me harder, Kaz. Stop babysitting the pussy."

Kaz slammed her ass onto his erection three solid times before she released a waterfall at his feet. The shit was sexy. The way her slit was squeezing him forced Kaz to cum sooner than he wanted. Both of them were sweating and breathing hard. Moving would have resulted in them ending up on the floor. So Kaz laid his head on top of hers until he was able to gain a little bit of strength in his legs. He carried her across the room, then gently placed her on the bed. Koko curled up like a baby, closing her eyes.

Walking into the bathroom, he removed the condom and threw it in the toilet, then relieved himself. After he washed his hands, he lathered a towel with soap before going to wipe Koko down. He was beyond tired as he returned to the bathroom to take a quick shower. When he was done, he walked to the door quietly so he wouldn't disturb her sleep. Soon as he touched the knob, her sleepy voice filled his ears.

"You gon' fuck and move, huh?"

"It's not like that. I don't know if I could keep my hands to myself if I lie next to you."

"Well, you will do your best by getting in this bed to cuddle with me."

"You're so bossy. But if me sleeping with you is what you want, you got it."

Kaz snuggled behind her, and they both drifted off to sleep.

Early the next morning, there was a soft knock on her bedroom door. She was sleeping good before the knocking woke her. Easing out of bed, she grabbed the robe from the bathroom before making her way to the door. Koko opened it slightly, and Marisol stood with a sad look in her eyes. The last thing Koko wanted was for the nanny to know she was sleeping with Kaz. It wouldn't have been a surprise to Marisol because she hoped her boss would follow his heart with Koko.

"I'm sorry to wake you, Miss Simmons. I'm looking for Mr. St. Claire. Did he by chance tell you where he was going this morning? He's not in his room, and there is an emergency back home."

Koko hesitated, then decided not to hide the truth. "He's here. I'll wake him and send him out pronto."

Marisol smiled as she nodded. Turning away from the door, she doubled back. "Give him a chance, Koko. He deserves a woman like you in his life. I have never seen his eyes light up the way they do when he's admiring you. Not to mention, Alessia loves you too."

"We'll see about that. Let me get Kazimir so you can tell him what's going on."

Closing the door, Koko walked to the side of the bed where he was sleeping soundly. She tapped him on the shoulder. "Kaz, wake up. Marisol needs to talk to you."

He stretched like a feline as he opened his eyes. Waking up to Koko every morning was something he could see himself doing the rest of his life. Her hair was disheveled, but she was still sexy as hell in her natural state. It was one of the attributes that had drawn him to her the first time he laid eyes on her.

"Good morning, Chocolate drop. What's going on?" he asked, sitting up.

"Good morning to you too. Um, Marisol said there's an emergency at your home."

"Tell her to come in here."

Kaz jumped up, scooping his pajama pants off the floor, as she did as he requested. A few minutes passed before the two women were walking into the bedroom. Marisol looked nervous, and Kaz didn't like that at all. In his mind, whatever happened involved Pax.

"Marisol, what happened?"

"Your phone rang several times, then I decided to answer when I didn't see you in the room. Kelly was hysterically crying, and I couldn't understand a word she said until she said the word *fire*. I had her calm down so I could hear her clearly. When she finally caught her breath, she revealed there was a fire at your grandfather's home."

Kaz made a dash out of the room to grab his phone. His entire body shook as he dialed Kelly's number, then paced the floor. The ringing in his ear heightened his anxiety because Kaz didn't know what he would do if something happened to his grandfather.

"Mr. St. Claire!"

"Kelly, what's going on?"

"The house is ruined. It's burned to a crisp. I was only gone for a short while…"

"Where is Pax? Is he alright?"

"Pax is fine. I took him with me, and I'm glad I did. The fire chief said there was a body found in the house, Mr. St. Claire. They will have to run tests to determine who the individual is because the body was burned beyond recognition. The police want to talk with you. When can you be back? Mr. Pax and I are at my place in Bolingbrook for now."

"I need you to send me your address, Kelly. Your spot is hot, and I would hate to kill your ex for harming you or my grandfather. I will send someone to take you to my penthouse in Chicago within the hour. Soon as I get off the phone with you, I'm going to get the jet ready. Thank you for looking out for Pax. I appreciate you, Kelly."

"No problem. The only reason he rode along was because he wanted to buy a gift for Barbara. I couldn't tell him no. He bought her a dozen roses, but he forgot about them soon after. Anyway, I'll see you soon. Safe travels, Mr. St. Claire."

Hearing that his grandfather still thought about Barbara made Kaz feel a little better, even though it reminded him of what Pax was going through. With the house being destroyed, Kaz needed to hurry back before Pax's behavior became too much for Kelly to bear. Being out of his element could cause him to act out from the unfamiliar place he was forced to be in.

Kaz turned around with a forced smile. "I need you all to go pack. We have to leave soon as possible. I have to call to get the jet ready," Kaz explained.

Marisol headed to the room she shared with Alessia, and Koko turned to go into her room.

"Chocolate drop, I want you to fly back with me. What I have to deal with can't wait. I promise to get you back home as soon as I can."

Koko bit down on her bottom lip while wringing her hands together. She was nervous because, at the end of the day, Kaz was still a married man. Going home with him wasn't the smartest decision for them to act upon.

"Kaz, I don't think showing up with you is a good idea. How would that look to your family? You are technically still married. What if your wife shows up?"

He walked across the room to stand in front of Koko. Gathering her into his arms, she stepped back so she could look him in the eyes when he responded. Kaz ran his hand down his face, then cleared his throat. He could see the worry on her face and knew he had to tell her the severity of what was going on with his family.

"Chocolate drop, my grandfather's house burned to the ground…"

"Oh no! Is he okay?" she asked.

"Pax is fine. I want you to meet him. It's part of the reason I suggested you fly out with us. You don't have to worry about being judged. Nicolette was served and has known from the start what it wasn't. No other woman has accompanied me to see my grandfather. You are special,

Chocolate drop. It's me, you, and Alessia from this day forth. In my eyes, you are my wife."

Kaz hugged her around the waist, then planted a kiss on the side of her head. "Go pack. Meet me back here in a half hour."

Patting her on the ass, Kaz made the call to his pilot, but he could still feel Koko's presence. He turned, blew her a kiss, then stated what he needed into the device.

Koko went into the room, throwing her luggage on the bed. Most of her clothing was already packed; she only had to gather the ones she had washed the day before. Once she finished collecting her toiletries, Koko went into the bathroom to take a quick shower. As the water cascaded down her body, she thought about the night she had with Kaz.

Koko never had a man caress her body in the manner Kaz had. It was all about her with him. She was pleased over and over before he even thought about pleasing himself. The way Kaz kissed her felt different. In a way, she wanted it to happen again. Koko was worried about how others would judge her for sleeping with a married man. She was really in her head, even though Kaz told her how he truly felt. Koko needed to talk to Horace. He would be able to help clear her head of all negativity.

Sliding on a pair of leggings, Koko reached for the shirt she left out on the bed and pulled it over her head. As she put on her socks, there was a light knock on the door. Kaz appeared, leaning on the frame.

"Are you almost ready?"

"Yeah, I just have to put on my shoes. I'm glad I brought my coat with me. I'm sure the temperature has dropped in Minnesota, so it's not too far off in Illinois."

"If you need to go shopping while you're there, I got you," Kaz said, walking further into the room. He bent down on one knee as he helped her put her socks and shoes on.

"Kaz, I have my own money, but thanks for the offer. Plus, I still have some of the money you transferred into my account for this trip."

"That means nothing, Chocolate drop. As long as you're my woman, the world will be at your fingertips. All you have to do is open up to receive what I have in store. I understand you want to uphold your own independence, and I'm not going to stop that. We're both going to win. Trust me when I tell you, your name is going to shine a lot brighter than mine because I'm going to make sure of it. Your man should be your biggest advocate. If he can't support what you're doing, he ain't the one for you. That's where I step in. That nigga fucked up when he didn't realize he had a precious jewel in his possession."

Tapping her on the leg, he stood tall as he reached for her hand. He gathered Koko into a hug and kissed her on the side of her neck, forehead, nose, then lastly her mouth. Using his tongue to part her lips, Kaz went in for the kill, making her knees weak. He took a step back, then went to the bed, zipping her luggage.

"You have everything, right?" Koko nodded. "Where's that damn vibrator?"

She giggled. "It's in my bag. I'm going to need it once I get home. You live eight hours away, Kaz."

"That means nothing. When you get the urge to cum, you hit my line, and I will either come to you or fly your sexy ass out. I won't rush you to pack up and move; just yet. But I will not be able to stay away from that modern day juicy juice you have between your legs, Chocolate drop. Just know, when I want it, I'm gon' get it. All you gotta do is say when, and I'm coming for you."

"You a mess. Don't we need to leave?" Koko asked.

"Yeah, let's go. When you can't find that muthafuckin' toy, don't call me talking shit. As a matter of fact…"

Kaz unzipped the bag and searched until he found what he was looking for, then closed her luggage again. He took the toy and threw it in the nearest garbage.

Koko stared at the can in shock until he grabbed her by the arm, leading her out of the room.

"Why would you do that?"

"You don't need that silicone shit when I got the best dick in the land. Stop playing with me, Chocolate drop. I don't just get rid of niggas behind you. Fake dicks can get it too."

# Chapter 16

Kelly tried her best to calm Pax down. He was cursing and throwing things around her apartment because he was ready to go home. Unfortunately, he no longer had a place to call his own. She understood his mood change, and it was the reason she stayed on top of the routine they were on. One slight change would result in the behavior Kelly was experiencing at that time. She felt bad for Pax, but there was nothing she could do other than wait for whomever Kazimir called to assist in the matter.

"Pax, come sit with me so you can take your medicine. It will make you feel better," Kelly said calmly.

He stopped pacing to glare in her direction. "Who are you, and when can I go home?"

"It's me, Kelly. Your Brown Suga."

Kelly walked toward him, but Pax backed up against the wall. She could tell his balance was off a little bit, and she hoped like hell he didn't fall. In his fragile state, he was bound to fracture something. That was the last thing Kelly needed to happen. Taking her phone from her pocket, she dialed Kaz's number while praying he would answer.

"Yeah, Kelly," he answered on the first ring.

"I'm sorry to call again, but I need you to convince Pax to take his medicine. Being in my home isn't good for him because he's not familiar with the atmosphere. Maybe if he hears your voice, he would calm down enough to do what's needed of him."

"Okay, I can try my best. I'm on the plane and should be there in a couple hours. Stephan should be there any minute. Put the phone on speaker so he can hear me."

Doing as he asked, Kelly increased the volume to the highest setting. "Okay, he can hear you."

"Paw Paw," Kaz called out.

Pax's eyes lit up at the sound of a familiar voice. It was common for dementia patients to recognize certain things over others. A smile appeared on his face, and that alone gave Kelly some relief. She walked closer to him and handed him the phone. He looked at the device until Kaz spoke.

"Paw Paw, hey man, I'll be there in a little while. I want you to take your medicine and be nice to Kelly, okay?"

"I want to go to my house, son. This is not my home. I gotta get back to Barb."

"Barb is fine. We'll talk about everything when I get there. I promise."

"Can't you see what's happening here? She's working for the enemy. They had her kidnap me from my home. There aren't any weapons in this barrack. They're going to kill me."

Pax's mind had gone back to his war days, and that was even scarier to Kelly. She could only imagine what he endured during his time in combat. His defensiveness could become dangerous for her and him.

"You're safe with her. I'm on my way, Pax. I love you."

"I love you too. I'll kill her if I have to, son. You better hurry."

"Take your medicine. It will make you feel better."

Kelly walked over with pills and bottled water. Pax hesitated before taking the items but soon did so. He took the medicine, then opened his mouth, showing he consumed them. Kelly reached for the phone and took his hand in hers. She walked him to the couch, where he sat down with ease.

"Thank you. He should be okay until you return," Kelly told Kaz once she had Pax settled. "Who do you think burned the house down, Mr. St. Claire?"

"I don't know, but I'm going to find out. Don't worry about anything. I'm on my way."

"Okay," Kelly responded before Kaz ended the call.

She was on her way to the kitchen when the doorbell sounded. Placing the water bottle on the island, Kelly made her way to the door. She looked out of the side window and was shocked to see her cousin Skylar standing on the porch. Kelly knew it was a mistake giving her the address to her place, but she never expected Skylar to show up. As she opened the door, her nerves worked overtime, causing her hand to shake a little bit.

"Sky—Skylar, what are you doing here?" Kelly stammered as she stepped onto the porch, looking around with caution.

"I need some money," she smirked. "Hopefully, this time you won't say no. I figured if I showed up in person, you would give me what's rightfully owed to me. See, Granny wouldn't leave her money to only one of her grandchildren. She didn't operate like that. I want my cut, and I want it now!"

Kelly reeled her head back because who the fuck did Skylar think she was talking to? It was diabolical for her cousin to come to her house causing a scene as if she were in the streets of Birmingham. Kelly lived on a quiet block where very few African Americans resided. Skylar and many others just like her were the reason she couldn't live around her people. On top of that, how the hell did Skylar travel all the way to Illinois to check her if she was so broke? Regardless, the bitch would be returning the best way she knew how; without a dime from Kelly.

"Are you serious? I emailed all of y'all the paperwork to show proof that Big Ma didn't leave y'all shit. What more do you want from me? Hell, at this point, go to the cemetery to voice your concerns. I don't have nothing for you. There was a reason the lawyer contacted me and me only. I was the only one there looking out for her."

Kelly's eyes stung as she fought the tears that threatened to fall.

"It was me who made sure Big Ma showed up to her doctor appointments. It was me going to her house every day after work to check on her. I didn't see none of y'all unless it was to ask for money. Do you know how many times she complained about helping y'all but still gave because she didn't want to see y'all struggling? No, you don't because y'all never gave a fuck. Taking is all y'all knew until she died. Now that she's not here to help anymore, y'all think I'm about to do the same thing. Well, you muthafuckas thought wrong because I'm not doing it. Get a job, go back to school, do something."

The emotions won. Tears fell down her cheeks, but Kelly swiped them away quickly. She hated her family for the way they ignored Big Ma during her illness. They didn't ask how she was doing but never missed a meal or a beat asking her to pay a bill. The shit was sad. Then they showed up at the funeral, falling out and fainting like they gave a flying fuck.

"Big Ma was good any time I went over to see her. You're blaming us for going to the one person we knew could help us in a bind. Girl, fuck you! If anybody got on her nerves, it was you. Always going over there with your problems and shit."

Kelly laughed because Skylar was trying her best to deflect the blame. Kelly wasn't going to allow it to bother her any further.

"Skylar, get the fuck away from my house before I whoop yo' ass. However you were able to travel here, you can take the same route back to Alabama and move around."

Stepping back into the house, Kelly was about to close the door in her cousin's face. Before she could, Skylar grinned evilly. The words she spoke next stilled Kelly momentarily.

"Fifty thousand is what I want. Or I'm giving Jacoby your address. How did it feel getting the text messages from him?" she asked, leaning against the porch.

"You really want to play in my face, huh? Hoe, you ain't shit. It's cool. Find somebody else to bribe. Fuck you and Jacoby. Go eat his dick since you holding on to his balls tightly. Do what you think is best for you, but I want you to remember the reason I ran away from him. You are not exempt from getting the same treatment I received; getting my ass whooped."

A car rolled down the street slowly, stopping in front of Kelly's home. The nerves in her body stopped operating, and Kelly couldn't move an inch. In her mind, Jacoby was the person about to get out of the G-Wagon that turned into her driveway. When the door opened, an unidentified man stepped out, and the Amiri sneakers hit the pavement smoothly. Adjusting the collar of his black bomber jacket, the handsome, caramel-complexioned man walked toward the entrance of the house. The breath Kelly held released itself, giving her lungs a much-needed break.

Skylar's eyes shined with excitement, her mouth hung open, and all she saw was dollar signs. The car itself had her pussy leaking. Kelly was out of the man's league, so Skylar knew he wasn't there for her cousin. It didn't stop her from asking the question she longed to know the answer to.

"Who the fuck is that?" she asked, starry eyed.

"None of your business. Get off my property, Skylar. You have worn out the welcome I didn't even give."

"Kelly, I'm not going nowhere until you cut me a check. You heard what I said about Jacoby. I'm not bluffing either. He won't hesitate to come because you owe him too. As far as him putting his hands on me, it won't happen. We not even on that type of time. But you, I wouldn't miss the moment to see him slap you around in real time."

Skylar opened her mouth to continue talking shit, but her words were cut off when the handsome man grabbed her by the neck, lifting her off the ground.

"I heard the lady say she wanted you to leave. What's the problem? You can't hear or something?"

Clawing at his hands, Skylar tried her best to release the hold he had on her without success. The rage in his eyes told her she needed to agree to leave before he cut off her air supply. She couldn't find her voice as she struggled to speak.

"Please…" she whispered.

"Please what? You were very loud when you threatened to invite someone to hurt her. Speak up, I can't hear you. Actually, I don't want to know what you have to say. Once I let you go, leave. Coming back around wouldn't be a good look for you. In fact, it would be a death sentence. Get the fuck from around here," the man gritted.

He released Skylar, and she fought to catch her breath by bending forward with her hands on her knees. She looked up briefly before taking off down the street. Skylar ran back to the car Jacoby rented for her and took off. Kelly may have been saved for the time being, but the next time she wouldn't be so lucky. Jacoby would get his revenge, and Skylar would get the money she believed was rightfully hers.

Back at the house, Kelly stared at the strange man, wondering who he was. It didn't take long for her to find out. With his hand held out toward her as he waited for her to take it, he introduced himself.

"I'm Stephan McCormick. I was sent by Kaz to escort you and Pax to his penthouse. You must be Kelly." She nodded. "What was that about?" he asked, pointing his thumb behind him.

"It's a long story. I am Kelly, but I think I'll be going back to being Kelis. It seems I'm no longer in hiding, so there's no use living under an alias anymore. Thank you for getting my cousin away from me. Now, I need to get far away from this house. It's not safe for me. I'll get Pax together so we can leave. Come on in."

She and Stephan entered the house and were met with a scene they weren't quite ready for. Pax stood in the middle of the living room butt naked, swinging his private part in a circle. Kelly turned away from him before laughing. He had never done anything like that before.

"Aye, Pax, what the hell you doing, man?" Stephan asked. "Put yo' clothes on so we can leave."

"Steph, how you doing? You taking me home?"

"No, I'm taking you to Kaz," he said, picking the old man's clothes from the floor. "You can't be getting undressed while a lady is in the room."

"I was hot. Then I had to see if I could still twirl this thang around like I used to."

Stephan laughed as he helped the man he considered a grandfather into his clothes. Pax was funny in his own way, but he had become hilarious as the days passed. Stephan hadn't been around lately because of the duties he had with his business. That would change, though, because Pax needed to know he had other people who loved him besides Kaz.

It took about ten minutes to dress Pax, but he got it done. Once he put his coat on, they were ready to head out. Kelly stepped outside while Stephan got Pax together. He didn't blame her. The sight of Pax playing airplane with his meat was horrible; even for Stephan. Someone had to put a stop to his shenanigans.

Guiding Pax out the door, Kelly locked up after retrieving her purse and phone. Walking to the expensive car, Stephan opened the door for her to get in.

"I think following you would be best. I don't want to leave my car here."

"That's up to you. The only thing I ask is that you keep up and don't go anywhere other than the destination I'm leading you to. One more thing, when we get to the penthouse, we have nothing but time to talk until Kaz arrives. Are you cool with that?"

"Do I have a choice?" Kelly asked.

"No, you don't. Well, get in your car and enjoy the ride."

Kelly got into her vehicle and waited until Stephan backed out of the driveway before following his lead. She couldn't believe Skylar tried to bribe her. Not only that, she was the reason Jacoby was able to contact her. At that point, Kelly wished she had beaten her ass to a pulp instead of letting her leave. Stephan choking her wasn't enough now that Kelly thought about it.

Her thoughts were getting the best of her as the silence began to suffocate her inside the car. Kelly connected her phone to the auxiliary cord when her phone rang in her hand. The words *Unknown Caller* appeared on the screen. Instead of declining the call, she answered.

"Hello?"

"You still look good, Kelis. It was a pleasure seeing you in your scrubs, knowing you've been keeping yourself up through the years."

The sound of Jacoby's voice sent chills down Kelly's spine. She automatically looked in her rearview mirror to see if she could spot him on the road behind her. Jacoby hinting, he had eyes on her terrified her to death. She couldn't even open her mouth to respond.

"You can stop trying to find me. Just know I can see you, baby. I have one question, though. How did you leave me for putting my hands on you but leave Alabama to get with a nigga who puts his hands on women too? Is it because the muthafucka got money?"

"Jacoby, you're talking out of your ass right now. I'm not with anyone, and it's not your business if I was. I left you because, yes, you didn't know how to keep your hands to yourself, but you also didn't want me. All the bitches you had on the side meant more to you than me. So we both got what we wanted. You were free to be with whomever you wanted, and I was able to move on with my life without worrying about waking up dead. Leave me alone."

Kelly ended the call and it rang again. She didn't answer. Finding a song on her playlist, she continued to drive while surveying her surroundings. The light changed before Kelly could go through behind Stephan. She noticed he pulled to the side, waiting for her, and she was relieved about that. As she sat, tapping her hand to the beat of the music, her car was rammed from behind. Her head hit the steering wheel, blurring her vision temporarily. Kelly touched her forehead and felt the wetness of blood on her fingertips. Before she could react, the driver's side window shattered. Shielding her face from the glass, Kelly's hair was pulled roughly.

"Bitch, get the fuck out of the car!"

Fighting for her life, Kelly did everything she could to prevent Jacoby from pulling her out of the car. She bit, scratched, punched and clawed at his hands, but nothing stopped him from dragging her out. She could hear people screaming for him to let her go but no one intervened to stop him from assaulting her.

*Where the fuck is Stephan?* Kelly wondered. "Please don't do this, Jacoby. I'm begging you," she cried.

"You gon' have to do more than beg. I'm going to punish you for leaving and for fuckin' another muthafucka. When I'm done, you gon' wish you were dead. Then afterwards, we will make sure you are good as new with yo' money."

Jacoby's grip on her hair tightened as he pulled her back toward his car. Kelly struggled to free herself from his grasp. With every tug she could feel her hair being ripped from the scalp. As she cried a voice rang out in the distance.

"Man, that's a female! How would you feel if I handled you like that?"

"Come try that shit, cracka." Jacoby laughed, popping the trunk from his key fob. "Pussy ass white boy."

That's all it took for the man to hop out of his vehicle. He didn't care about it being in the middle of the street either.

The stranger approached Jacoby, punching him in the jaw. The two fought like boxers in a heavyweight fight. Stephan pulled up, throwing his car in park, then jumped out, blocking the other side of the street. He stopped to help Kelly to her feet.

"Get in the car now!" Stephan removed a Glock from the holster hidden underneath his jacket.

"Stephan, let's just go. He's going to kill me," she pled.

"Not before I kill him." Stephan turned to walk away but Kelly grabbed his arm.

"There are too many witnesses. You will go to prison, and I can't have that on my conscious."

"I'll be the judge of that. Now, get in the car."

Before Stephan could join the fight, a few Bolingbrook police cars pulled on the scene. He placed the gun back in its rightful place while watching as they intervened. The man who came to Kelly's aid was led down the street while another officer attended to Jacoby. Standing on the side of Jacoby's car, Kelly watched as the bystander pointed in her direction. Her nerves were all over the place as one of the officers headed her way.

"Tell them everything they need to know. Leave nothing out," Stephan said, giving her a half hug. "I'm right here with you."

His reassurance wasn't enough to calm Kelly. She looked to her left and Jacoby was eying her. If looks could kill, she would've been dead as fuck. Kelly knew she had to do what was right to save herself. Without a shadow of a doubt, he would remove her from the face of the earth. The only choice she had was to turn him in so he'd spend time in jail.

The officer approached slowly. "Hello, ma'am. I'm officer Shapiro. What's your name?" he asked.

"Kelis Gray."

"Miss Gray, what happened here today?"

"I was driving, minding my own business, when Mr. Lockport called my phone. I haven't seen him in years, but he received my number from my cousin. We exchanged words and I ended the call. When I stopped at the light, my window shattered before I was pulled from my vehicle and dragged along the pavement. His intentions were to put me in the trunk of his car. If the man in the white shirt hadn't intervened, he would've succeeded in what he wanted to do."

"So, he was attempting to kidnap you?" the officer questioned.

"If that's what you want to call it." Kelly responded. "He was taking me against my will."

"That would be considered kidnapping, Miss Gray." Writing on the notepad he held, he looked up. "What is your relationship with Mr. Lockport?"

"There isn't a relationship. I left him a few years ago because of the physical abuse he put me through. I moved here from Alabama and started a new life without him. Now, we're back at square one. You don't have to ask; I want to press charges. I refuse to run from him again."

"I have to move my car. I'll be right back," Stephan whispered in her ear.

The officer followed him with his eyes. "Who is that?"

"He is a friend of my employer."

"And your employer is whom?" the officer asked.

"Kazmir St. Claire."

"The CEO of St. Claire Candies?"

"Yes. I'm the caretaker for his grandfather. We were taking him to one of Mr. St. Claire's properties because his house was burned down today."

"Okay, I won't hold you too much longer," he replied as he wrote on the notepad. "I need a contact number for you." Giving the officer what he requested, Kelly waited for what was next. "We will press charges on your behalf so you won't have to come to the station. You will receive a call providing you with a case number. Mr. Lockport will be getting arrested today."

"Thank you so much. Is the other guy being arrested, too? He was only trying to protect me. He didn't do anything wrong."

"I will make sure to pass that information along. You are free to go, Miss Gray."

Stephan pulled up and stepped out of his vehicle. He had his phone to his ear and he appeared to be deep in conversation. Kelly took in his appearance and realized the man was beyond handsome. Whoever was in a relationship with him was lucky because he was for sure a protector. The man didn't know anything about her and he was sticking his neck out for her.

Kelly turned to the officer. "Would it be possible for me to talk to the good Samaritan?"

The officer talked into his walkie talkie, informing his partner to release the guy who helped her. He also told him to walk him over to where they were. Kelly took a quick look back at Stephan and he was still on the phone. He was staring at Jacoby as if he wanted to tear his head from his body.

The man was escorted over to Kelly and he wore a grim expression. Soon as he was in front of her, he held his hand out. "Hello, I'm Brock. Are you okay?"

"I will be," she replied, shaking his hand. "I'm Kelis. Thanks for what you did for me."

"No thanks needed. I only did what was right. No man should ever put his hands on a woman. He's lucky the cops showed up because I was ready to kill him. I have daughters and a wife. God only knows what would happen if some dirt bag handled them like that. Please, get away from him. He doesn't love you, sweetheart."

"I been realized he didn't love me; it's the reason I left years ago." Kelly chuckled. "He found me and now we're here. I appreciate you so much. I would like to compensate you for your actions. Do you have Zelle, Apple Pay, or Cash app? I don't have any cash on hand."

"That won't be necessary. You being safe out here is enough payment for me. That guy is dangerous. Learn how to shoot so the next time he approaches you, put him out of his misery. Try to enjoy the rest of your day, Kelis. Keep your head up."

Brock gave her a side hug then walked toward his car. It was rare for anyone to intervene in a situation that had nothing to do with them. Kelly was lucky he was in the right place at the right time. Without Brock's help, there was no telling where she would've been had Jacoby placed her in his trunk. Stephan pushed off his car, following Brock. They talked for a few before Stephan handed him a wad of bills then shook his hand before walking back toward Kelly.

"Did you get everything you need from the police?" he asked.

"They will call me with the case number when it's available. Hopefully, this is the end of the bullshit."

"I called someone to pick your car up. I want to get it checked out to make sure the asshole didn't have a tracker on it. Get everything you will need from your vehicle. You're riding with me. We'll talk about all of this once we get to Kaz's place."

Kelly didn't feel comfortable discussing her past with someone she didn't know, but Stephan probably wouldn't allow her not to do so. Kazmir was going to give her the third degree once he found out what took place. She walked back to her car, got in, then drove it down the street to a vacant lot to move it out off the street. Stephan pulled in behind her as she gathered her purse and phone from the passenger seat. She then grabbed a thick manilla envelope from the back. Kelly hoped like hell rain wasn't in the forecast because her window was no longer intact There was nothing of value in the car and she doubted if anyone would steal an old Nissan Maxima.

Embarrassment was an understatement. Kelly was mortified that so many people saw the way Jacoby dragged her down the street by her hair. Allowing herself to go back into depression wasn't an option because she had come too far to go backwards. She was prepared to fight hard to keep Jacoby behind bars without fear. Kelly got into the backseat of Stephan's car, sitting quietly as they drove to their destination.

# Chapter 17

Horace struggled to open his eyes because the pain he was enduring was excruciating. His back and side felt as if it was burning. Then on top of that, something was sticking his right arm repeatedly for whatever reason. Horace could tell he was in a bed but it wasn't his king size purple mattress.

"Damn, I can't get this needle in. The veins keep moving." He heard a female mutter.

"You better figure it out or get somebody else in here that knows what the fuck they're doing. You're about two seconds from getting punched in your shit." Horace's head rolled slowly in the direction of the voice and opened his eyes. "Just stop," he snapped.

The brightness of the lights caused him to force his eyelids closed again. Horace took a deep breath and started coughing. He felt a hand on his shoulder but shrugged it off while he tried to get himself under control. The aches in his body made him forget about the needle that was so hard for the nurse to insert in his arm. He knew he was in the hospital and why. Horace was glad he made it to see another day. It was the pain he wasn't fond of.

"Mr. Miles, I'm going to sit you up a bit so you can drink some water."

The bed elevated slowly as his coughing subsided. Taking the cup, he took a sip. The water tasted like fine wine to him because his throat was extremely dry. The nurse took the cup after Horace drank all he wanted and sat it back on the nightstand.

"How are you feeling?" she asked.

"I'm in pain. How long have I been here?"

"Three days. You were put under heavy sedation after surgery. You were shot in the back; missing your spine by an inch. You are one lucky guy. The bullet came out of your side. It didn't hit any main arteries, but there's a little damage to muscles and two of your ribs were broken. The good news is you lived to see another day."

"Lucky is an understatement. God was on my side. I'm blessed to still be here."

The nurse pulled a fresh pair of gloves on her hands while Horace watched curiously. The conversation about his blessings were a thing of the past because he wondered what the fuck she thought she was about to do. He was willing to forgive her for the way she poked and probed at his veins earlier, but he may have to follow through with slapping the shit out of her for attempting to stick him again.

"What are you about to do?"

"Insert your IV," she said straight forwardly.

"No, the hell you not! Go find somebody else to do it. Obviously, you need more training." Horace looked down at his arm with a frown. "My arm is turning purple. Go get someone who is more skilled to handle this task. I would hate to hit you in the top of your head for touching me."

"You don't have to be so nasty. Threatening to harm me is not the way to say I hurt you. I'm new here and couldn't find your vein. I won't try to insert the IV again." She pivoted to leave but stalled before facing him again. "Your phone is on the nightstand, next to the bed. Call your people because no one has called inquiring about your rude ass."

She left with an attitude, but Horace didn't care. His arm was bruised and throbbing from all the sticking she had done. He couldn't wait for the next nurse to come in because he had a few choice words for them. The oxygen tube in his nose was irritating him, so he took it out as the door opened. The nurse rushed over to the bed in record time.

"Mr. Miles, I need you to keep the tube in. Your oxygen levels aren't where they're supposed to be," she said, putting it back in its place. "I'm Melinda. Let me see your arm so we can get this IV in so the fluids are flowing again. Oh my," she exclaimed lowly as she studied the damage done.

"Oh my is right," Horace retorted. "Yeah, the amateur you sent in here to use me as a guinea pig did that shit all wrong. I'm here to tell you, I won't be a pin cushion for any of y'all. Either send in a nurse with experience or tell me when the fuck I can go home. Being that I've been shot and had surgery, I know I won't be leaving anytime soon. With that being said, don't send another intern in this room."

"I understand your anger, but could you be a little bit more respectful? It won't happen again, I promise," Melinda said, pulling a pair of gloves over her hands. "Your right arm isn't the ideal place to insert the needle. I'm gonna have to use the other one." She grabbed the pole with the bag of fluid hanging from it and maneuvered her way to the other side of the bed.

"That's fine. Long as you know what you're doing, I don't have a problem with you performing your duties," Horace said, watching her every move. "Speaking of disrespect, it was well deserved because she nor anyone else who doesn't know what they're doing should perform a task on a patient without adequate training. So, hopefully, it will not happen again in room 508. I won't promise to be nice because one thing I don't play about is my health. If something isn't being done correctly, I will speak on it. I'll ask questions and refuse service from said participants. It's not me being difficult, but protective of myself."

"Noted," Melinda replied as she expertly slid the needle into his vein on the first try. "For the duration of your stay, I will make sure a skilled nurse is appointed to assist you."

As she finished her task, there was a knock on the door. Two detectives entered the room before anyone could give them permission. Melinda gathered the used materials to dispose of. Tapping Horace on the arm, she gave him a grim, lazy smile before walking around the bed. She threw the items in the garbage, then instructed Horace to hit the button if he needed any assistance as she left him and the detectives alone.

"It's good to see you're finally awake, Mr. Miles. I'm Detective Martinez. How are you feeling?"

"Like I got shot," Horace responded sarcastically.

Adjusting himself until he was comfortable, Horace followed Martinez with his eyes as he sat in the chair closest to the bed. Detective Martinez stared sternly at him as if he was trying to calculate Horace's thoughts. Seconds ticked away, making Horace uneasy. He waited patiently for the interrogation to begin.

"Mr. Miles, tell me what happened the day you were shot."

"I remember going to my friend's apartment to finish cleaning because she had to go out of town at the spur of the moment. Next thing I know, I'm here."

"So, you don't know who shot you?" Detective Martinez asked.

"No, I do not."

Horace refused to give Cyrus up. It wasn't because he was afraid; he had something in store for his ass once he was well enough to retaliate. Telling the law what really took place was something Horace wasn't willing to do. Snitching wasn't in his blood, but whoopin' ass has always been in his DNA. There was no way Cyrus would believe he had spooked Horace in any way. His hands were the reason Cyrus had to pull his gun in the first place. He was getting beat by a gay dude, and that fucked up his ego.

"What's your friend's name?"

"Kameeko Simmons. I'm sure you knew that already. Hell, you've probably talked to her as well."

"Actually, I haven't. She's next on my list. Do you know when she is due back?"

"No," was all Horace gave him, closing his eyes.

"Well, here's my card. If you miraculously remember any new details that occurred the day you were shot, give me a call. I'll be waiting. In the meantime, rest up."

The detective placed the card on the nightstand, then stood to leave. His partner opened the door, but Martinez didn't move to leave. In his mind, he knew Horace was holding back information; he just didn't know why.

"There's a lot of crime going on around the world and in the state of Minnesota. Especially the inner city. Allow us to do our job. I promise to prosecute the person who shot you to the fullest extent of the law," Martinez stated.

"I've already told you I don't know who did it. I believe the police will do what's needed to find whoever is responsible for my injuries. You will have to do the legwork because I can't help you. Would you please tell the nurse my pain levels are at ten? I need relief."

Turning his head, Horace closed his eyes again, indicating the conversation was over. The detectives left soon after, and Horace's mind went back to the day Cyrus shot him. Thinking about what occurred pissed him off because why did he have to shoot if he was so tough? Cyrus' actions proved he wasn't shit without a gun. Melinda returned, giving him medicine through his IV. He kept his eyes closed because he wasn't in the mood to converse. Within minutes, the pain subsided, sending him into a deep sleep.

Horace was awakened hours later when a new nurse tapped him on the shoulder. His eyes fluttered open as he glanced at the window. The sky was dark, and his mouth felt like there was cotton in it. Turning his head, he cleared his throat before trying to speak.

"Can you pass me some water, please?" he croaked.

"Sure," the nurse said, reaching for the pitcher. She walked over, adjusting the bed so Horace was sitting upright, then placed the straw into his mouth. "I brought you something to eat. You can't take any medication on an empty stomach. So, I picked you up a burrito when I went out for lunch. The meatloaf, mashed potatoes, and corn didn't look good enough to eat, in my opinion." She rambled.

Removing the straw from his mouth, Horace belched loudly. "Excuse me, and thanks," he whispered. "Did you buy all of your patients' dinner?"

"No, only you," she laughed. "Melinda told me how you snapped earlier. I'm trying to be on your good side."

"I'm with you when you're right. You didn't have to go out of your way, though. What's your name?"

"Oh, I'm sorry. My name is Diane," she said with a smile. "You don't know how many times I've told them about sending interns into a room alone with patients. They fucked around and found out, I see."

"Definitely. One thing I don't play about is me," Horace chuckled.

He and Diane chopped it up while she took his vitals and flushed his IV line. The burrito she bought smelled good as he unwrapped it. Horace paused when his phone rang on the side table. Diane took the liberty of handing it to him. His face lit up instantly when he saw Koko's name on the display.

"Hey, Ko. How's your trip going?"

Horace tried his best to hide the pain shooting through his back. Diane noticed his discomfort and helped him unwrap the burrito. She pointed for him to eat, then held up the medication he knew he could only get if he finished the burrito. Nodding, Horace took a hefty bite while listening to his friend on the other end of the line.

"My trip was going great until it was cut short. I just landed in Chicago, so drop your location because I miss you, and there's so much I need to tell you."

Horace forgot he was supposed to be in Chicago until Koko mentioned it. He didn't want her to know he was in the hospital, but there wasn't any other way to spin the narrative. She wanted to see him, which was impossible, being he never made his way out of Minnesota. Hell, he hadn't even talked to Malcolm. He would make that call as soon as he finished the conversation with Koko.

"What are you doing in Chicago?" he asked to buy a bit of time.

"I'll explain soon as I get to you. Make sure there's plenty of liquor available. We're going to need it." The other end of the line had gone silent. "Horace, can you hear me?"

"I'm here," he sighed. "Koko, I didn't go to Chicago. I'm still in Minnesota."

"Is Malcolm playing games? Give me his number so I can cuss him the fuck out! You were looking forward to that trip too." Koko was fuming as she talked about Malcolm as if he was the problem.

"Hold up, sis. It's not what you think. Malcolm didn't cancel the trip. I never made it out of your apartment. Actually, I did, but I was carried out on a stretcher."

"Wait, what happened? Are you okay?"

"The past three days have been a blur…" Horace glanced over at Diane as she hung on to his every word. "Would you mind leaving so I can finish my conversation? I don't care for the way you're all in my mouth. I'll hit the call button when I'm ready for my pain medicine." He waited until the door closed completely behind Diane before he tuned back in.

"Who was that?"

"The nurse who's taking care of me." Horace grunted as he moved to adjust himself on the bed. Taking another bite of his burrito, he swallowed before resuming his conversation. "I'm fine, Koko. The day you left, I went back to the apartment to clean as you asked. Cyrus showed up and shot me in the back."

"What?" she gasped.

"We fucked your apartment up. I apologize in advance. He was mad because I told him you were out of town riding new dick. He wasn't too happy to hear the tea, but he can't blame nobody except himself. Cyrus is a pussy, though. He shot me after I beat his wannabe tough ass. The police will be contacting you at some point because the incident happened at your place."

"You have to tell me everything you told them, friend. I don't want to go into this blindly. Did you tell them Cyrus was the one who shot you?"

"Hell nawl, I didn't! I want to get that bitch myself. When the detective asked if there was anyone who wanted to hurt you, I said no. The last thing I want is for Cyrus to get locked up again."

"Horace, I think you should allow the police to do their job. Cyrus can be dangerous at times."

"Chocolate drop, we are cleared to exit the jet. Is everything alright?"

While Koko explained what happened to who Horace assumed was Kaz, he listened as he finished eating. The way that man spoke to his friend let Horace know something happened beyond friendship between the two of them. When Kaz asked for her phone, Horace wasn't ready for what was about to be said.

"Hey, Horace, as you know, Koko told me about the situation. I need to know if Cyrus said anything about hurting her?"

"No, he didn't say anything like that. He did say she will always be his, though."

Kaz chortled. "Okay. We will be there in a couple days. Keep telling the police you don't know anything."

"Kaz, I don't want you to get involved," Koko all but pleaded.

"I'm already involved. Not only did the muthafucka have a hand in stealing from me, which he denied. He fuckin' shot me! Cyrus is a menace to society and thinks he's untouchable. Call me the terminator because his ass is done! If you want to protect the bitch nigga, I can put you on the next thing smokin'. Then you can warn him that the grim reaper is coming for his soul. After I handle my business here, I'm heading to Minnesota to shake shit up. I'm tired of muthafuckas testing me and the people I give a fuck about!"

"I'm not trying to protect him! It's you I'm concerned about," Koko snapped. "You have so much to lose. Killing isn't even who you are, Kazimir!"

"That's where you're wrong. I see I'm gonna have to school you on how to separate the two. Kazimir keeps Kaz at bay until he can't! Sorry, baby, you fuckin' with a street nigga now."

The call dropped, leaving Horace flabbergasted. He witnessed the well-dressed man who owned a lucrative company turn into a nigga who was ready to tear somebody's head clean off their neck. Koko didn't want to deal with Kaz because of his marital status. Finding out he was deep in the streets would definitely cause her to fall back.

# Chapter 18

The car ride was quiet. Koko didn't appreciate how Kazimir blew up at her. Under no circumstances would she ever attempt to protect Cyrus. Whatever happened to him was well deserved, and he brought it on himself. She wasn't going to tolerate the tone Kazimir used when he addressed her. She had gone through a tedious few years with Cyrus, and she refused to start a new relationship with the same bullshit waiting to make its appearance.

Kaz drove while periodically glancing at the side of Koko's face. Her jaw clenched and unclenched as she stared out of the window. He knew she was upset with him, and it had a lot to do with the way he revealed his involvement in the streets. Kaz had the chance to tell her the truth when she questioned him in the hotel the day he was discharged from the hospital. Telling her about his life as the plug would've lessened their chances of being in a serious relationship. Now the truth was out, and Kaz felt he lost her anyway.

He was doing a bit above the speed limit in order to get downtown faster. The traffic wasn't too bad, and that was a plus for Kaz. His mind was in several places at once, but his main focus was getting to Pax. The thought of his grandfather's house burning down didn't sit right with him. Pax worked his ass off to have the home built for him and Barb, then he welcomed Kaz with open arms after his parents were murdered. He planned to find out what happened and who the fuck took part in destroying his family's property.

Glancing in the rearview mirror to make sure Marisol was keeping up, Kaz had Alessia ride with her so he and Koko could talk openly. Kaz didn't want the tension between them to affect his daughter. Plus, he didn't know how Koko would react to what he had to say. Clearing his throat, Kaz prepared himself for the conversation he was about to embark on.

"I apologize for not telling you about my illegal business."

Koko remained silent as she admired the beautiful skyline of the city she was born in. She didn't want to discuss the situation at the present time, so she kept her mouth closed. Her silence only pushed Kaz to continue speaking.

"As I said before, the less you know, the better."

"Kazimir, you're missing the point," Koko said, speaking up. "You didn't have to tell me because I already knew. When you said the less you know, the better, that in itself told me all I needed to know. Even though I made a vow to never get involved with another man in the streets, your mentality is different from the rest. The problem I have with you is the tone you used when addressing me while on the phone with Horace. Please don't let my softness fool you. I will not tolerate anyone trying to reign dominance over me."

"That was not my intent, Chocolate drop. I was upset when you told me not to get involved. Cyrus is going to get dealt with on the strength of his involvement in shooting me. The way he's harassing you is just the icing on the cake. I apologize for the way I spoke to you, and it will never happen again. This is not the way I want us to begin our lives together. We have so much to learn about one another, and I can't wait to travel down that road with you. It's too soon for us to be at odds with one another."

"Apology accepted. The moment you find out what's going on with your family, I'm going to head back home. Horace needs me."

Kaz stared at Koko as she tapped away on her phone. He had a feeling she was booking her flight as she talked. Kaz wanted her to leave with him, but he wouldn't stop her if going home alone was what she really wanted to do. But he had to try his hand at convincing her to wait it out.

"Chocolate drop, would you please wait to travel back with me? If something happens to you and I'm not around, I don't know what I would do. So, do not book that flight."

Koko slowly looked to her left, and Kaz was focused on the road. She had no clue how he knew she was on the airline app booking a flight. All she had to do was press the button, and she would be on the next plane out of Chicago in a few hours. Closing out of the app, Koko planned to book the trip as soon as she was out of Kaz's sight. She wanted to leave so she could gather her thoughts and prepare for whatever life was about to throw at her. The knot in her stomach was huge, and she knew what Cyrus did to Horace was only the beginning. The devil was busy, and he was spreading his evil ways throughout the world; especially in Minnesota and Chicago.

Kaz exited the expressway as his phone rang. Steelo's name appeared on the car's display, and he answered from the steering wheel.

"Lo, what's going on?"

"Where you at? I just saw on the Citizen's app Pax's house burned down. Everything okay?"

"I don't know yet. I'm on my way to the penthouse now. Give me a minute, and I'll let you know once I get more information about the situation. I have to meet up with the officers in charge of the case. A body was found, but it's not my grandfather. The only person it could possibly be is David."

"Kaz, I need you to clear yo' head. There were cameras all around the property, and you should have all the answers in the palm of your hand. No matter if the house is no longer standing, the footage is still available. You will know exactly who died and what caused the fire."

The thought of the cameras he had installed didn't cross Kaz's mind. Steelo was correct; his mind was overwhelmed with everything that had been taking place in his life. He would pull up the app as soon as he got settled in the penthouse. Forgetting he was in the middle of a conversation, Steelo's voice brought him out of his thoughts.

"I found some shit on Cyrus." Kaz glanced over at Koko briefly to calculate her reaction. She stared straight ahead as if she wasn't soaking in every word. "He was released a few days ago, but nobody has seen him."

"You in Minnesota?" Kaz asked.

"Yeah, I wanted to get on this before shit hit us first. We have a problem, though. Word on the street is some muthafucka is selling laced pills that's dropping folks like dominoes. The spots are hot, and I shut everything down until I find out who's pushing that shit in our territory. I'm glad I followed my first mind and came up here. Otherwise, we would be dealing with the police. We don't need that type of heat. You got enough going on in your personal life."

"What the fuck! Have you talked to Lowkey? If not, find his ass because he should be on top of shit over there. He should've been the one calling me about this because it's crucial!" Kaz pushed the button on the remote clipped to his visor as he steered the car into an underground garage.

"Look, I'm about to see what's up with my people. Let me know if you find out anything before I get there in a day or two. Keep your head on the swivel because somebody is trying to ruin the operation."

"Fo sho. You do the same and hit my line if need be."

Pulling into an empty slot, Kaz watched as Marisol parked next to him. He spotted Stephan's ride and was glad his good friend came through in the clutch. Kaz cut the engine and exited the vehicle. He rounded the car, then assisted Koko out by the hand.

"Thank you," she said, pulling away.

Kaz wrapped her into his arms before she could walk away from him. The perfume he became fond of on her skin invaded his nostrils. He kissed the top of her head, then released her. Kaz noticed the shift in Koko's mannerisms toward him, and he felt the distance she was forming between them. There was no way he would allow that to happen. The feelings he had for the woman standing in front of him may have been too soon for some to understand, but Kaz knew without a shadow of a doubt that Kameeko Simmons was the woman he needed in his life. He planned to prove how much in due time.

Koko made her way to Marisol's vehicle to assist with Alessia. The little girl was sleeping soundly, so she reached inside, removing her from the car seat. When she turned with the child in her arms, Kaz was there to take the weight off.

"I'll carry her," he said softly, taking Alessia from Koko.

The ride to the top floor of the building was silent. Marisol sensed the tension between her boss and the woman he was smitten over. She gave Koko's hand a light squeeze with a smile. Looking over at her, the gesture was bleakly reciprocated as the elevator doors parted. Kaz stepped off first as they entered the spacious apartment. There were four people sitting in the living room as if they were waiting for his arrival.

"Marisol, take Alessia to her room and check on Pax for me, please."

"No problem. Koko, are you coming too?" she asked.

"She can sit with me. I need my daughter away from the conversation that's about to take place. Thank you for everything, Marisol. I appreciate you."

Kaz waited for Marisol to round the corner before leading the way into the room. Nodding at Stephan, he guided Koko to the sofa next to Kelly, then took a seat in an empty chair beside her. The two suited men were indeed police officers. He wondered how long they'd been present in his home because the overweight one looked very agitated.

"Mr. St. Claire, nice to meet you. I'm Detective Denver," he said, standing to shake Kaz's hand. "I'm glad you were able to get home quickly. I would like to discuss what took place at your grandfather's residence. He couldn't tell us much, so that leaves you to fill in the pieces."

"Of course, he wouldn't have been able to share anything because he struggles with remembering what happened an hour prior to anything he does. In case you didn't know, my grandfather was diagnosed with dementia. To be frank, I don't know how he could help because he wasn't home when the fire took place, which is a great thing to me. On top of that, I can't help much either because I was thousands of miles away when the incident transpired."

Detective Denver looked down at the notepad he held as he contemplated what he wanted to say. After a brief moment, his partner decided to step in to take over the questioning. Looking Kaz from head to toe with a distasteful glare, Kaz could sense his judgment without him uttering a vowel. When he dressed for the flight back to Chicago, Kaz decided to dress down in a black jogging suit with a pair of black and red Jordans.

"There's no need for the wisecracks. We are dealing with a serious situation, and answers are needed. The no-snitch rule is not something you should go by. You people use drug money to finance your lavish lifestyles—"

"You people? Drug money? No-snitch rule? What the fuck are you talking about?" Kaz hissed.

"Everyone in this room knows you can't afford the way you're living while working a nine to five. Stop the bullshit, St. Claire! Your name may be classy, but your image screams drug dealer! Now, what the fuck happened at the house? Who was burned in the fire? Do not lie because we have an idea who the victim is."

Kaz fought hard to refrain from beating the fuck out of the fat, sloppy, disrespectful pig. The muthafucka sat there sounding dumb while assuming he had his life figured out down to a science. Instead of physically putting his hands on the fucktard, Kaz decided to slap him with pure facts.

"Who do I have the pleasure of sharing the same air with today?" Kaz asked calmly.

"McGraw. What does that have to do with what I stated?"

"Actually, it has everything to do with it. You have the nerve to sit in my home and talk shit about me that you based off the color of my skin and the attire I have on. See, McGraw, I believe you should've asked some of your colleagues about the family you were coming to speak with. As far as me purchasing anything with drug money, you are totally wrong."

"I know your kind, boy!" McGraw yelled.

"A boy is something I haven't been in a long time. Respect me in my shit or get the fuck out. The power trip you're on may work with others, but it won't work on me. McGraw, your MAGA is showing. I'm here to tell you, your President will get you fucked up! I don't give a damn what your perception is of me. I'll be the one to tell you, all Black people are not the same."

"I own my business, so drug money is something I know nothing about," Kaz lied. "In fact, I'm quite sure your fat ass has eaten plenty of sweets from St. Claire's Candies. Ain't shit illegal going on over here. Now, you can leave," Kaz concluded, then turned to Detective Denver. "I'll talk to you, but he needs to get out of my home."

Detective Denver sighed as he looked between Kaz and his partner. One could tell he didn't know who to side with. McGraw sat with a smirk because he had no plans of leaving. In his mind, the police were the rulers.

"Wait for me in the car. There is too much tension between the two of you," he said, addressing McGraw.

"We are the fucking cops! We make the demands, not him!"

"McGraw, go wait in the car!"

Struggling to stand to his feet, McGraw huffed as his face flushed with anger. He walked slowly toward the elevator, then turned, glaring in Kaz's direction.

"I don't give a fuck who you claim to be. I'm on your ass, nigger," he snarled.

Stephan jumped up in time to halt his friend's movements. If he hadn't, Kaz would've been handcuffed for felony assault against an officer. He struggled to get out of the hold Stephan had on him but just couldn't get to McGraw.

"Let it go. He's trying to rile you up. We know what the fuck this is about," Stephan whispered. "Think about Alessia and Pax, man."

"I'm cool," Kaz said, pushing Stephan off of him.

He stepped forward, then Koko grabbed him by the back of his sweatshirt. Kaz turned his head, and their eyes locked. He forgot she was there, but the look in her eyes calmed him instantly. That's when he surveyed the room, seeing the look of fear on Kelly's face. The detective had him acting out of character in front of the women who meant everything to him, and Kaz didn't like it.

"Escort yo' boy out of my crib before something drastic happens to him."

The detectives left the premises, and Kaz finally sat down in deep thought. Koko sat next to him, holding his hand. Her support meant everything to him, even after the debate they had in the car earlier. The elevator doors opened a few minutes later, and Detective Denver entered.

"Mr. St. Claire, I apologize on behalf of my partner."

"Nawl, he should've issued that shit himself. You're too old to be apologizing for another grown ass man. The Black man is the most hated in this dreadful world, but I won't ever sit back quietly while a proud racist tries to belittle me in front of anyone. In fact, I'm going to defend the shit whenever I witness it. McGraw better tread lightly when it comes to me because his threats and hate hold no weight this way."

"As you should," Detective Denver replied. "I've spoken to him about his actions several times, and it's who he was raised to be. There is nothing I can do about that. But when I was outside, I received a call from the medical examiner's office. The remains found inside of the rubble were identified as David St. Claire through dental records. Would you mind telling me more about him and his relation to you and your family?"

Shaking his head, Kaz wanted to punch the officer in his shit for deflecting the way his partner disrespected him. He wasn't going to allow what took place to slide; Kaz was going to address the bullshit at a later date. The information Detective Denver revealed wasn't a shock because he suspected David was the person who had perished in the fire. He dreaded the fact of having to tell Pax that his only living son was now deceased. Although David did wrong for many years, the love his father had for him never wavered. Pax had to practice tough love so he would do better with his life. Kaz, on the other hand, hated the ground his uncle walked on. If he hadn't stepped in and took over his grandfather's estate, everything Pax worked hard to achieve would've been taken from him.

"I know this is hard to process," Detective Denver's voice cut into Kaz's thoughts, "but the more I know about your relative, the better the investigation could be."

"David is my uncle. He hasn't been around much, and the last I heard, he was drowning in gambling debt. I can't begin to explain much more about the way he lived his present life. Nor can I tell you why he was at the property the day of the fire."

"Is it possible someone was out to harm him?"

"I don't know the answer to that. Again, I haven't been in communication with David since I took over my grandfather's company. I'm afraid there's nothing more I can tell you. David and I live separate lives."

"There's one last question I have for you. Is there any reason you would want your uncle dead, Mr. St. Claire?"

Kaz clenched his teeth tightly as he balled his hands into fists. Which part of he was out of town didn't the detective understand? He was being accused of a serious crime against his own family, and Kaz didn't appreciate it.

"Detective, why would I want my uncle dead? Oh, maybe because he was robbing my grandfather blind behind his back? No, that couldn't be it because I gave him hundreds of thousands of dollars to get his life back on track. Hmmm, or you believe he didn't have a place to live after I kicked him out of the big house. No, that wouldn't have been a problem either because I made sure he had a home of his own that I paid for. Don't ever play in my face by insinuating I killed my uncle. Even though he fucked my grandfather over, I would never want anything to happen to him other than him getting his life in order. To answer your question, I had nothing to do with what happened at that house!"

"Okay. The investigators found pieces of surveillance cameras in the rubbish. We will find out what happened, and you better hope there's no evidence of you or anyone associated with you on the footage. Once the main box is located, we will have all we need to bring charges."

The good cop act was gone, and Detective Denver revealed everything he had been holding in. They suspected Kaz from the start and couldn't wait to put cuffs on his wrists. He couldn't be any different from his father. Kellan was a man the police wanted to take down with a passion. He was selling drugs in the streets of Chicago, making money hand over fist. Denver and McGraw didn't like the fact that a Black man in the hood was bringing in more money in a day than their salary for the year. When Kellan objected to the offer to join forces, it pissed both Denver and McGraw off. They tried for years to get him locked up for life, but nothing ever stuck because Kellan was smart enough to keep his hands clean. The night Denver received the call that Kellan was dead, he celebrated as if he'd gotten a promotion.

"Like McGraw said, we have our eye on you. It doesn't matter if you run a lucrative business, Kazimir. The drugs running through the streets are still being put there by a St. Claire. The apple doesn't fall far from the tree, and I will bet my last dollar Kellan taught you all you needed to know about the drug game. Hopefully, you don't have the same outcome he did."

Kaz reacted out of anger when his father was mentioned. He punched Detective Denver in the mouth. Kelly screamed out soon as the detective crashed into the table, sending glass all over the room. The death of his father was still raw even though it happened years prior. No one was ever convicted of his murder, and from the way Denver spoke, it was clear the police had a lot to do with his death.

"You muthafuckas killed my father!" Kaz spazzed, kicking the officer in the head.

"Stop, Kaz. It's not worth it. You will go to jail for this shit!"

Koko grabbed him by the back of the shirt as she tried to stop Kaz from hurting the man any further. It didn't work. He snatched away, picking the detective up by the collar.

"If I find out you had a hand in my father's death, I'm going to kill you myself!" Kaz dragged Denver to the elevator, then shoved him inside. After pressing the button for the lobby, he stepped off then locked access. "Call your backup because this is a charge I'm willing to take. You muthafuckas are barking up the wrong tree. I'm not my father, but I see you hate me off the strength of his power," Kaz laughed. "Get the fuck on, and you bet not ever come back! Whatever new information that may arise, appoint someone else to the case. I won't be able to control my anger a third time."

"Kazimir, I hope you enjoy jail because that's exactly where you're headed. Scum like you are a threat to society. I will have a cell ready for you. As a matter of fact, I'm going to have a few potted plants placed inside so you'll feel at home."

"Fuck you, pig! I'll be out within the hour, so whenever you send yo' folks to lock me up, I'll be ready."

Kaz backed away and allowed the elevator door to close, taking a deep breath. When he turned around, the first person he saw was Pax standing in the hall with a confused expression. Walking slowly toward him, Kaz embraced his grandfather and dropped his head on his shoulder. Seeing the people in the living room, Pax forgot all about the commotion between Kaz and the man in the suit. He locked in on Koko over his grandson's shoulder.

"Kellan, who is that beautiful, chocolate goddess over there?" he asked, smiling from ear to ear. Pax shoved Kaz gently as he inched a little further into the room. "Simona is going to kick your ass," he laughed. "Didn't I tell you to stop bringing these women to my house? If you can't take 'em where you lay your head, then you shouldn't be with 'em."

"Paw Paw, it's me, Kazimir."

"Hahaha! That's even worse because that white woman gon' kill you. I told you to leave her alone from the jump. See, that's the woman you should've married. Dark and lovely, just like my Barbara. Hello, gorgeous," he smiled at Koko.

"Hi. How are you, sir?"

"I'm great now that my boy has finally brought a beauty to meet me. I automatically welcome you to the family, but I want you to be careful because the Italian ice this man married isn't going to go away quietly. Please encourage him to divorce her first so you won't be labeled as a homewrecker. I'm a realist, and I want you to know this is not his real home. It's just the one he goes to when he wants to be a single man."

"Paw Paw, how are you tarnishing my name in my presence?" Kaz laughed. "Do you think I'm dumb enough to bring her around without telling her the story of my life? Koko knows all about me being married."

"Koko, huh?" he voiced coolly as he grabbed her hand, kissing the back of it. "The name fits because you are like divine chocolate. I would call you brown suga, but there's already one in the family. Brown suga, come over and meet my new granddaughter, Koko."

"Nice to meet you," Kelly greeted Koko with a hug. "Pax, it's time for you to take your medication."

"I'm not taking anything until someone tells me why those people were here yelling at my boy."

Kaz thought he had more time before revealing the truth to Pax. The old man's senses kicked in whenever they wanted, and Kaz wished they would've held off until the next day. There was no way Pax would allow him to ignore his request. An uneasy feeling fluttered in Kaz's stomach, and his nerves were getting the best of him. There was nothing in the world that could have him in that state other than his paw paw. He didn't know how the news would affect him, but there was no getting around it.

"Paw Paw, have a seat. There's something I need to tell you."

Kelly assisted Pax to the sofa, taking a seat next to him. She cradled his hand in hers in case she had to calm him. Pax glanced over at the broken table, then attempted to stand.

"No, stay seated."

"Brown suga, what happened to the table?"

Kaz sat next to his grandfather. "Paw Paw, the man you saw was a detective. He was here to talk about your house."

"I can go home?"

"Unfortunately, not. Your house burned to the ground. There's nothing left. I promise to find a new house for you to live in. Until then, you will stay here with me."

"Kaz, I don't want to live here. Hell, this ain't even where you sleep every night. What do you take me for, a fool? The home I built from the ground for my Barbara is the place I want to go back to!"

"Paw paw, I wish I could turn back the hands of time. If that was possible, my parents would be alive, you would be in the greatest health, wouldn't have to take medicine, and need a caretaker. I would've never married Nicolette either. On top of all of that, David would be here to clean his life up instead of being in the county morgue."

The last statement was one Kaz didn't mean to spill the way he had. The hurt displayed on Pax's face hurt his heart. He wanted to tell him about David in a way he would understand; however, it came out with a slip of the tongue. Kaz cursed himself for not controlling the words that flowed from his mouth effortlessly.

"Did you just say my David is dead? I may be losing my mind, but it's not totally gone. I can comprehend a little bit."

"Paw Paw, David was in your house when it burned. The police came to tell me. That's why they were here."

"Why was he in my home and I wasn't? This isn't making sense to me. I'm still alive, but the only child I had left is dead? How can that be?"

"It's true. David was identified through dental records. He was burned beyond recognition. I'm going to find out what happened, Paw Paw. I promise."

Pax sat silently as his eyes brimmed with tears. The elder man had outlived both of his sons. In his heart, he wished he had gone before them because it was never easy for a parent to bury a child. Kaz would be the last of the St. Claire bloodline. Pax had to use his last breath to make sure he was safe. He didn't know how that would be possible with his failing health. There were many things his grandson didn't know about his father and mother's murder, so he had no idea how he would be able to save him after he revealed the truth.

"Kaz, David did wrong, and we don't know all he was into. The same goes for your father too. Just leave it alone because the very people who came here to tell you David was dead is the same motherfuckers that killed your father. I don't have proof, but in my heart, I believe the police was one hundred percent responsible."

Pax confirmed what he'd already suspected. Kaz wasn't going to allow any of that to deteriorate his grandfather's health any further. It was hard not to show emotion, but on the inside, Kaz was piping hot. Everything presented to destroy him was turning him into a nigga whose soul was turning cold. There was going to be a whirlwind of hell coming through Chicago soon as he found out who was behind the fire. Plus, he had to be ready whenever Anthony decided to approach him on behalf of his wicked ass daughter.

***

Nicolette sat at the table in her father's kitchen, going through the paperwork she took from Kazimir's office. After going back and forth with him via text, she had already made up her mind to leave the home she had been living in for the past three years. It was obvious Kazimir wanted out of the marriage, but that didn't mean she would give it to him easily. Nicolette wanted to know more about the man she made a vow to love til death, and it was a shame it had taken him filing for divorce for her to do it. In her mind, she thought they would have stayed together at least until Alessia left for college. That shit only happened in movies, obviously.

As she read the papers from a bank statement, Nicolette found out he had an account for her daughter which held three million dollars. Rustling through the papers quickly, she couldn't believe there wasn't anything with her name attached for the same. When she saw just how much her husband was worth, she gasped. The man was far richer than she thought. Her shock turned to anger when she happened upon a deed for a penthouse located downtown.

"Daddy!" Nicolette yelled.

Anthony rushed into the kitchen to see what was wrong. "What is it?" he asked.

"Kazimir has a place downtown that I knew nothing about. I bet that's where his money is. There's no way he has every dime in the bank. This motherfucker is really living like a bachelor while married."

No matter how many times her husband reminded her about why they were initially married, Nicolette always had high hopes that their union would eventually turn into true love. It never happened, then that bitch came along with her cake making skills, getting his attention. The anger had her on the brink of tears as she sat looking over the address to what she knew he used to sleep with other women.

"He's still out of town, right?" her father asked, bringing her back to their conversation.

"Yeah. Far as I know."

"Good. We're going to that address to see what he has of value stashed there since we didn't get anything except jewelry from the house. I still can't believe you never thought to gain access to his accounts. What type of wife were you for the past three years?"

"One who sat back comfortably as her husband took care of her and the daughter that wasn't biologically his. I wouldn't have to worry about his money if you hadn't spent mine."

Anthony slapped his daughter in the mouth, drawing blood. Her hand automatically went to her face to protect it from any assault that may follow. Glancing down at her fingers, they were covered in blood. Never in her life had her father ever put his hands on her. The most he'd done was yelled. His actions scared her to death, and she didn't know how to react to it.

"That was my money! I worked my ass off for it until shit went south. I had no choice but to use it to pay off my debt! So, keep your smart-ass comments to yourself, little girl. I made a way for you to be set for life, but your dumb ass didn't take the time to suck and fuck properly."

Anthony didn't care how what he said made his daughter feel. He felt she should've been knee-deep into that man's pockets, and whenever he decided to be done with her, she would have been overly compensated afterwards. Did he expect to be dead broke years after having everything? No, but who does when the money was used irresponsibly? Anthony told Nicolette a partial truth about her trust, and that truth was, he had to use it. He just didn't have any intentions of telling her what he used the money for. It wasn't her fucking business, was his thought process on the matter.

"Was there a key for the penthouse?"

She wanted to say no but knew better than to do so. Holding up the key, Anthony reached to snatch it from her hand, yet Nicolette drew back. There was no way she was giving him the key to run off with. Besides, she had no plans of even taking him along when she did decide to go.

"Bitch, what is your problem? Give me the fucking key!"

"We will go together. I hate to say this, Daddy, but I don't trust you to do right by me. You have shown me I come second to whatever you have going on in your life now."

He grabbed her long brown tresses, dragging her out of the chair. She screamed for him to let her go, but her cries went in one ear and out the other. He stood over her with his fist drawn back but never threw the punch. The same man who killed a man for violating her was now the demon that got a kick out of whooping her ass. For the couple hours she'd been in his home, Nicolette noticed her father's on and off behavior. She didn't want to believe he was on some type of drug, yet that is where her mind was leading her. Nicolette was scared. The evil in his eyes was on full display, and she was glad she hadn't mentioned the money and bank card she took from Kazimir to him.

"Get the fuck up and go wash your face! I'll be waiting in the living room so we can go."

Stepping over his daughter's body, Anthony left without uttering an apology. Nicolette's head was throbbing from the way he pulled her hair. She went into the bathroom, and the waterworks fell immediately from her eyes. The relationship she had with her father was immaculate until he forced her into marriage. They'd gone from talking every day to speaking only when she needed to complain about how Kazimir wasn't being the ideal husband. He would get mad, but that was the extent of his actions until that particular day.

Nicolette looked at herself in the mirror, and seeing the blood in the corner of her mouth pissed her off. She retrieved a clean towel from the rack, then opened the medicine cabinet to get the peroxide. Cleaning the cut, she came to the conclusion that she was not going to the penthouse with her father. She had to find a way to get out of the house without him seeing her. Wiping her face one last time, Nicolette tossed the towel in the wash bin and opened the door quietly. As she rounded the corner, her suspicions were confirmed. Anthony sat on the sofa nodding out. There were a few pills on the coffee table, and she assumed he had taken at least one of them.

The opportunity to get out of the home unnoticed presented itself, and she took it. Going back to the kitchen, she hurriedly collected the papers and her purse after putting her phone inside. She grabbed her keys and headed for the back door, leaving her father where he sat. Not bothering to hit the locks from the fob, she unlocked the door of her BMW from the keypad so she wouldn't draw the attention of her father. When she was safely inside, she hurried to push the start button and threw the gear in reverse to back out of the driveway.

Nicolette cried silently the further she got away from her father's home. The one person she thought would be by her side, turned on her. It was the drugs. She knew that had to be the issue, but until she could get her father the help he needs, She would have to love him from a distance. Going against Kazimir on her own would be a hard task to accomplish. However, Nicolette was ready to fight for what she believed she earned the entire three years she was disrespected by her husband. He owed her, and if that meant going to his hoe spot to collect, so be it.

The nerves in her body were running wild as she drove along the route toward downtown. Nicolette wished she had someone with her for backup, but unfortunately, she had to tackle the shit alone. Kaz being out of town made it a little better because she could get in and out without any confrontations. Her stomach growled, so she decided to stop for something to eat before going to the penthouse. Nicolette got off the expressway at Randolph Street and made her way to the restaurant on Green Street where they served turkey tips.

She found a parking spot not far from the entrance, then prepared to pay the meter for at least an hour. Going inside, she placed her order with a drink, taking a seat at the bar. There were televisions on the walls with sports on every one of them. Nicolette was a football girl, so she was glad she could watch a game on the screen in front of her. The sound of her phone gained her attention briefly. She looked down at all the texts and missed calls from her father. His words were all over the place and didn't make any sense. It was a clear indication that Anthony was still trying to get beamed up like Scotty.

Taking a sip of the strawberry lemonade, the waitress sat in front of her, someone sat in the seat next to her. Nicolette closed out of the text thread and opened a solitaire game app to take her mind off the things her father said in the messages.

"How may I help you?" the waitress asked from behind the counter.

"I would like a chopped brisket sandwich, mac and cheese, and a bourbon sweet tea. I'll also take a glass of water as well."

The deep baritone intrigued Nicolette, forcing her to see who was behind it. The guy sitting next to her was well dressed and handsome. His hair was cut low and he had waves that would make anyone who stared too long dizzy. The diamonds in his watch glistened in the sunlight, and his nails were freshly manicured without a speck of dirt underneath them. His appearance gave off boss vibes, and he wore it well.

"Do you like what you see?" he asked.

"Shit," Nicolette muttered to herself. She was caught red handed, eye-fucking the stranger. Clearing her throat, she took a long sip of her drink before turning back toward him. "I don't know what you mean."

"You were staring, so I assumed you were admiring the greatness that's sitting before you."

"When you assume, you make an ass of yourself. I can't lie; you're handsome, no doubt, but your arrogance makes you ugly. I hope you enjoy your lunch."

She grabbed her glass, purse, and phone, then went to find a table far away from the bar to sit. Nicolette went back to playing her game while waiting on her meal to arrive. When the waitress came over a few minutes later, the aroma of the turkey tips hit her nostrils, making her mouth water. Closing out of the app, she took a small bottle of sanitizer from her purse to cleanse her hands. Not wasting a moment, she started to eat.

A shadow fell over her face as a figure blocked the sunlight that was beaming down on her. Chewing slowly, Nicolette glanced up, becoming annoyed at the sight of the stranger standing beside the table she chose to get away from him. Acting as if he wasn't there, she picked up a French fry, placing it in her mouth.

"Aren't you going to invite me to join you?" he asked with a smile.

"No, I don't even know you," Nicolette replied politely as she could. "Why would I want someone who's full of himself to sit with me?"

"It has never been against the law to have confidence in yourself."

Ignoring the fact she didn't want his company, he set his plate on the table and took a seat across from her. Nicolette was able to get a good look at him, and he was easy on the eyes. No wonder his arrogance was loud. The man was fine as fuck. He wasn't Kazimir St. Claire by a longshot. Yet, he was a strong second.

"I'm Arvon Young. Who do I have the pleasure of meeting today?"

"Nicolette. Mrs. Nicolette St. Claire," she fielded the question, putting emphasis on the Mrs. while flexing her left hand so he could see the rock on the ring finger.

Arvon took note of the fact she was married. However, it didn't stop him from pushing forward. Nicolette was beautiful, and he wanted to get better acquainted.

"Is there any chance you're part of the St. Claire family who owns the candy company?"

"The one and only. I see you're familiar," she smirked. "It doesn't surprise me. My husband is very well known in this city. Many find it very surprising that he has a wife. Are you one of those people, Mr. Young?"

"In fact, I am. Kazimir is a businessman who never discussed his personal life. I just assumed he was single," Arvon stated with a shrug.

He took a huge bite of his sandwich as he stared Nicolette down. He and Kazimir had done business together in the past as well as hung out with beautiful women afterwards. It wasn't Arvon's business to tell the woman about her husband's infidelities. He wouldn't be the one to crush her world; yet, he was ready to be there when she needed to relieve some stress the moment her husband started to neglect her.

They ate in silence as if they were sitting at separate tables alone. After a while, Nicolette waved the waitress over and asked for her check and a to go container. She was ready to get out of there. Even though her marriage to Kazimir never felt like one for real, she had never stepped out on him, and she wasn't going to start that day. Arvon was handsome and looked as if he had a lot going on for himself. Something told her he was well acquainted with her husband. That was too close for comfort, and she wasn't going to deal with anyone who knew Kazimir on any level. Plus, she made a vow. Until they were divorced, she was going to be the faithful wife she promised to be, even if he wasn't doing the same.

The waitress came back with the container, then walked off. Nicolette became annoyed because she didn't bring the check. Standing to her feet, she was about to yell out when Arvon spoke before she could open her mouth.

"I've already taken care of your tab. Enjoy your day, Nicolette," he said, slipping a business card into the outside pocket of her purse. "I'll be waiting on your call."

"Don't hold your breath, Arvon. I'm a married woman." Picking up the container she filled with her food, she collected her belongings, then paused. "Thank you for lunch."

Nicolette walked out of the restaurant without looking back. She could feel Arvon staring a hole into her back as the door closed behind her. The loyalty she had for Kazimir angered her but at the same time gave her the courage she needed to go find what she felt was rightfully hers at the penthouse. She was no longer nervous and was ready to complete the mission. Then she would wait for the opportunity to get her daughter back.

# Chapter 19

Kaz sat and talked with his grandfather for over an hour to make sure he was alright after hearing the dreadful news about David. It was never easy learning the passing of a loved one. Paw paw was literally sad for a limited time before his mind blocked out the pain. Kaz ordered enough food to feed an army to make sure everyone ate before he headed out for a few. He watched Koko as she tapped away on her phone, which prompted him to sit next to her. Kaz knew soon as he left, she would be leaving Chicago.

"You okay?" he asked.

"Yes," she replied as she turned to look him in the eyes. "Kaz, you have a lot going on, and I don't want you worrying about being here to entertain me. I think it's best for me to head back home."

"I understand where you're coming from, Chocolate drop. I don't want you to go home alone because there's no telling what Cyrus will do. I stressed my concerns already. Horace will be okay for one more day. Just stay here for the night, and I will make sure to accompany you back to Minnesota safely tomorrow. I have to go home and get my laptop so I can look at the cameras that were in paw paw's house. I need to know what happened. Promise me you'll be here when I return."

"Go take care of your business, Kaz. Before you leave, would you bring my luggage in? I want to take a shower."

"There are T-shirts in the middle drawer in my bedroom. Take a shower and relax. I'll make sure to bring your bags inside when I come back."

"Kaz—"

Leaning in, he cut off her words with a passionate kiss. Koko didn't kiss him back because she couldn't allow his antics to cloud her judgment about going home. Her plans of leaving were still in effect. She had a business to run, and since she wasn't in California anymore, it was time to get back to it. When his tongue invaded her lips, instinctively, she welcomed it. Koko found herself getting caught up in her feelings and stepped out of his grasp. She saw a hint of disappointment in his eyes, but Kaz didn't speak on it.

"Go ahead and get comfortable," he said, stroking her cheek. "Kelly, would you mind showing Koko to my bedroom? I'll be back shortly, Chocolate drop."

Koko forced a smile as she followed Kelly from the room. Kaz stood to his feet. His gaze never left the woman he found himself falling hard for. He couldn't wait to return so he could hold her in his arms.

"She got you, huh?" Stephan laughed lowly. "Love looks good on you, man."

Glancing down, Kaz noticed Koko's phone on the sofa. He picked it up, and it wasn't locked. Something in his gut told him to share her location on his device, and he did just that. If she decided to leave, he would be ready to move in and bring her back where she belonged. With him.

"Yeah, I won't lie. I've been bit by the bug. My marital situation has her holding back, though, which is understandable. I would want her to end what she has going on before we could move forward too. So, I get it. But I've produced the papers and explained countless times how the marriage was arranged from the start."

"You can talk til you're blue in the face, Kaz. A woman like Kameeko wants to see the action behind the words.

Once the divorce is finalized, I'm sure she won't have a problem moving forward."

Nodding in agreement, Kaz tapped the phone into the palm of his hand as Stephan's words resonated in his brain. Koko was running from the feelings she was having a hard time fighting. That said a lot about why she was ready to go home so soon.

"Aye, when I come back, I need you to ride with me to the house. We can finish talking on the way."

"Cool. You can tell me a little bit about Kelly. I tried to get her to open up, but she's not budging," Stephan said, leaning against the wall.

"Hold on a sec."

Kaz walked to his bedroom and eased the door open. Koko locked eyes with him soon as he entered. She was sitting cross legged in the middle of his bed while Kelly sat on the floor. He smiled, seeing the two women getting to know one another. It would be great for both of them to find true friendship and have someone to talk with when needed.

"You left your phone on the couch. I didn't want you to be freaking out because you couldn't find it."

"Thank you. Now would you leave already so you can return?" Koko joked.

"Yes, ma'am. I'm heading out now."

Kaz left the room and closed the door. To hear Koko tell him to basically hurry was a relief because she wasn't thinking about leaving without him. Walking past Stephan, he made his way to the elevator and pushed the button. Stephan didn't miss a beat he was right there with his friend.

"What did you want to know about Kelly?" Kaz asked when the elevator doors closed.

"The type of life she lives. What type of woman is she? What do you know about the nigga she was with because she's going to have a problem with him," Stephan replied, holding on to the rail.

"What nigga?" Kaz asked as they stepped out into the garage.

"Her boyfriend."

"Kelly doesn't have a boyfriend. This I know for sure." He paused as he hit the fob on his keyring and made his way to his vehicle.

Kaz started the car the minute he sat down and backed out of the parking spot soon as Stephan was safely inside. He listened as his friend recited the incident he witnessed with Kelly. The way his jaw clenched was a clear indication that he was pissed as the details resonated in his ears.

"You mean to tell me that pussy tried to put her in the trunk?"

"Yeah. A dude jumped out of his car and stopped him from completing the mission he was on. By the time I made a U-turn to get back to her, the police were already on the scene, and the nigga got his ass whooped in the process."

"Pax wasn't in the car with her, was he?"

"No. After he was standing in the middle of Kelly's dining room ass naked, I figured he needed to ride with me. She drove her car so she would have a way to get around. I recall her stating the car wasn't safe at her place. Now, I know why."

"Wait, what?" Kaz laughed. "Why was Pax naked?"

"Hell if I know. I was making sure the bitch Kelly was arguing with on the porch got her ass off the property. I had to yoke her ass up. She's lucky that's all I did to her."

"Who was she?"

"That's something you would have to ask Kelly. All I can remember her saying was the name Skylar. Oh, she also mentioned Jacoby, who I realized after the fact is the muthafucka who snatched her up."

Kaz was livid and couldn't wait to get more information on the Skylar chick. He knew there wasn't much Kelly could tell him about Jacoby, being she hadn't heard from him in years. His list was getting longer by the day, pulling him deeper into the street shit he had successfully gotten away from. The business side of him was nonexistent, and there was no telling when Mr. St. Claire would resurface.

In deep thought, Kaz stopped focusing on the traffic ahead of him, not realizing what was taking place on the road until the blare of a horn brought him back to reality. He had to swerve to avoid hitting a car in the left lane. Had he collided with the vehicle, it would've been a catastrophe.

"Aye, you have a lot on your mind right now. Pull on the shoulder and I'll take over. You almost caused a bad accident."

"You don't think I know that!"

Driving was the last thing Kaz needed to be doing in the mindset he was in. He knew Stephan was right and didn't attempt to argue with him. Instead, he signaled to get over safely. Kaz stopped the car on the shoulder, then got out of the vehicle. Stephan met his friend at the rear of the car.

"Everything gon' be good, bro. The devil is busy, but this shit won't last much longer. You have to believe and remain faithful."

Kaz stared at his friend briefly before he spoke what was on his heart. "I hear what you're saying, and I appreciate every word. To be honest, that righteous shit won't work on me today. Nothing or nobody can deter me away from what I have to do in order to protect mine. This world has too many sensitive niggas in it, and it's time to eliminate a few of them. Please save the you have too much to lose speech. I don't want to hear it."

Walking to the passenger side of the vehicle, Kaz left Stephan standing there and got inside without another word. The ride was deafeningly silent while Kaz tapped away on his phone. He had to make sure his business ran smoothly because he didn't have any plans of returning until his home life was back to normal. Once he was sure his management team had everything under control, Kaz proceeded to think about every incident that disturbed his peace.

Nicolette came to mind, and it dawned on him, she hadn't called nor texted talking shit about him not bringing Alessia back. It was odd because she was adamant about what she wanted the last time they communicated. Kaz took that opportunity to give her a call. Listening to the phone ring caused a high level of suspicion for him. Soon as the voicemail kicked in, he hung up to send a text.

**Kaz:** *Nicolette call me.*

The bubbles appeared the moment the message was marked read. Whatever she had to say was taking her quite a while to send. Waiting patiently, Kaz glanced out of the window, taking in the scenery. The ping of his phone brought his attention back to his soon-to-be wife.

**Nicolette:** *Fuck you, Kazimir! I told you to bring my daughter home! Let's see how your precious company suffers once you're seen on every news station being arrested for kidnapping in sunny California.*

Kaz chuckled because she wouldn't be tough if she knew he was back in the state. Keeping his cool, he replied back with a simple question.

**Kaz:** *Where are you?*

**Nicolette:** *Maybe under a man like you're lying under a bitch that's not your wife!*

**Kaz:** *Do what you do, baby girl. I just wanted to make sure you were alright. Someone set Pax's house on fire, and my uncle David is dead. I don't know who's behind it, and at this point, it's not safe for my family to be out and about right now.*

**Nicolette:** *Oh, now I'm your family LOL. Fuck you like I said.*

**Kaz:** *I'll see you soon, Nicolette. We have things to discuss. Have your lawyer ready when I return. It's obvious you didn't read the papers I sent to you.*

**Nicolette:** *Fuck them papers too! There won't be a divorce long as I don't sign. Marriage is forever when I'm* *involved. You're going to get that woman hurt while you're trying to replace me.*

**Kaz:** *I never intended to replace you. The woman God created to be my better half happened to cross paths with me at an unforeseen time of my life. You and I were never meant to be. It was a forced encounter that never went beyond I do. I've realized it was a mistake. When will you get on board? This is your opportunity to find the man who will love you the way you desire. That man is not me, sweetheart.*

Nicolette never responded to the last message, and Kaz was fine with that. She wanted war when all he hoped for was peace. Throughout the entire exchange, Stephan watched his friend out of his peripheral vision.

"Everything cool?"

"It will be. Nicolette is on bullshit. That's nothing new, though. She's not trying to sign the divorce papers, talking about I'm trying to replace her. I don't know why she wants to pretend we were in love and fucked all day, every day for three years. In fact, it was the complete opposite. I've never fucked her. Not even once. Hell, I don't think I've ever kissed her on the lips."

"Kaz, there's no way she's acting the way she is and you've never hit. You have said it since the day y'all got married, but right now, I don't believe that shit."

"Believe it," Kaz said, shaking his head. "I had in-house pussy, but I went outside to fuck," he laughed. "That alone should shed light on any doubts you may have. Look at it this way, I've never lied to her about where my dick has been. Nicolette didn't care long as I continued to take care of her and Alessia. She only started talking out the side of her neck when Koko entered the picture."

"Be careful. You don't know what she's capable of. With a father like Anthony, Nicolette could be the devil in disguise."

"Stephan, she has already shown her evil side thinking I have no knowledge of her wrongdoings. She has been abusing Alessia, and that alone is why I want my daughter away from her. Not to mention the reason Nicolette and her father have to die."

"Wait, she's been hitting Alessia?" Stephan asked, taking his eyes off the road for a second.

Kaz filled him in on everything he found out about Nicolette and Anthony's plan. Stephan was shocked as he listened to the details. Alessia was the niece he never had and couldn't imagine anything happening to her. He knew now that Koko wasn't the main reason Kaz was walking away from his marriage. It was the safety of his daughter.

"What do you plan to do? You know the law is going to force you to give Alessia back, right? You are not her biological father," Stephan stated as he turned into Kaz's driveway.

"She's not going back. I'm the only father she knows. Plus, my name is on her birth certificate. Trust, I got this."

Kaz got out of the passenger side of his car before it could come to a complete stop. He wanted to grab his laptop and leave before Nicolette showed up. The last thing he wanted to do was argue with her over shit she already knew. As he walked through the house, he noticed little things that were out of place. The moment he entered his office, Kaz knew shit wasn't right.

Going further into the room, he surveyed the scattered papers that were thrown on the floor. His laptop sat open on the desk, and the bottom drawer was left agape. It was where his important papers were kept for his personal records. Nicolette had been snooping, and he didn't like the fact she had invaded his space.

"What the hell happened in here?" Stephan asked as soon as he entered.

"I don't know, but I'm gon' have to kill this bitch."

Leaving Stephan in the office, Kaz jogged up the stairs, and as he expected, the master bedroom looked like a tornado hit it. There were a lot of Nicolette's makeup brushes, along with perfume and other miscellaneous items, lying on the floor next to her vanity. When he went to the closet, confirmation hit him in the face. The bitch had packed up and made her exit. If Nicolette thought her leaving was going to hurt him in any way, she was sadly mistaken. That shit was like a breath of fresh air. Kaz knew her shenanigans were soon to follow, but he was ready for whatever she thought was about to take place.

He would have to come back at a later date to clean up the mess. He took a quick glance around and chuckled because Nicolette was a joke. Everything that took place in his absence was on camera, and he was sure there would be valuable evidence for him to present in court. While she thought she was going to get back at him for something her father involved her in, Nicolette was digging her own grave fuckin' with him. Kaz went back downstairs to his office. He packed up his laptop while Stephan sat reading a document.

"Aye, this is the information for your penthouse. What was she looking for that for?"

"She wasn't looking for it because she didn't know about it. She just happened to come upon the paperwork while being nosey." He opened the drawer, and the spare key was missing. "Let's go," Kaz said, rushing out of the door. "The bitch may be on her way there. The key is gone. I just left everybody I give a fuck about in that damn place."

Just as they were about to walk out of the house, Kaz received a text.

**Koko:** *I want you to know that me and Alessia is going out for a walk. I never want to do anything without your permission.*

**Kaz:** *Baby, don't leave the penthouse. Nicolette may be lurking around. I can't take the chance of anything happening to y'all. I'm on my way back now.*

**Koko**: *Okay. I'll find something to do with her for the meantime. See you soon.*

Stephan left out of the house first, then Kaz stepped on the porch behind him, resetting the code on the keypad and revoking Nicolette's access to his place. He jumped into his vehicle, and Stephan put foot to gas soon as the door closed. Knowing Nicolette found out about the penthouse wasn't a problem because she didn't know the half about him. She only knew what he wanted her to know. The problem was, she was liable to do something to hurt him in the worst way possible. There was nothing like a woman scorned, but did she really have a reason to be? Kaz didn't think so because he was upfront from the gate, and for her father, she agreed to be his wife with conditions.

He sat back and shot Steelo a text to see how things were going in the Twin Cities. He hadn't heard anything, so there couldn't be any new information he needed to know about. Kaz could feel the demon activating inside of him slowly. Closing his eyes, he said a silent prayer, thinking it would stop him from converting back to the devil he used to be. He didn't like the man he used to be back in the day because there was so much blood on his hands, and it took years to cleanse his sins. Now, he was easing back toward the dark tunnel he fought hard to get out of. It was inevitable, especially when his family was threatened.

Stephan was pushing the pedal to the metal, weaving in and out of traffic because Kaz's silence told him his homie was in another world. That meant death was on the horizon, and he didn't want him to go backward. Kazimir was a monster when he had to defend himself and the people he cared for with his whole heart. Getting them to the penthouse was a must so he could see with his own eyes that his family was safe. Stephan's logic was short lived soon as Kaz's phone rang in his hand.

"Aye, Bernard, what's going on?" he asked the front desk clerk from his place. Kaz's anxiety hit the roof of the vehicle because he was never contacted by anyone there.

"There's a woman here trying to go up to your place. She claims to be your wife, and she has a key. I wanted to make sure it was alright with you before letting her up."

"Stall her. She does not have permission to even be there. I'm about ten minutes away. If you need to do so, call the police and have her ass locked up. Hold off on getting the law involved, though, because I want to deal with the bitch myself."

"I don't know how long I'll be able to do that because she is being very belligerent."

"Trust me. She will continue to rebuttal long as you tell her she can't go up. I'll be there shortly."

Kaz hung up and looked at Stephan. "Floor this muthafucka. The bitch is trying to make entry."

"I told you she was going to be a problem. You want to tell me the truth now?"

"What truth, nigga?"

"That you never fucked her. She is doing the type of shit a woman would do when the dick is taken away. Nicolette is in her if she can't have you, nobody can era."

"I've. Never. Fucked. Her! She isn't going insane behind my dick. Hell, if that was the case, she would've been acting up long ago. Nicolette knows her money train has exited the station. She should be good because her daddy got money, right?"

"If your reasons are correct, it doesn't seem as if he has too much to fall back on. That would be a question you could ask when we pull up."

"Stephan, I know you're not that green to the game. Nicolette is not going to flat out say her family is broke. She's going to argue me down that Koko is the reason I filed for divorce. Is she wrong? No, but keep in mind, I didn't want to marry her in the first place. Pops is the reason I went along with the bullshit, and I would lay my life on the line for him. The marriage went on far too long, and Koko just so happened to come into my life and made me realize I needed real love in my life. Case closed."

The moment Kaz clarified his thoughts, he searched his contacts and found the one he needed. He gave his driver a heads-up that he wanted to take a road trip with him and his family to Minnesota the next day. He would need him to fuel up the bulletproof RV and make sure everything was cleaned and stocked for the ride. There was no way Koko was going back home alone, and he couldn't leave his Pops and Kelly after what took place while he was away. Thinking about David getting killed only fueled the fire inside of him more. Kaz wanted to find the muthafucka who thought it was a good idea to set his childhood home ablaze and kill his uncle in the process.

All of his thoughts came to a halt soon as the view of his second home appeared. Stephan parked in the front and turned on the hazard lights, but Kaz had already jumped out and was heading toward the entrance. Lo and behold, Nicolette was still there causing a damn scene. When Bernard noticed Kaz entering, it was like he let out the breath he was holding in. Nicolette yelled while calling the man every name but a child of God.

"I keep telling you I'm his wife and have every right to go up to that expensive ass apartment! Why do you think I have a key, dumb ass?"

"You have the key because you stole it. Nicolette, why are you here causing problems?" Kaz asked calmly as he could.

"How did you know I was here? Did this man call you?" she demanded to know while glaring at Bernard.

"In fact, he did. That's part of his job. Give me my damn key; not now, but right muthafuckin' now," Kaz sneered.

"I'm not giving you anything until you give me my daughter. She is the only reason I'm even here."

"It's not going to happen. Alessia isn't safe in your care. You proved that shit in more ways than one. If you want to battle me about it, call the police. My daughter is not going anywhere with you unless the judge tells me otherwise, which I highly doubt."

"Kazimir, you must have dementia like your grandfather because you do know she's not your daughter, right?" Nicolette laughed. "What judge in their right mind would take a child from their mother and give them to a man that's not her father? Not one that I know of. Keep dreaming."

"You can laugh now, but I promise, you will cry later. I'm the only father she has ever known. She calls me Daddy because I treat her as such. If anyone asks her who her daddy is, my name would roll off her tongue with ease. I'm more of a parent to her than you will ever be. You know what? Fuck all that because you ain't talking about shit. Give me my muthafuckin' key before I snatch yo' head off ."

Bernard came from around the desk and stood in between the two of them. He was afraid things would get out of hand and result in physical harm. He didn't want to see the man he admired go down for assaulting the rude woman.

"Mr. St. Claire, I'm going to call the police. Ma'am, if you don't want that to happen, I advise you to leave the premises now."

"Fuck you, and fuck him too! I will get my daughter, Kazimir. Your name won't be able to save you from the pain I will cause you and your family. Trust me."

Nicolette bumped into Kaz as she stormed toward the door to make her exit. Before she could touch the glass, she was snatched by the back of her neck like a pitbull. He had the urge to snap her fuckin' neck right then and there, but the witnesses had grown from just three people at that point. Kaz wrestled the key from her hand, then shoved her away from him. She was lucky he was able to contain himself from doing bodily harm because that would've been bad publicity for St. Claire Candies.

"Don't ever bring yo' ass back here, Nicolette. And don't think about going back to the house because you no longer have access. You removed all of your belongings, so there is no reason for you to be there. Oh yeah, I hope you found everything you were looking for in my office. What I need is locked away on the laptop you left behind when you couldn't get into it. I'll see you in court. Remember to say your prayers. You're going to need them."

Nicolette pushed the door open, but Kaz's voice stopped her in her tracks.

"And another thing, if you ever threaten my family again, you will come up missing. That's a promise, not a threat."

She left without another word but didn't leave right away. Nicolette stood staring at Kaz through the glass wickedly. Ideas raced through her mind to the point she couldn't keep up with them all. The end result was Kazimir would pay for putting his hands on her. The pain he was going to feel would be far worse than losing his perverted ass uncle and his grandpa's house.

# Chapter 20

Koko was sitting on the couch watching *Zootopia 2*, thinking about the text she received from Kaz. She didn't know what his wife was capable of, but she wasn't about to go against his wishes by taking Alessia out. In fact, she was waiting for the drama to present itself at the elevator, but it never happened. As the movie came to an end, she looked down and noticed Alessia was sleeping like a baby. The sound of the doors parting averted her gaze to the entrance. Koko rose from her seat slowly, ready to beat the fuck out of the bitch she thought was entering without permission, she sighed with relief when she saw Kaz.

"Hello, Chocolate drop. Why do you look ready for combat?"

"I thought your wife was the one coming in here. She was about to be carried out on a stretcher."

Kaz laughed because he could hear the seriousness in her voice. Stephan walked in a few seconds later, and her face lit up at the sight of him. Koko bypassed Kaz and hugged Stephan tightly.

"Kameeko, you got me all the way fucked up. How you gon' show this muthafucka love before me?" Kaz requisitioned.

"Jealousy don't look good on you, bro. You know Koko is family to me, right? I get all the love firsthand."

"I know she is fam, but did you know she's my woman, and you could lose a limb just by standing close to her?" he smirked.

"Go give that nigga a hug or something before we tear this room up."

Koko laughed as she made her way to Kaz. Wrapping her arms around his waist, she looked up at him with a smile. "So, when did I become your woman?"

Kaz bent down to whisper in her ear. "The moment you allowed me access to your sugary walls. I like it there, and no other nigga will ever experience that the way we did. Now, give me those lips."

Slipping his tongue into her mouth soon as their lips connected, Koko could feel the moisture between her legs. Every time Kaz kissed her, she got turned on immediately. She didn't want it to go too far because they had company. Stepping out of the hold he had on her, Kaz pulled her back in, then pecked her a few times before allowing her to be free. Through her chocolate skin tone, he could tell her cheeks were burning with desire, and she wanted him just as bad as he wanted her.

"Um, what's going on with Alessia's mother? Is there anything we should be cautious about?" she asked, breaking the silence.

"I took care of that. Nicolette better find her something safe to do and leave mine alone," Kaz replied, going over to the couch where Alessia slept soundly. "How was her day?" he asked, lifting the little girl into his lap once he sat down.

"She was upset because we couldn't go out, but I changed her mood with a movie, popcorn, and pizza. I hope it was okay for me to give her those things."

"You never have to worry if I'm alright with anything you do for my daughter. The way she clings to you tells me all I need to know. She loves you, beautiful. If you were doing anything to harm her, she wouldn't want anything to do with you. I can see you being in her life for the long run. Hopefully, mine too."

"I mean, you already said I'm your woman. It seems to me I don't have a choice because you have already set claim."

"Damn right I did. You are officially the future Mrs. St. Claire. There are just a few things I have to close the doors on, and I will be making you my wife expeditiously."

"Woah! I am agreeing to be your woman, but it's too soon to talk marriage. We have so much to learn about one another, and I think we have nothing but time to accomplish that. You and I both have past relationship issues we have to resolve. You understand, right?"

"Of course, I understand what you're saying, and you are absolutely correct. What I want you to know is, we will get married and become one in more ways than one. Waiting on the woman I feel is the best thing since sliced bread is small to a giant. Being with you is where I want to be. We're going to move mountains and build together."

Koko could feel the affection Kaz had for her, and it was mutual. She sat watching how attentive he was with Alessia, and it warmed her heart. After the miscarriage, Koko was afraid to get pregnant again, but being around Alessia and Kaz had her rethinking her decision. She didn't want it to happen until the relationship flourished into something great with a promise of longevity. But she could see herself having Kazimir's child and experiencing motherhood from the start.

"How was Paw Paw while I was gone?" he asked, cutting into her thoughts.

"He was kind of fussy when it was time to eat earlier. Alessia was a good great-granddaughter. She convinced him to eat all of his food by playing airplane with him. He laughed the whole time, playing along with her antics. He has been in his room for a few hours, sleeping, I believe. Kelly has been checking on him periodically."

Kaz got up with Alessia in his arms. He asked her to get his laptop bag he'd dropped in the middle of the floor when he came inside. When he maneuvered it on his shoulder, Kaz kissed the top of Koko's head, then headed to the back of the condo toward the room he had set up for Alessia. She followed his every move until he disappeared around the corner. Stephan sat smiling as he watched Koko's reaction to his friend.

"You can stop playing hard to get. What Kaz wants, he gets, and he want you. There's no turning back."

"Who's playing hard to get? Not me. I'm not about to jump into a marriage and barely know the man that will be my husband. You heard my explanation, and he understood."

"He will go along with whatever you suggest because that's the type of guy Kaz is. But rest assured, he is not going to sit around waiting for things to happen too long. He is going to make it happen. Believe that."

"No one can rush me into anything I'm not comfortable with. That could work with a woman who needs a man to provide and give. It doesn't stand a chance with me because I know how to live and survive without a soul doing anything for me. Know the difference, Steph."

"It doesn't matter if you can provide for yourself or not. When a man has his mind set on being there and doing for a woman, he's going to do it. Especially when that woman has something going for herself. Don't get me wrong, even if she doesn't have all her ducks in a row and is trying, a real man is going to help her get where she's trying to go in life."

"Many men don't think that way and would watch a woman struggle long as they can still have sex with her. It's part of the reason I decided to go hard in my craft so I will never have to depend on anyone to get me out of a bind."

"You're going off track, Koko. Kaz isn't that type of guy, and he would never just want you for what you can provide in the bedroom. Trust me. Not to put his business out there, but he can get pussy any day of the week if he chooses to. That's not the case because he hasn't entertained another woman since meeting you. I can vouch for him there. All I can say is, be ready when he decides to sweep you off your feet."

Kelly walked into the room heading for the kitchen, causing Steph to stop what he was saying. Drool was present in the corner of his mouth as he watched her disappear behind the counter. Chuckling while shaking her head, Koko reached out and dabbed at his mouth.

"What you do that for?" he asked.

"You almost slobbered on yourself. I had to catch it before it slid down your chin. Go talk to her. I'm going to wash your cooties from my fingers, then go discuss going home tomorrow with Kaz."

"Yeah, do that. I need to learn a little more about that woman in the kitchen. She seems to be someone who needs a lot of tender loving care," he whispered.

"I don't know Kelly's story, but there's definitely one to be told," Koko said, rising from her seat. "How long are you hanging around here?"

"It hasn't been a walk in the park for her, that I do know. The man baby who had her heart fucked up, and I'm going to be the superhero to mend it back together," he smirked. "Far as how long I'll be here… who knows. Maybe I'll see you at the dinner table later," he winked.

"You are a mess. Be her friend first, Stephan. Don't try no hanky panky on the first night."

"Yes, mother," he joked as Koko left him alone.

She decided to wait for Kaz in his bedroom but was met with a surprise once she stepped inside. He was sitting up in bed, shirtless, with his laptop in his lap. The anguish on his face made her a little afraid to proceed further into the room. As she backed up, Kaz looked up and removed one of the earbuds from his ear.

"Where you going?" he asked.

"I was going to give you some privacy to finish what you're doing. It looks like there's something that needs your undivided attention. I don't want to be a bother."

"Come here, Chocolate drop," he said, motioning her to the bed. "You can never be a bother. I'm going over the footage from my house. Watching Nicolette going through my shit pissed me off, and I now regret not smacking her ass up when I saw her downstairs."

"Kaz, what would putting your hands on her accomplish? Nothing. You did the right thing by telling her to leave without physically putting your hands on her," she responded while climbing onto the bed.

"Koko, I'm not the type of man who will hit a woman. But Nicolette is going to make me kill her muthafuckin' ass. She not only took the key to this place and was on her way here to see what she could take while I was out of town, but she stole from me. I had to cancel the cards she took. The money was chump change, and hopefully, she will be able to make it stretch because she's not getting another dime from me. From the looks of it, she found the documents for the account I have set up for Alessia too. There's nothing she can do with them other than get angry every time she reads them."

Koko couldn't believe the lengths his wife had gone through to steal from him. All she had to do was tell her lawyer what she wanted out of the divorce, then handle it that way. Nicolette was doing the most, and poking the bear was a bad idea in her opinion.

"I have a question. Is there a reason you didn't make sure your wife was okay along with Alessia?"

"Yes. Alessia has been my responsibility since I took on the role of being her father. Nicolette, on the other hand, was only a business deal. I didn't agree to love her at all. The agreement was for me to marry her so she wouldn't be a woman who had a baby out of wedlock. I held up my end of the bargain. She's stretching that shit like I'm out here cheating on her. I never consummated the marriage. To me, that shit was a dud and don't count."

"Understood. So, what have you found other than the fact she stole things from you?"

"Nothing. She moved her things out of the house, and it was the best decision she has made thus far. Nicolette was one step closer to being out of my life for good. I'm about to see if I can retrieve the footage from Paw Paw's home. Finding out who killed my uncle is something I need to know. There is no telling what he had done to get himself killed, but my grandfather could've been killed if he hadn't left with Kelly. So, whoever did it signed their own death certificate when they put his life in jeopardy."

Listening to Kaz talk about getting revenge for what happened to his family brought a little bit of discomfort to Koko. She understood his mindset and why he wanted to hurt whomever was responsible, but she knew if he went to jail for the crime, holding him down wasn't something she would be able to do. She sat quietly while he searched his laptop, becoming more frustrated as the seconds ticked away.

"Fuck!" Kaz bellowed, running his hand down his face. "Where is the footage?"

"It's not there?" Koko asked

"No. I should be able to run it back even if the system was destroyed. It's not coming up."

He reached over to get his phone from the nightstand, then placed a call. As he waited for whomever to answer, Kaz caressed Koko's thigh. The tingling sensation immediately jumpstarted her yoni. It wasn't the best time to be horny with the mindset he was in, but human nature had a mind of its own. She inched away from him a little bit, and Kaz gripped her flesh, pulling her back. The stern look he delivered halted her movements.

"Where you trying to go?"

"Nowhere. I was giving you some space."

"Kaz, my man, I'm not going anywhere," Eduardo replied in his thick Spanish accent. "You need something?"

"My bad, that wasn't meant for you," he laughed. "Aye, my grandfather's house was burned down, and the surveillance equipment was destroyed. I tried pulling up the footage from my laptop, but it's not coming up. Didn't you say the footage would save no matter what damage was caused?"

"Yeah, that's correct. Give me an hour or so, and I will override the system. I'll send all the files to your email since you are out of town."

"No, I'm back. Don't send it via email. Save it to a flash drive and bring it to the penthouse, or I can come to you early tomorrow. I'm due to hit the road to Minnesota; however, I need to know what happened at Paw paw's crib."

"Fo sho. I'll have that for you soon as possible. Rest your mind for a minute, and I'll bring it to you. It's not a problem."

"Thank you. Call me when you're on your way so I can meet you downstairs."

Eduardo agreed, then hung up. Knowing the footage would be retrieved took a lot of weight off his shoulders, and he was eager to see who was behind the fire. In the meantime, he had to take his mind off killing a nigga. Glancing over at Koko, she was looking at him with a small smile.

"What are you smiling for?"

"My initial plan was to come in here to tell you I needed to go home, and you already have a time and date for me to do so."

"I told you we were going together. There was no way I could send you back alone. I've repeated that line so many times I'm starting to feel like a parrot. We're driving out in the morning. The whole family is going. Is that okay with you?"

"Even your grandfather?" she asked.

"Yes. I don't want anyone left behind. The person who killed David and burned down the house is still out there. I can't take a chance of something else happening. Plus, Nicolette is pissed for many reasons, especially because I won't return Alessia to her. There's no telling what she's bound to do."

"Kaz, I don't have the room at my apartment for everyone to be comfortable," Koko explained.

"You won't need to worry about that. As a matter of fact, let me book a hotel while we're talking about it."

Kaz went to the Hyatt website and booked a suite along with a single room for Stephan. His friend wasn't going to be left behind while he was trying to get in good with Kelly. The matchup was one he wanted to see work because she needed a man to be there and love her correctly. The nigga who ran her away from the only place she knew had fucked her up badly. Kaz couldn't wait for the day he met his punk ass face-to-face. He had a beatdown with his name on it whenever the time presented itself.

"We're all set," he said, closing his laptop, then placing it along with his phone on the nightstand. "Now, it's about me and you."

He gathered Koko in his arms and kissed the side of her neck. She talked a lot of shit about not wanting to jump into marriage, but that didn't have anything to do with her opening her legs to him. If he was going to be her husband one day, she had to make sure they meshed in the bedroom on all levels. Practice made things perfect, right? At least that was how Koko felt things would play out between them. She was in for a long night of lovemaking, and she was ready to open up to Kaz like never before.

***

Kaz kissed Koko's face, to wake her. He saved her for last since he had worked her over something fierce the night before. After putting her to sleep, he got out of bed to sit in the living room. So many thoughts were in his head, preventing him from closing his eyes to relax. Eduardo called, informing him that he needed more time to retrieve the footage. He promised to have it for him upon his return to Chicago. That in itself had him a little edgy. Koko was his calm before the storm, and he wanted to absorb as much of her as he could before they entered her stomping ground. There was a huge possibility she would have a lot of turmoil of her own with Cyrus' bitch ass.

She stirred, then stretched like a feline as he planted another kiss; this time to her lips.

"What time is it?" she asked groggily.

"Seven thirty. Everyone is getting ready so we can get on the road. It's your turn now, Chocolate drop."

Kaz had already showered and dressed hours before. He took the liberty to lay out her clothes, and he took all the bags to the bus. Troy showed up bright and early to be sure he was outside waiting when his boss was ready to roll. Koko sat up with a yawn. She was beautiful even in her sleepy state. Kaz admired her beauty, then leaned in for a kiss. Turning her head, she waved him off while covering her mouth.

"I have morning breath. I'll make sure to kiss you long as you like after I freshen up."

"Your dragon breath isn't a concern for me. I'll respect your wishes, but I'm going to hold you to what you promised. I can't get enough of your lips; both of them," he smirked.

Koko smiled as she shoved him in the middle of his chest. The image of his head between her legs and her hands pushing his face deeper had her squeezing her thighs together. If they didn't have to leave, she would've initiated another round of the amazing sex she knew he could provide. Instead, she got out of bed and headed to the bathroom to handle her hygiene.

The thought of going back home tried to sour her mood. It wasn't happening. The only person she wanted to lay eyes on was Horace. Anyone else in the state could kiss her ass.

Every step she took felt like walking on a cloud. She had Kaz to thank because the lovin' he dished out had her happier than the day her career was established.

She showered and pulled her hair into a ponytail before getting dressed in the olive-green sweatsuit Kaz left out for her to wear. After brushing her teeth, Koko made her way out of the bathroom in search of her shoes. The man who was trying his best to cuff her stood outside the door with her Chucks in hand.

"Thank you, Mr. St. Claire," she smiled.

"No problem, Mrs. St. Claire," he replied seriously.

Koko took the shoes without responding to the name he threw back at her. She was going to let him have that shit for now. There was no reason to correct him because it would've been a losing battle. She also didn't want to ruin the high he had her on. They would be on the road at least eight hours, and tension was the last thing needed for a long road trip.

Alessia appeared in the doorway, rubbing her eyes.

"Daddy, I'm sleepy," she whined.

"I know, sweetheart. Soon as we get downstairs to the RV, you'll be able to go back to sleep. Remember, we're taking Koko home."

"Koko, I want you to live with me."

Alessia walked into Koko's outstretched arms, hugging her tightly around the waist. Bending down to Kiss the top of the little girl's head, Koko couldn't think of a single word to say in response to what Alessia had said. Instead, she chose to stay quiet, expecting another subject would come forth. Hoping and wishing didn't work because she wasn't letting up. Alessia wanted a response.

Looking at Kaz for help, Koko pleaded with her eyes for him to intervene. He laughed lowly as he stood shaking his head. His daughter was being extra, and he liked it. Hell, he wanted Koko to live with him too.

"Alessia, Koko doesn't live here. She will come back to visit whenever she has time. We will go see her too. Maybe one day we will be able to live together. For now, we will stay in touch by phone and visits. Is that alright?"

"No!" she pouted, still holding on to Koko.

Lifting her up so she was sitting in her lap, Koko cradled Alessia in her arms. "Your dad is correct. I will still be in your life. I'm not going anywhere. We can talk about it more on the ride to my place. Right now, we have to go. Let's get your coat so we can head out."

Koko stood, carrying Alessia toward the door as she glared at Kaz. She didn't realize being around his daughter would have such an impact on her departure. It was a sad situation when her own mother acted as if she didn't give a damn about her daughter. The pull in her heart did something to Koko, and it had her thinking about her decision to go back home. There was no getting around it, being that her business was in Minnesota, not Chicago.

The ride on the elevator was silent. Koko thought about solutions to make things easier for her to continue being in Alessia's life. The proposal to expand her business Kaz presented months earlier invaded her mind. She hadn't given it much thought until that moment. Alessia had a lot to do with her contemplating her relocation, but the sex with Kaz played a major part as well. The chemistry the two of them had in the bedroom was immaculate. Koko wanted to make sure intercourse wasn't the root of their connection. She needed more than that to establish any type of relationship. Alessia was definitely a strong add-on, but she didn't need to be in Kaz's life to manage a bond with her. It was already established.

Soon as they boarded the RV, Kaz led her to the bedroom to lay his daughter down. The bed looked comfortable and was calling her. She toed off her shoes, then did the same for Alessia before laying down beside her. It didn't take long for the both of them to fall asleep.

Kaz waited patiently for Koko to come back to sit with him, but she had yet to return. They were already on the highway when he got up to look for her. He smiled as he stood in the doorway, watching the two ladies that had his whole heart sleeping soundly. Leaving them to rest, he went back to his seat up front.

Pax grabbed his arm as he walked down the aisle.

"That pretty girl got you by your nuts, son. It's time for you to get rid of the pale woman and follow your heart. I haven't seen your face light up like that in a long time."

Sitting across from his grandpa, Kaz smiled because Pax was speaking with a sound mind. Kelly must've been able to get him to take his medicine before leaving the penthouse, which was a good thing for them all. The last thing he needed was Pax acting a fool while they were confined inside.

"You're right. She is something special. I told her she would be my wife one day, but she turned me down. For now."

"Do you blame her? I wouldn't want to commit to a married muthafucka either. Son, you have to close one door before opening another. I forget her name, but she doesn't look like the type of woman who's going to play second fiddle. If you wait too long, she's going to leave your black ass to play games with your damn self," Pax shook his head.

"She reminds me of my Barbara. That woman didn't tolerate my bullshit. She let me know how she felt every time I fucked up. I was on my last leg with her, and she laid down the law. I bet I got my shit together quick because she meant that much to me. I'm saying all this to say, if you want to be with her, you are gonna have to make some changes. Leave all those hoes alone and concentrate on her. That includes letting that wife of yours know her time is up."

"Paw Paw, I did all that the moment I decided to get to know Kameeko."

"Kameeko. That's a beautiful name for a beautiful woman," he smiled. "I'm glad you did because she looks like she can whoop you, my boy. I can sense the hurt she has endured in her life. She seems guarded, and it's gonna take more than dick to break the barrier."

Kaz started coughing uncontrollably when spit went down his throat wrong. He wasn't prepared for what his grandfather said. In fact, he was shocked.

"What makes you think I'm sleeping with her?" he asked.

"Hell, everybody who slept at your place last night knows you're sleeping with her! If you want privacy, you may want to soundproof your bedroom. That woman has a set of lungs on her. Shit, she had me thinking you were her daddy in real life."

Kelly and Stephan laughed loudly as they looked back at Kaz. It told him all he needed to know; he and Koko had the whole house in their business the night before. It never crossed his mind they were louder than an NBA YoungBoy concert. He was relieved Koko was asleep and not present to witness them joking about their encounter. She would've been embarrassed for sure.

"I hope you were clapping your hands behind that door. It damn sure better not have been her ass cheeks."

"Paw Paw, leave it alone. I don't want to hear anything else about what you heard. Remember, I'm a grown ass man and I have needs. I apologize for carrying on the way I did. It was disrespectful to you and everyone else."

"What you apologizing for? Shid, I used to get it in just like that before my bones became brittle. It's all about the stroke of your back. You had that girl bellowing out her best falsetto. It was music to my knees. I think my willie stood at attention for the first time in a long time."

"That's enough! All jokes aside now," Kaz scolded his grandpa. "Are you hungry?"

"Yeah. What you got for me?"

Kaz got up to fix Pax a plate. He made sure there was enough food for breakfast and lunch catered for their trip. Putting a couple of pancakes, eggs, and turkey sausage on a plate, he grabbed a small bottle of orange juice and syrup to finish it off. Making sure he had silverware and napkins, Kaz took the food down the aisle. He ignored Stephan waiting to get him a plate with a sly smirk. Saying something to him was on the tip of his tongue, but he didn't want to get his grandpa started again.

Kaz sat in the back of the RV and reclined his seat. He took the time to get some sleep for a few minutes. His nap turned into several hours. He was awakened by Koko kissing him passionately on the lips.

"I think when we arrive at the hotel, we should go out and have some fun. I want to go out to eat and maybe listen to some live music," she whispered.

"How are we going to do that, Chocolate drop? We can't just leave Kelly to care for Paw Paw while we're out. It wouldn't be fair. You should've told me your plans before we left Chicago. I would have brought Marisol along."

"If it's alright with you, I can have Stella come sit with Alessia and your grandfather for a few hours."

"Who is Stella?" he quizzed.

"Jackie's mother. She's like a second mother to me. I trust her."

Kaz sat up fully, turning to address Koko. "Hell no. You may trust her, but I don't trust her grimy ass daughter. Nah, it's not going to happen."

"If I tell her not to say anything to Jackie, she won't. They will be safe with her. I promise."

"I'll let you know by the time we get to Minnesota."

Leaving Kaz to rest and think about what she planned, Koko walked to the small kitchen to get something to eat. They were about two hours out of Minnesota, and she was well rested. Alessia was still sleeping, so Koko wanted to make sure she was ready when she woke up. Piling enough food on the plate for both her and Kaz, she went back to where he sat so she could feed him. Seeing him with his eyes closed, she realized why she was so attracted to him. Kazimir St. Claire was sexy as fuck. She couldn't wait 'til they were alone to ride what she had fallen in love with; his magic stick.

# Chapter 21

Nicolette camped outside of the penthouse so she could follow Kazimir whenever he left. The man she vowed to obey and cherish stayed the entire night with another woman. Nicolette didn't know until she saw them leaving bright and early in the morning. The plan to follow him was put into effect the moment she saw that Black bitch cradling her daughter while cheesing in her husband's face as they walked out of the building. They looked like a happy family, and she didn't like it. Nicolette told Kazimir to bring her baby home, and instead of doing that, he had his bitch playing mama to the child she pushed out.

The shit had Nicolette hotter than fish grease. She couldn't believe Kaz wanted to divorce her for such a basic bitch. It couldn't have been about pussy because he hadn't given her a chance to show him what hers felt like. Her thoughts were running off topic as she sat in wait. Strumming her fingers on the steering wheel, if she had been able to destroy the vehicle in front of her with just a deadly stare, it would already be up in flames. The brake lights lit up, and Nicolette started her car and put it in gear.

Staying where she was until a few cars passed, Nicolette merged into traffic. She could keep her eyes on the vehicle since it was so big. Her first thought was Kaz taking his bitch to the cabin he had in Spring Grove. The weather was nice enough for him to snuggle with his hoe by the fireplace. If she had anything to do with it, both of them would die soon as they stopped at their destination. By law, she was still his wife, and Nicolette felt she was entitled to whatever Kaz would be leaving behind. Since he wanted the divorce to live life with someone else, she had plans to kill his ass in the process.

The driver got on the expressway, and Nicolette wasn't too far behind. She hit the power button to turn the radio on and continued to cruise. Her assumption was correct; they were heading in the direction of the cabin. Several ways of killing the couple came to mind, and she stored every last one of them for later use. Kaz would have to go first because she wasn't strong enough to do anything more than shoot him. Now, the homewrecker was going to go through a world of torture. Nicolette couldn't wait to make her suffer. Her phone rang, and she sighed loudly. Without looking at the screen, she answered the call through her earbud.

"Hello?"

"Nicolette, where are you?" her father's voice boomed in her ear.

He'd been calling her since he realized she was no longer in his home. Nicolette ignored his calls for hours because she didn't want to hear his fucking mouth.

"Does it matter where I am? You don't give a damn about me. The only reason you're constantly calling is to see if I was able to get my hands on any of Kazimir's money. Well, the answer is no."

"What do you mean, no? Did he have anything in there of value?"

"Dad, I didn't get the opportunity to go up to the place. Security protects the residents like they work for the Secret Service. The man at the front desk threatened to call the police on me. He actually called Kaz, and he showed up, took the key from me, then told me to get the fuck off his property."

There was a long pause on the other end of the line. Anthony was fuming because he felt Nicolette should've found a way to get into that apartment by any means necessary. He needed money, and he needed it fast. The debt he had wasn't going to pay itself, and the St. Claires were his only way out of the mess he had gotten himself into.

"Were you able to get Alessia?"

"No, she wasn't with him. I believe she was upstairs with Kazimir's mistress."

"She is the only way we will get our hands on any money, Nicolette! You need to get that child back, and soon too."

"Anthony, I agreed to get Alessia for you, but now I'm trying to get my baby back for me. You will not use my daughter for a payday. I won't be an accessory to you murdering my child. When I do get my baby from Kazimir, I'm leaving this fucking city. You and Kazimir can kiss my ass."

"Bitch, I want you to hear me and hear me good. If you don't follow the program, you will come up missing too. I have a policy on your daughter. What makes you think I don't have one on you too? Bring that child to me by tomorrow. Or else."

Anthony hung up, and what he said brought tears to Nicolette's eyes. Her father was someone she didn't know anymore. The drugs had taken over, and she couldn't see him coming back from the hold they had on him. Even though Anthony didn't outright say he would harm his daughter, Nicolette heard the threat loud and clear. That alone was the reason she was leaving Chicago just as she stated. Getting her things out of his house was going to be a challenge, but she would figure it out.

As she continued to drive, Nicolette wiped the tears from her eyes and turned the radio up to get her mind off the conversation she'd just had with her father. The drive shouldn't be more than an hour and a half, so she would be able to survive. With everything that was going on and seeing her husband entertaining another woman, she wished she had given Arvon a chance. Hell, she still could once she had her baby back. His number was still in her purse.

The longer she drove, the more she wondered if Kazimir was going to the cabin. Grabbing her phone, she put the address in the GPS to see how much longer it would be for them to get there. According to the device, they were no longer on the road to Spring Grove. Nicolette had no clue where they were going. She was down to a half tank of gas and didn't know if she would have enough to drive wherever they were leading her. She would have to pray about it because there was no way the RV wasn't full of gas.

Continuing to drive, Nicolette allowed her playlist to keep her company. Every thirty minutes, her father would call her phone, but she declined them all. There was nothing he could say to make what he said to her right. The text messages came soon after, but she didn't bother to read those either. Summer Walker's new album was playing, and it had her thinking about everything Kazimir put her through during their marriage. She wanted to make him pay for wasting three years of her life without providing the love she craved.

It seemed as if they were riding the highway for an eternity, but it was a little over three hours. She had no clue where they were heading. She started reading the signs, and one informed her that she was leaving Wisconsin. They had to be driving like a bat out of hell because it usually took four hours or so to get into the state, and they were driving out of it.

Nicolette thought long and hard, then remembered the day she saw Kameeko at Stephan's event. She had done a little research on her and found out that she was from Chicago but resided in Minnesota. It clicked at that moment; they were headed to that bitch's house. Glancing at the gas gauge, she didn't panic seeing she was at a quarter tank. At the rate they were going, she would make it. They were probably going to make it to Minnesota; if that's where they were going, in a matter of two hours. The Altima she drove didn't use too much gas, and Nicolette was glad she kept it simple when she chose it as the vehicle she preferred.

Robbed You came on, and Nicolette fumed, wishing she would've taken a little bit of money from her husband just as her daddy suggested. She just didn't think he would want to leave because he met a bitch he actually thought he was going to fall in love with. Over her dead body. She would kill him and her before they lived happily ever after.

*I should've known you wasn't all the way in it*
*I should've known you wasn't standing on business*
*If I waited for just another minute*
*I would've been sinning*
*Losing my mind by the second*
*Playing with my time, my shit is precious*
*I need all of that back and then some*
*Cause with all the things you've done*
*I should've robbed you*
*I should've popped you*
*Putting your trust in these no good bitches*
*Could've had 'em on my payroll, swear they would've listened*
*I could've robbed you*

The more she listened, the angrier she became. Summer depressed the fuck out of her, so she changed the music, then reached for her purse. Retrieving the card Arvon put in her purse, she decided to send him a text. Her life couldn't stop just because one man didn't want to treat her the way she deserved. As soon as she handled her business, she was going outside to get fucked before leaving Chicago for good.

**(773)555-0023:** *Hi, this is Nicolette. I met you earlier. You bought my lunch. I wanted to thank you again because it was kind of rude how I left.*

Nicolette kept driving as she waited for a text back. She was about fifteen miles in from the time she reached out when her phone rang. The number was unfamiliar, but she remembered the last two digits being part of Arvon's number. Turning the music down, she answered.

"Hello," she said with a smile.

"Well, you had to think for a couple hours before calling me, huh?"

"It's not like that. You know my husband, and I didn't feel right indulging in conversation with you because of that alone."

"What do your husband have to do with me? If he leaves you out here to get cuffed by another, that's on him. So, what are you up to?"

"I'm on the road picking my daughter up from my sister."

The lie rolled off her tongue with ease. Nicolette wasn't going to tell him she was going to kidnap her child from her husband. Arvon would never call her again. She would appear insane, and he would run in the other direction. They talked for the remainder of her commute. She hadn't laughed with a guy like that in a long time. Arvon was a great conversationalist, and she really enjoyed the conversation. She was so caught up in what he was saying, she almost missed the RV getting off the highway.

"Oh shit!" she exclaimed aloud as she signaled to get in the lane to make the exit.

"Are you okay?"

"Yeah, I almost missed my exit. Um, I'll call you once I'm headed back to the city. It was nice talking to you."

"Same here. Make sure you hit me up. I want to take you out."

"Will do."

Nicolette kept her eyes on the vehicle that was turning the corner. She cursed under her breath because the light turned red, and she was stuck. There was an opening at a McDonald's, and she pulled into the parking lot, then bypassed the traffic. The RV was further up the street, but she could see it over the other vehicles in front of her. The driver made a left turn at another light, and Nicolette swerved into the left lane and pushed the gas pedal. The car she cut off blew its horn like a mad person, but she didn't stop. She went through the light on yellow and slowed down so she wouldn't get a ticket.

Seeing the RV turn into the Hyatt parking lot, Nicolette drove past to make sure she wasn't seen. When she pulled back in on the other side of the building, she parked a short distance away from the entrance. Kazimir exited and made his way inside, but no one else got out of the RV. Nicolette opened her door to get out but made the decision to wait a little longer before she made her move.

Reaching into her glove compartment, she removed a cloth and a bottle of chloroform. She found the chemical in her father's bathroom and knew it would be useful at some point. The time had come, and Nicolette had her mind set on using it on someone that day. Bouncing her leg with anticipation, Nicolette kept her eye on the entrance of the hotel, then movement from the RV caught her attention. Kelly got off, then held her hand to assist Pax out. She was saying something that prompted Nicolette to lower her window.

"Come on, Pax. I know it was a long ride. You can rest when we get to the room. I promise."

"I wanna go to my own damn house, Brown Suga! I'm not a fucking orphan that can be bounced around from house to house. Take me home!"

Nicolette chuckled because she knew Pax didn't have a home to go to. Kelly looked like she wanted to cry because the old man didn't budge. He was giving her a hard time, and she didn't know what to do about it. The stress disappeared from her face soon as Kazimir came out of the building. He looked as if he was on his way to a photoshoot for activewear. The black jogging suit he wore clung to his muscled chest, and his bowed legs were an added bonus.

"Hey, Paw paw, what's wrong with you?" Kaz asked as he neared his grandpa.

"No, what the hell is wrong with you bringing me here? I want to go home, Kellan. How many times have I told you I don't want to be involved with the shit you're doing out here in these streets?"

"Paw paw, it's me, Kazimir." He stepped onto the bus, hugging his grandpa. "I would never bring you anywhere you will be harmed. I'm not my father."

"Oh, Kaz," the older St. Claire said with tears rimming his eyes. "My Kellan is gone, my David is gone, I haven't seen Barbara in a long time. I just want to go back home to her."

"I know. Your house was destroyed in the fire. Remember I told you that? You have to live with me for a while until I get you back into another home. We had to come bring Koko home, and then we will head back to Chicago. It wasn't safe for me to leave you there. Do you understand?"

"No, but I guess you know what's best."

"Not always, but in this instance, I think I do. Come on. Go with Kelly and Stephan so I can get our bags, okay?"

Pax nodded, then allowed Kelly to escort him off the RV. Kaz gave Stephan the key to both his room and the suite he had for the rest of the family. They walked toward the hotel while Kaz and the driver exited with some of the bags. When they were out of eyesight, Nicolette made her move. Everyone was off the bus except Koko and Alessia. It would be her only chance of getting her daughter without being noticed.

Jumping out with the soaked cloth, Nicolette rushed to the RV. As she climbed the steps, Alessia could be heard giggling. She followed the sound of her daughter's voice and stood in the entryway. Koko had her back toward the door, having no idea her worse nightmare was standing behind her. Without a word, Nicolette reached around placing the cloth against Koko's mouth and nose. Her body went limp instantly, then she fell to the floor. Alessia screamed as she watched in horror. She hated to do it, but Nicolette did the same to her daughter just to quiet her.

Lifting the toddler into her arms, Nicolette raced to the front of the RV and made a beeline for her vehicle. She placed Alessia in the back and didn't worry about strapping her in. She rounded the car, then started it just in time to drive off quietly. Glancing in the rearview mirror, she could see Kazimir walking slowly back to the RV.

"Yeah, go find your precious bitch passed out where I left her. I told your ass not to fuck with me." Nicolette laughed as she merged into traffic and hauled ass back to the highway in the direction of Chicago.

**To be continued...**

## Lock Down Publications and Ca$h Presents Assisted Publishing Packages

***Due to an increase in the price of services we have increased our prices. The prices below reflect the price increase as of 11/1/24.***

| **BASIC PACKAGE**<br>**$699**<br>Editing<br>Cover Design<br>Formatting | **UPGRADED PACKAGE**<br>**$1000**<br>Typing<br>Editing<br>Cover Design<br>Formatting<br>Upload eBooks to Amazon<br>Upload Paperback to Amazon |
|---|---|

| **ADVANCE PACKAGE $1,400** | **LDP SUPREME PACKAGE $1,700** |
|---|---|
| Typing<br>Editing (line editing/content)<br>Cover Design<br>Formatting<br>Copyright Registration<br>Proofreading<br>Upload eBooks to Amazon<br>Upload Paperback to Amazon | Typing<br>Editing (line editing/content)<br>Cover Design<br>Formatting<br>Copyright Registration<br>Proofreading<br>Set up Amazon Account<br>Upload eBooks to Amazon<br>Upload Paperback to Amazon<br>Advertise on LDP's Amazon and Facebook Page |

***

Other services available upon request.
Additional charges may apply

**Lock Down Publications**
P.O. Box 944
Stockbridge, GA 30281-9998
**Phone:** 470 303-9761
**Email:** lockdownpublications@gmail.com

# Submission Guideline

Submit the first three chapters of your completed manuscript to ldpsubmissions@gmail.com. In the subject line add **Your Book's Title**. The manuscript must be in a Word Doc file and sent as an attachment. Document should be in Times New Roman, double spaced, and in size 12 font. Also, provide your synopsis and full contact information. If sending multiple submissions, they must each be in a separate email.

Have a story but no way to send it electronically? You can still submit to LDP/Ca$h Presents. Send in the first three chapters, written or typed, of your completed manuscript to:

**LDP: Submissions Dept**
P.O. Box 944
Stockbridge, GA 30281-9998

*DO NOT send original manuscript. Must be a duplicate.* Provide your synopsis and a cover letter containing your full contact information.

Thanks for considering LDP and Ca$h Presents.

# NEW RELEASES

BLOODLINE OF A SAVAGE 1-3
THESE VICIOUS STREETS 1-3
RELENTLESS GOON 1-3
SOULLESS GOON 1&2
**BY PRINCE A. TAUHID**

THE BUTTERFLY MAFIA 3
**BY FUMIYA PAYNE**

A THUG'S STREET PRINCESS 1&2
**BY MEESHA**

CITY OF SMOKE 1-3
**BY MOLOTTI**

GET IT IN SLUGS 1 &2
**BY B. STALL**

STANDING ON HER BUSINESS 1&2
**BY DG SANTANA**

STEPPERS 1,2&3
THE REAL BADDIES OF CHI-RAQ 1-3
**BY KING RIO**

THE LANE 1-3
**BY KEN-KEN SPENCE**

THUG OF SPADES 1&2
LOVE IN THE TRENCHES 1&2
CORNER BOYS 1&2
ONCE YOU GO GANGSTA
PROTÉGÉ OF A LEGEND 1- 3
**BY COREY ROBINSON**

TIL DEATH 3
**BY ARYANNA**

THE BIRTH OF A GANGSTER 4
**BY DELMONT PLAYER**

PRODUCT OF THE STREETS 1-3
**BY DEMOND "MONEY" ANDERSON**

MONEY HUNGRY DEMONS 1-2
**BY TRANAY ADAMS**

TRAP STARS
**BY B. SHELLY**

HUB CITY MENACE 1-4
**BY J. WHITE**

A THUGGISH PASSION 1&2
LAND OF DA HOOLIGANZ 1-4
KILLAZ ON STANDBY 1&2
FRESH OFF DA PORCH 1-3
SECURE DA BAG
AMBITIONS OF A SLIDER
FOR MY ENEMIES SAKE
SOULLESS GOON 1&2
FO'EVA ROLLIN 1-4
**BY ASSA RAYMOND BAKER**

THE LEVEL UP 1&2
**BY LUXURY KING**

HUNGRY FOR MONEY 1&2
**SLIMBOS**

QUEEN OF NAPTOWN 1&2
THA TAKEOVER 1-3
**BY KEITH CHANDLER**

DRILL CITY 1&2
**BY ZAY'TOWVEN**

LOVE ME OR LET ME GO
**BY R. FACEY**

SAVAGE DREAMZ
**BY KING DAVID**

MONEY AND DEAD HOMIES
**BY DERRICK SUMMERS**

WHITE BOYS
**BY BANDEMIC**

A THUGS STREET PRINCESS 3 Coming Soon
**BY MEESHA**

BETRAYAL OF A G 2
**BY RAY VINCI**

SAVAGE FAMILY EMPIRE 1&2
SOULLESS GOON 1&2
THE DIRTY SIDE OF MONEY 1,2&3
**BY PRINCE**

BY THE TRUCKLOAD 1-4 COMING SOON
T SOULLESS GOON 1&2
IPPIN' THE SCALES 1-4
BAD BITCHES WIT GUNZ 1-3
PROBLEM SOLVED 1-3
THE GIRLRILLA AND HER N*GGA
THE SINGLE LADIES
**BY CHRISTOPHER "DIESEL" HORNEZES**

# AVAILABLE NOW

RESTRAINING ORDER 1 & 2
**BY CA$H & COFFEE**

LOVE KNOWS NO BOUNDARIES 1-3
**BY COFFEE**

RAISED AS A GOON I, II, III & IV
BRED BY THE SLUMS I, II, III
BLAST FOR ME I & II
ROTTEN TO THE CORE I II III
A BRONX TALE I, II, III

DUFFLE BAG CARTEL I II III IV V VI
HEARTLESS GOON I II III IV V
A SAVAGE DOPEBOY I II
DRUG LORDS I II III
CUTTHROAT MAFIA I II
KING OF THE TRENCHES
**BY GHOST**

LAY IT DOWN I & II
LAST OF A DYING BREED I II
BLOOD STAINS OF A SHOTTA I & II III
**BY JAMAICA**

LOYAL TO THE GAME I II III
LIFE OF SIN I, II III
**BY TJ & JELISSA**

IF LOVING HIM IS WRONG…I & II
LOVE ME EVEN WHEN IT HURTS I II III
**BY JELISSA**

PUSH IT TO THE LIMIT
**BY BRE' HAYES**

BLOODY COMMAS I & II
SKI MASK CARTEL I, II & III
KING OF NEW YORK I II, III IV V
RISE TO POWER I II III
COKE KINGS I II III IV V
BORN HEARTLESS I II III IV
KING OF THE TRAP I II
**BY T.J. EDWARDS**

WHEN THE STREETS CLAP BACK I & II III
THE HEART OF A SAVAGE I II III IV
MONEY MAFIA I II
LOYAL TO THE SOIL I II III
**BY JIBRIL WILLIAMS**

A DISTINGUISHED THUG STOLE MY HEART I II & III
LOVE SHOULDN'T HURT I II III IV
RENEGADE BOYS 1-4
PAID IN KARMA 1-3
SAVAGE STORMS 1-3
AN UNFORESEEN LOVE 1-3
BABY, I'M WINTERTIME COLD 1-3
A THUG'S STREET PRINCESS 1,2&3
EMBRACING THE LOVE OF A BOSS
**BY MEESHA**

A GANGSTER'S CODE 1-3
A GANGSTER'S SYN 1-3
THE SAVAGE LIFE 1-3
CHAINED TO THE STREETS 1-3
BLOOD ON THE MONEY 1-3
A GANGSTA'S PAIN 1-3
BEAUTIFUL LIES AND UGLY TRUTHS
CHURCH IN THESE STREETS
**BY J-BLUNT**

CUM FOR ME 1-8
**AN LDP EROTICA COLLABORATION**

BLOOD OF A BOSS 1-5
SHADOWS OF THE GAME
TRAP BASTARD
**BY ASKARI**

THE STREETS BLEED MURDER 1-3
THE HEART OF A GANGSTA 1-3
**BY JERRY JACKSON**

WHEN A GOOD GIRL GOES BAD
**BY ADRIENNE**

THE COST OF LOYALTY 1-3
**BY KWELI**

BRIDE OF A HUSTLA 1-3
THE FETTI GIRLS 1-3
CORRUPTED BY A GANGSTA 1-4
BLINDED BY HIS LOVE
THE PRICE YOU PAY FOR LOVE 1-3
DOPE GIRL MAGIC 1-3
**BY DESTINY SKAI**

A KINGPIN'S AMBITION
A KINGPIN'S AMBITION II
I MURDER FOR THE DOUGH
**BY AMBITIOUS**

TRUE SAVAGE 1-7
DOPE BOY MAGIC 1-3
MIDNIGHT CARTEL 1-3
CITY OF KINGZ 1&2
NIGHTMARE ON SILENT AVE
THE PLUG OF LIL MEXICO 1&2
CLASSIC CITY
**BY CHRIS GREEN**

GANGSTA CITY
**BY TEDDY DUKE**

BACK IN BLOOD
SEX, MURDER AND GOD 1&2
COUNTDOWN OF A KILLA 1&2
GUNS DOWN, BOTTOMS UP 1&2
**BY LO-LIFE**

A GANGSTER'S REVENGE 1-4
THE BOSS MAN'S DAUGHTERS 1-5
A SAVAGE LOVE 1&2
BAE BELONGS TO ME 1&2
A HUSTLER'S DECEIT 1-3
WHAT BAD BITCHES DO 1-3
SOUL OF A MONSTER 1-3
KILL ZONE

A DOPE BOY'S QUEEN 1-3
TIL DEATH 1-3
IMMA DIE BOUT MINE 1-6
DYING FOR LIKES 1&2
KILLA CREW 1&2
**BY ARYANNA**

A DOPEBOY'S PRAYER
**BY EDDIE "WOLF" LEE**

THE KING CARTEL 1-3
**BY FRANK GRESHAM**

THESE NIGGAS AIN'T LOYAL 1-3
**BY NIKKI TEE**

GANGSTA SHYT 1-3
**BY CATO**

THE ULTIMATE BETRAYAL
**BY PHOENIX**

BOSS'N UP 1-3
**BY ROYAL NICOLE**

I LOVE YOU TO DEATH
**BY DESTINY J**

I RIDE FOR MY HITTA
I STILL RIDE FOR MY HITTA
**BY MISTY HOLT**

LOVE & CHASIN' PAPER
**BY QAY CROCKETT**

TO DIE IN VAIN
SINS OF A HUSTLA
**BY ASAD**

BROOKLYN HUSTLAZ
**BY BOOGSY MORINA**

A DRUG KING AND HIS DIAMOND 1-3
A DOPEMAN'S RICHES
HER MAN, MINE'S TOO 1&2
CASH MONEY HO'S
THE WIFEY I USED TO BE 1&2
PRETTY GIRLS DO NASTY THINGS
**BY NICOLE GOOSBY**

LIPSTICK KILLAH 1-3
CRIME OF PASSION 1-3
FRIEND OR FOE 1-3
**BY MIMI**

TRAPHOUSE KING 1-3
KINGPIN KILLAZ 1-3
STREET KINGS 1&2
PAID IN BLOOD 1&2
CARTEL KILLAZ 1-3
DOPE GODS 1&2
**BY HOOD RICH**

BROOKLYN ON LOCK 1 & 2
**BY SONOVIA**

THE STREETS ARE CALLING
**BY DUQUIE WILSON**

STEADY MOBBN' 1-3
THE STREETS STAINED MY SOUL 1-3
**BY MARCELLUS ALLEN**

WHO SHOT YA 1-3
SON OF A DOPE FIEND 1-4
HEAVEN GOT A GHETTO 1&2
SKI MASK MONEY 1&2
**BY RENTA**

GORILLAZ IN THE BAY 1-4
TEARS OF A GANGSTA 1/&2
3X KRAZY 1&2
STRAIGHT BEAST MODE 1&2
**BY DE'KARI**

SLAUGHTER GANG 1-3
RUTHLESS HEART 1-3
**BY WILLIE SLAUGHTER**

GOD BLESS THE TRAPPERS 1-3
THESE SCANDALOUS STREETS 1-3
FEAR MY GANGSTA 1-5
THESE STREETS DON'T LOVE NOBODY 1-2
BURY ME A G 1-5
A GANGSTA'S EMPIRE 1-4
THE DOPEMAN'S BODYGAURD 1&2
THE REALEST KILLAZ 1-3
THE LAST OF THE OGS 1-3
**BY TRANAY ADAMS**

MARRIED TO A BOSS 1-3
**BY DESTINY SKAI & CHRIS GREEN**
TRIGGADALE 1-3
MURDA WAS THE CASE 1-3
**BY ELIJAH R. FREEMAN**

KINGZ OF THE GAME 1-7
CRIME BOSS 1-4
**BY PLAYA RAY**

FUK SHYT
**BY BLAKK DIAMOND**

DON'T F#CK WITH MY HEART 1&2
**BY LINNEA**

ADDICTED TO THE DRAMA 1-3

IN THE ARM OF HIS BOSS
**BY JAMILA**

YAYO 1-4
A SHOOTER'S AMBITION 1&2
BRED IN THE GAME
**BY S. ALLEN**

TRAP GOD 1-3
RICH $AVAGE 1-3
MONEY IN THE GRAVE 1-3
CARTEL MONEY 1&2
**BY MARTELL TROUBLESOME BOLDEN**

FOREVER GANGSTA 1&2
GLOCKS ON SATIN SHEETS 1&2
**BY ADRIAN DULAN**

TOE TAGZ 1-4
LEVELS TO THIS SHYT 1&2
IT'S JUST ME AND YOU
**BY AH'MILLION**

LOYALTY AIN'T PROMISED 1&2
**BY KEITH WILLIAMS**

KINGPIN DREAMS 1-3
RAN OFF ON DA PLUG
**BY PAPER BOI RARI**

THE STREETS MADE ME 1-3
**BY LARRY D. WRIGHT**

CONFESSIONS OF A GANGSTA 1-4
CONFESSIONS OF A JACKBOY 1-3
CONFESSIONS OF A HITMAN
CONFESSIONS OF A DOPE BOY

**BY NICHOLAS LOCK**

I'M NOTHING WITHOUT HIS LOVE
SINS OF A THUG
TO THE THUG I LOVED BEFORE
A GANGSTA SAVED XMAS
IN A HUSTLER I TRUST
**BY MONET DRAGUN**

QUIET MONEY 1-3
THUG LIFE 1-3
EXTENDED CLIP 1&2
A GANGSTA'S PARADISE
**BY TRAI'QUAN**

CAUGHT UP IN THE LIFE 1-3
THE STREETS NEVER LET GO 1-3
**BY ROBERT BAPTISTE**

NEW TO THE GAME 1-3
MONEY, MURDER & MEMORIES 1-3
**BY MALIK D. RICE**

CREAM 2-3
THE STREETS WILL TALK
**BY YOLANDA MOORE**

THE STREETS WILL NEVER CLOSE 1-3
**BY K'AJJI**

LIFE OF A SAVAGE 1-4
A GANGSTA'S QUR'AN 1-4
MURDA SEASON 1-3
GANGLAND CARTEL 1-3
CHI'RAQ GANGSTAS 1-4
KILLERS ON ELM STREET 1-3
JACK BOYZ N DA BRONX 1-3
A DOPEBOY'S DREAM 1-3

JACK BOYS VS DOPE BOYS 1-3
COKE GIRLZ
COKE BOYS
SOSA GANG 1&2
BRONX SAVAGES
BODYMORE KINGPINS
BLOOD OF A GOON
**BY ROMELL TUKES**

CONCRETE KILLA 1-3
VICIOUS LOYALTY 1-3
BLOODY MONEY BAGS
**BY KINGPEN**

THE ULTIMATE SACRIFICE 1-6
KHADIFI
IF YOU CROSS ME ONCE 1-3
ANGEL 1-4
IN THE BLINK OF AN EYE
**BY ANTHONY FIELDS**

THE LIFE OF A HOOD STAR
**BY CA$H & RASHIA WILSON**

NIGHTMARES OF A HUSTLA 1-3
BLOOD AND GAMES 1&2
**BY KING DREAM**

HARD AND RUTHLESS 1&2
MOB TOWN 251
THE BILLIONAIRE BENTLEYS 1-3
REAL G'S MOVE IN SILENCE
**BY VON DIESEL**

MOB TIES 1-7
SOUL OF A HUSTLER, HEART OF A KILLER 1-3
GORILLAZ IN THE TRENCHES
OOPS CRY TOO 1-3
THE DAUGHTER OF A CARTEL BOSS 1&2

**BY SAYNOMORE**

BODYMORE MURDERLAND 1-3
THE BIRTH OF A GANGSTER 1-4
**BY DELMONT PLAYER**

FOR THE LOVE OF A BOSS 1&2
**BY C. D. BLUE**

KILLA KOUNTY 1-5
TENDER 1&2
**BY KHUFU**

MOBBED UP 1-4
THE BRICK MAN 1-5
THE COCAINE PRINCESS 1-10
STEPPERS 1-3
SUPER GREMLIN 1-5
A GANGSTA'S SON
THE CONNECT'S SECRET
**BY KING RIO**

MONEY GAME 1&2
**BY SMOOVE DOLLA**
A GANGSTA'S KARMA 1-5
**BY FLAME**

KING OF THE TRENCHES 1-3
**By GHOST & TRANAY ADAMS**

QUEEN OF THE ZOO 1&2
**BY BLACK MIGO**

GRIMEY WAYS 1-3
BETRAYAL OF A G
**BY RAY VINCI**

XMAS WITH AN ATL SHOOTER
**BY CA$H & DESTINY SKAI**

KING KILLA 1&2
PAPER, ROCK, SNAKES
**BY VINCENT "VITTO" HOLLOWAY**

BETRAYAL OF A THUG 1&2
**BY FRE$H**

COUNTDOWN OF A KILLA 1&2
SEX, MURDER AND GOD 1&2
GUNS DOWN, BOTTOMS UP 1&2
**BY LO-LIFE**

FOR THE LOVE OF BLOOD 1-4
**BY JAMEL MITCHELL**

HOOD CONSIGLIERE 1-3
NO TIME FOR ERROR 1&2
REAL
**BY KEESE**

THE PLUG'S RUTHLESS DAUGHTER 1,2&3
REDEMPTION IN THE STREETS
**BY TONY DANIELS**
BORN IN THE GRAVE 1-3
CRIME PAYS 1-3
**BY SELF MADE TAY**

MOAN IN MY MOUTH
**BY XTASY**

TORN BETWEEN A GANGSTER AND A GENTLEMAN
**BY J-BLUNT**

LOYALTY IS EVERYTHING 1-3
CITY OF SMOKE 1-3
**BY MOLOTTI**

HERE TODAY GONE TOMORROW 1&2

**BY FLY ROCK**

WOMEN LIE MEN LIE 1-4
FIFTY SHADES OF SNOW 1-3
STACK BEFORE YOU SPLURGE
GIRLS FALL LIKE DOMINOES
NAÏVE TO THE STREETS
**BY ROY MILLIGAN**

PILLOW PRINCESS
**BY S. HAWKINS**

THE BUTTERFLY MAFIA 1-3
SALUTE MY SAVAGERY 1&2
**BY FUMIYA PAYNE**

THE LANE 1&2
**BY KEN-KEN SPENCE**

THE PUSSY TRAP 1-5
**BY NENE CAPRI**

DIRTY DNA
**BY BLAQUE**

SANCTIFIED AND HORNY
**BY XTASY**

## BOOKS BY LDP'S CEO, CA$H

TRUST IN NO MAN
TRUST IN NO MAN 2
TRUST IN NO MAN 3
BONDED BY BLOOD
SHORTY GOT A THUG
THUGS CRY
THUGS CRY 2
THUGS CRY 3
TRUST NO BITCH
TRUST NO BITCH 2
TRUST NO BITCH 3
TIL MY CASKET DROPS
RESTRAINING ORDER

EMBRACING THE LOVE OF A BOSS 2 | MEESHA

RESTRAINING ORDER 2
IN LOVE WITH A CONVICT
LIFE OF A HOOD STAR
XMAS WITH AN ATL SHOOTER

www.ingramcontent.com/pod-product-compliance
Lightning Source LLC
LaVergne TN
LVHW020705110826
845149LV00012B/2120

* 9 7 8 1 9 7 1 7 7 0 2 0 8 *